DREAMWALKERS

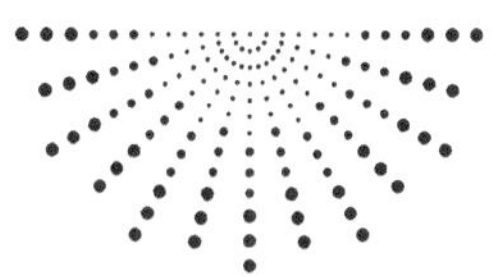

LESLIE RUSH

Midnight Tide
PUBLISHING

Cover credit: Sevannah Storm

Second Edition 2025

ISBN 978-1-964655-52-9

Midnight Tide Publishing

www.midnighttidepublishing.com/

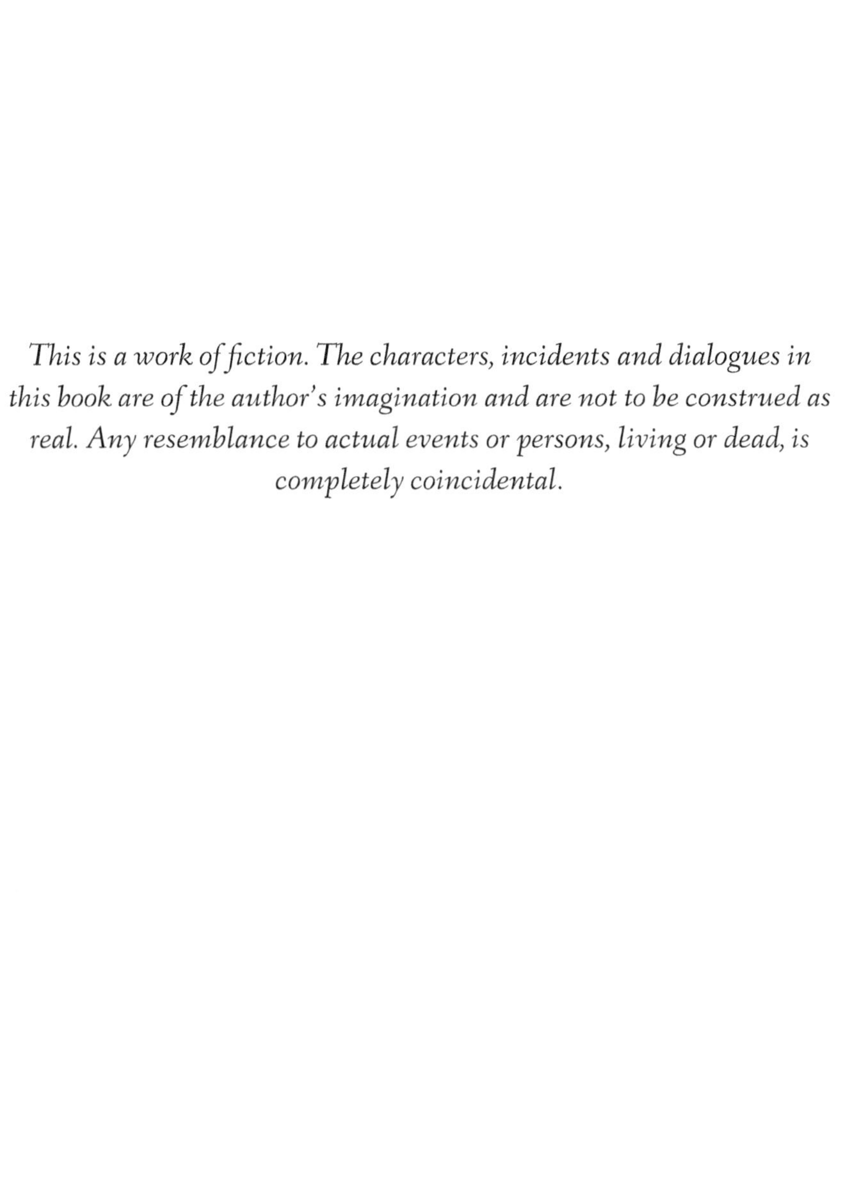

For my husband.

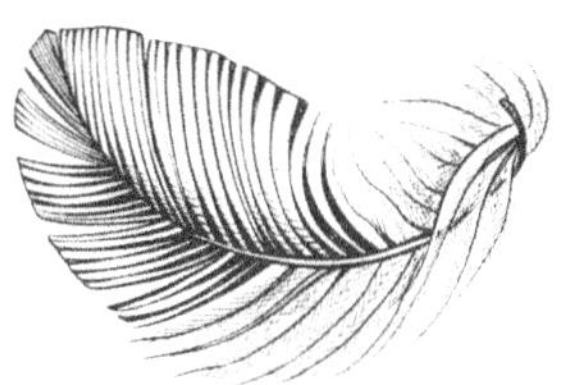

PROLOGUE

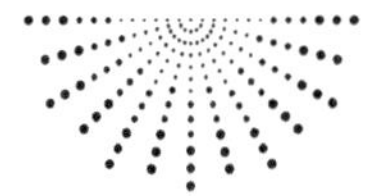

Transcript [FILE 201 130614 SANTA FE (03:27)]

Raven: Requesting Stargate SIT REP.

Trigger: We found them. Asset validation complete. ET mission complete 0140 hours.

Raven: Copy that. I'm going in. Initiate target acquisition.

CHAPTER ONE

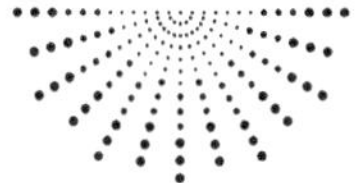

THE WORST THING about living in the Land of Enchantment is that it hardly ever lives up to the promise of that name. When we first moved here, I thought there would be actual magic, like the sky might change color at my command. A nighthawk with my father's voice would teach me all the secrets and show me how to fly. Even though New Mexico looked mostly like desert, I figured that was just a clever disguise. The magic was hidden, but I would find it.

Seven years later, the Land of Enchantment still sounds great and sells a lot of T-shirts, but the magic is hard to find and slippery when you do. There are enchanted spots, if you know where to look, and when the sun sinks into its fiery cauldron of color every evening, I almost believe. But controlling the skies and the animals, flying wherever I want to go? I can still only do those things in my dreams, and since Mom won't let me get my driver's license, the only flying I'm doing is on my bike.

Fortified with coffee, yogurt, and a handful of pecans, I'm doing my pre-flight backpack check when Brian shuffles in, still in his faded Spider-Man pajamas. I don't know how my little brother can tell, but he always can. He takes one look at me and shakes his head.

"That dream again?"

"Yeah. Third time this month." It's the one dream I can't control —a lightning-cracked nightmare, a ravenous storm of panic and rolling thunder. Normally I would have gathered it in before it took shape, the way Dad taught me, but I never feel this one coming until it's too late.

"I'm glad I never dream," Brian announces, opening the refrigerator. "Oh, gross. Almond milk again." Yawning and scratching his sticking-out-all-over brown hair, he pours a bowl of Raisin Bran Crunch, dumps the last of my cream over it, and plops onto a chair to dig into the cereal.

"You do too. Everyone dreams. You calculate the secrets of the universe in your sleep. I'm just lucky you don't remember them, or you'd beat me to graduation for sure." I'm only half-teasing. Brian's not even ten, but Genius Boy will be finished with high school before he's twelve.

"I told you when we were taking Pre-Cal to let me help you." Brian slurps an enormous mouthful from his spoon, wiping off his cream mustache with the back of his hand.

"I'm a senior now," I remind him. "Even if you did get all of the math and science DNA in our gene pool, I don't think you can catch up with me." Even if he *did* get an A in his online class, while I got a C in an actual class with an actual teacher.

Brian spies my paint box. "Are you finishing the sign today?"

"Uh-huh." At least when I paint, I can control light and color the way I do in my dreams. No math required.

I splort a blob of sunscreen onto my arm. I may have Dad's dreams and his thick, black hair, but my skin is like Mom's, and even an early morning bike ride is a menace in the New Mexico desert.

"You can't wear that shirt." Brian's eyes narrow.

"Yes, *mother*." I check my backpack for gum.

"She'll make you cha-ange," Brian sings through another crunchy mouthful.

"Bet she doesn't—and you don't have any money anyway."

"Bet you five Macaroonies she does."

The backpack is good to go: Phone. Sunglasses. Paint box. Dad's iPod. A couple of cheese sticks. And, best of all, a long, skinny, spicy, non-organic beef stick consisting primarily of fats, nitrates, and forbidden-by-Mom deliciousness. A heart attack in stick form. Yum.

Brian sees the snacks sticking out of my backpack and snakes his hand in, which emerges clutching my prized beef stick. He eyes me hopefully. "Are there any more of these cat tails?"

"In the garage. Who knows, maybe they'll feed you something good this year. Remember the Spaceman Sticks?"

Gagging noises erupt as Brian crosses his eyes and dies in his chair. Last summer, the Space Campers got samples of astronaut "food." Tang—an orange-flavored drink powder—and this truly disgusting thing called a Spaceman Stick. It looked kind of like Brian's cat tails, but it was chewy and sweet. Its grainy texture and vitamin-chocked taste was too gross even for the eight-year-olds.

"Okay." He sighs, putting the cat tail back in my bag. Just in time.

Mom, silent as a ninja, appears in the doorway. "Don't dawdle, Brian. The bus will be here in half an hour." She pauses. "And that shirt, Vivian. It's certainly true, but not for work."

Busted. Summer Hawk, Psychic Tarot Life Coach, can spot inappropriate at 7:00 AM without even using her magic powers.

"Okay, I'll change when I get there." Personally, I think my "KARMA'S A BITCH" T-shirt is totally appropriate. Mom's shop is a collection of vintage clothing, New Age books and supplies, Native American crafts, jewelry, and assorted work from local artists. Christened "Déjà Vu," it's where all things—from "experienced" clothing to crystals, carvings, and tarot cards—are either reincarnated from an old life or designed to help each customer find a new one. Now that school is out, I get to work there a few days a week instead of just Saturdays.

She hands me the shop keys. "Okay. Be careful riding, Vivi. Oh—Una should be coming today. Jewelry and probably clothes from Santa Fe."

Brian fakes a cough and holds up his fist, releasing his fingers one at a time, reminding me of my cookie debt. I grab my backpack and drop the keys in the outside pocket. As I pass Brian, I flick my finger on the back of his head in farewell.

"See ya, Brainiac."

"See ya, Vivisection."

Cruising through the desert blast furnace usually scorches out the last remnants of that renegade dream, but today I'm headachy and crooked, like a locker with a wonky corner that won't close right. Part of me is still trapped in that forest at the edge of the cold, rain-slashed abyss, and I can almost hear his voice, feel the name on my lips, when it happens.

It's not my fault.

Brakes screech wildly, and out of nowhere a white van veers into me, punches me off my bike into the air, slamming me to my knees in the dirt. A cloud of fumes and dust belches into my face, pelting me with gravel as the van speeds away.

"Hey!" I yelp at the vanishing van and try to stand. The world tilts sideways and pain shoots through my knees, buckling me back to the spinning ground. Slower this time, I roll over and sit up, spying my backpack in a clump of ragweed a few feet away. Where's my bike?

"Are you all right?"

Startled, I turn and squint into the sun at a tall shadow that looms out of the impossibly blue sky. He offers his hand, but I wave it away, scrambling for my dignity as I stand up, ignoring the throb of protest from my knees. Mr. Helpful is good looking, with a tropical vacation tan. He's wearing expensive casual clothes and has suspiciously perfect hair—like a forty-ish model on his way to shoot a commercial for the black Escalade purring a few yards behind him on the shoulder.

"Yeah, I think so," I reply, brushing off my jeans. I glare in the direction of the vanished van and spot handlebars poking up from the irrigation ditch on the edge of the field.

My favorite T-shirt is now coated with dirt, but other than the knees and a skinned elbow, I'm okay. The last thing I need is some helpful stranger calling 911—or worse, calling Mom.

"What an idiot! He just ran right into you! I can't believe he didn't even stop to see if you were okay." He shakes his head and removes his Ray-Bans, revealing icy blue eyes that don't quite match the concern in his voice. "I wish I'd gotten his license plate number."

"I guess the law doesn't apply if you have government plates," I grumble.

"Government?" Mr. Helpful pauses. "Are you sure? Looked more like Texas to me."

Yeah, well, that van wasn't farting fumes and spewing rocks in *his* face. I saw what I saw. With all the military bases, Border Patrol, and ICE offices around here, half the vehicles on the road have those plates.

"Well, thanks for stopping, but I'm fine. Really." I start toward my bike, knees whimpering.

"No, no, let me." Mr. Helpful cuts smoothly in front of me, stepping down into the ditch. He lifts the bike and climbs back out in one effortless motion. Right on cue: a movie-star smile, like we're on camera and this is his good deed for the year.

"Here you go." He frowns slightly, wiggling the handlebars. "Looks a little crooked."

I take the bike, and sure enough, the handlebars are knocked out of alignment. He's looking at me intently, and I'm suddenly glad the bike is between me and Mr. Helpful. Maybe it's the lingering unease from the dream, or the fact I just got tossed onto the shoulder like a bag of trash, but his attention creeps me out.

Eyes still on me, he tilts his head in the direction of the Escalade. "Can I give you a ride? I'm sure your bike can fit in the back."

Like I'm getting in a car with a total stranger? That's a whole bunch of no. I may have banged up my knees a little, but my brain still works.

"No, that's okay. It's not far. I can fix it. But thanks anyway." I hop on my bike and pedal painfully away. I feel his cold eyes following me until the Escalade turns around, crunching over the gravel. By the time I reach the edge of the Magic Forest, Mr. Helpful is nowhere in sight.

The crisp whizzing of the wheels and the echoing chorus of cicadas settle my thoughts as I spin through my favorite part of the ride. Valley Road winds through a dozen tiny towns separated by acres of jalapenos, cotton, and pecan orchards along the Rio Grande, and in this area the ancient pecan trees reach across the road, creating a canopy of dappled shade that lasts for more than three miles. It's not magic every day, but for these few minutes, the temperature drops ten degrees, and I'm no longer pedaling through the relentless red and gold desert, but cruising through a cool, green, eight-minute oasis of shade.

Shafts of sunlight pierce through the branches, dancing like the tiny chips of lightning that follow me back from my dreams. I emerge from the trees, zooming past the twenty-foot statue of the World's Largest Pecan toward the ancient adobe homes landscaped with sagebrush and wildflowers that surround Historic Zia Square. By the time I park my bike in the back, the throbbing in my knees has settled into a dull ache.

"Déjà vu" literally means "previously seen," and our shop has seen a lot. It was a house a century ago, but it's been reincarnated a few times. There's an entire wall of sturdy shelves and mysterious, drippy stains on the floor from when it was first a library, then an ice-cream parlor. The low ceiling and deep, shaded porch looks out onto the grassy center of Zia's tourist zone. Mom says the tiny bathroom was a luxury when most houses here still had outhouses. *Outhouses.*

Yeah, no. This is why I'm grateful I live in the 21st century. Toilets that flush, air conditioning... much better.

The antiquated kitchen greets me with the seasoned aroma of a hundred years of coffee and wooden floors. I prop open the heavy swinging door from the ice cream parlor days and pluck a clean T-shirt from the tourist stack—black with green and red chiles all over it, and "BITE ME" in big, white, satisfying letters. My project for today is to paint new life into the sign that hangs over the front door.

But first things first: the tiny bakery across the square is open, and, well, there are priorities. I cross over to Noonie's, home of delicious baked goodies and sandwiches of all kinds, but most famous for Noonie's Macaroonies. Tiny cookie bombs of OMG that are the heart of our secret food stash in the garage. Mom puts out Macaroonies for our customers almost every day. She says they buy things because they feel welcomed but I think they buy things because they feel guilty for eating the cookies. I don't blame them one bit. Three dozen should bring on plenty of guilt and refill our secret stash. Plus the five extra for Brian.

By the time I hear Mom's car, it's 9:00 and we are ready to go. I hit the switch that throws pools of light onto the artwork hanging on the back wall and unplug the iPod, cutting off Metallica's "Enter Sandman" in mid-grind. Just in time, Spanish guitar strums lightly through the main room.

But instead of Mom breezing through the back door, there is a light knock, and an unfamiliar voice calls out: "Hello? Summer? You here?" I stick my head through the kitchen doorway and see a short, sturdy woman peeking through the screen. A small red truck is backed up to the porch with the tailgate down and cardboard boxes in the bed.

"Hi! Are you Vivian?" She has dark hair and eyes, amber skin, and a huge smile. "Una Wolfsong. Your mom told you I was coming, right? I finally get to meet you?"

"Hi! Yes. Come in." I open the door. "She'll be here any minute. In fact, I thought you were her."

Una steps inside and sets her large woven bag on the counter. She looks about thirty-five and smells like sun and cantaloupe. "No one would make that mistake twice." She laughs.

This is true. Mom is slender and graceful, like a desert willow, and Una looks more like a short, round chile pequin bush. She has a great laugh, and I like her immediately.

"Would you like something to drink? There's tea and coffee. Water?"

"Water would be nice, thank you." She takes a few rolled-up flannel jewelry bags out of her tote. "It looks like a busy summer for you."

"I'm not sure when Mom will need me yet. Saturdays for sure. Probably a few days during the week." I open the fridge and grab one of the waters I'd brought from home. "Depends on how many readings she can book, I guess."

Una's black eyes gleam. "A mother-daughter team?"

"No way." I snort. "I leave that to the experts." Which would definitely not be me.

Una shakes her head. "You never know. You could learn. Your mother is very talented. They say these things run in families, right? She reads the cards, and you could learn to read palms."

"Mom is good with the cards," I admit, "but I don't have the, uhh, 'gift.'" Because I'm pretty sure you have to actually believe in this stuff to be "gifted."

Una chuckles as if I'd said that out loud. "Vivian, it's not really *magic*. You learn what the lines mean and you look at who your client is. Figure out what they're worried about. Two plus two."

Riiight. Advanced people-reading for suckers.

"I guess." I don't want to be totally rude, but—

"Everyone wants to know about their health, money, and of course, love. Your job is to help them believe in themselves. *That*'s the real gift."

Her eyes are twinkling as she steps closer to me and holds out her hand. "Here, I'll show you. It's easy. Give me your right hand."

Oh no.

I learned a long time ago not to let Mom's friends test out their so-called "powers" on me. Some of them hint that because I'm part Apache, I must have some inside knowledge of the spirit world. Not! I don't even let Mom read my cards, although I suspect she lays them down on my behalf anyway.

But Una doesn't believe in this stuff, either. She just wants to show me how it's done, right? And she's Apache too. Not one of the weirdos from Mom's classes trying to see if I'm some kind of magic Indian. Most important of all, there are no witnesses.

I hesitate, then stick out my hand. "Okay."

Her strong, warm fingers unfold my cool, reluctant ones. She gives me a conspiratorial wink and then closes her eyes. Taking a deep breath, she composes her face, transforming it with a serene, angelic smile.

"Ah," she intones gently, opening her eyes and poring over my palm. "You will have a long life with many adventures." She traces one line and announces, "You will have many admirers, but there will be only one true love."

Well, so much for that.

"Umm, Una? I don't even have *one* admirer, much less anything resembling true love." Last year's Homecoming Dance disaster doesn't count.

"Oh, there's no doubt. You do. You will." She leans in, tracing another line up to the base of my fingers, and stops in one spot. "Hmmm," she says softly, cocking her head as if listening to something only she can hear.

"What? What is it?" I ask. She doesn't answer. All right, I admit it. Despite my complete and total lack of belief in supernatural "woo," I'm practically holding my breath. She's really got the act down—this is total BS, but I still want to know.

"You have a hidden talent. A talent you may have just barely discovered." Something unreadable flits across her eyes.

"I'm a half-decent artist," I venture. Maybe Una sees my paintings on the walls of a shop someday. Hopefully a shop that isn't my Mom's.

Una shakes her head. "No, that isn't it. It's something else." She has this oddly satisfied look on her face, as if she finally heard what she was listening for—which makes me even more curious. Outside, Mom's Camry arrives and turns off.

"Well, what is it?" I ask, trying to seem like I'm not anxious.

Una straightens up to her full 4'11", eyebrows raised. "See? Like I said, anyone can do it."

"Hey, now wait a minute," I protest. "That's pretty vague! What about right now? What's happening this summer?" I'm joking, of course.

Aren't I?

"Oh, that's easy." The car door shuts, and Mom calls out hellos to the shop-neighbors. Her footsteps creak on the back porch.

A sly smile plays on Una's lips. "You will meet a mysterious, handsome stranger."

Mom is in the office with Una when I step into the blazing sunshine to unload the truck. The two smaller boxes rattle and clunk—probably crafts from the Hopi reservation. The big one is heavy and solid, packed full of vintage clothes. I wrestle with it, awkwardly sliding it to the edge of the tailgate, when a cold, spidery tickle slithers up the back of my neck.

I jolt upright and look around, but the back porches and doorways behind the square are deep in morning shadow. A flicker of movement under the ancient mulberry tree behind the Slushee Stop catches my attention—then nothing. My radar on full alert, a chill creeps around my shoulders, but I can't see anything past the sun's brutal glare. It's probably 95 degrees already. Aren't hallucinations a symptom of fatal heat stroke? Ugh. I hoist the box off the tailgate and

stagger through the back door, turning around one last time to see...
no one.

[FILE 201 130614 SANTA FE (09:27)]

Raven: WTF was that?

Trigger: SNAFU. I was looking at the GPS. Didn't see her. Visual just now, she's unharmed

Raven: You know there's no room for error this time. No more mistakes!

Trigger: HUA. Heard, understood, acknowledged.

CHAPTER TWO

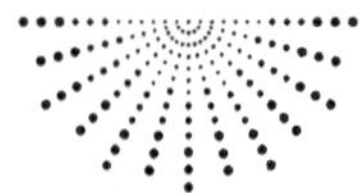

"Did you drag that in by yourself?"

I'm shoving the big box across the kitchen floor with my foot when Una returns from the office. "My nephew took some melons over to the fruit stand, but he was supposed to help unload."

I shake my head. No melons, no nephew, no help—no problem. Mom already told me about the nephew. The orphan. I can't even imagine the most horrible thing in my life happening *twice*. Their family is White Mountain Apache, like Dad's side of the family, and Mom said our fathers knew each other in Bosnia. I know he's older than me, but my brain keeps picturing a Wimpy Kid-looking waif. That clothing box is so heavy and awkward, any real help from her sad, scrawny nephew would be, as Brian would say, not likely.

It's not until after lunch that I get a chance to inventory the new-old stuff Una brought. I haven't seen much of Mom. She has readings booked for the whole day, but she emerges to run the register, so I can grab lunch. I duck into the kitchen and eat my cheese sticks, an apple, and my secret beef stick. Disguising my cat-tail breath with six cinnamon Macaroonies, I tuck the remaining cookie stash safely in my backpack.

Mom stretches her arms over her head, bracelets tinkling, gauzy sleeves fluttering like a fairy queen. She checks her skirt pocket for cash and heads for the front door.

"I'm getting a tuna wrap. Back in twenty." It will probably be more like forty, but I don't mind. She needs to walk around and clear her head. No matter how breezy Una is about doing these readings, they can be really draining for Mom. I know I said I don't believe in this stuff, but she really is good, and *her* mom was famous for it for a while. But the psychic powers skipped right over my DNA—just like the math.

This quiet won't last long, so I dig into the boxes. Just as I thought: the clunky ones contain touristy crafts—beaded barrettes and key chains, friendship bracelets, dream catchers, and arrowheads tied on leather cords. I pop open the big box of clothes, which is stuffed full of colorful tops and skirts—the kind my friend Lorena always wants me to save for her—and a couple of vintage jean jackets. All pretty typical, except for a glamorous peach silk nightgown that looks like something from one of Brian's old movies. Below that is a carefully wrapped blanket woven in a tight geometric pattern of red, black, and white wool, which will fetch a good price for sure.

Then I feel something from heaven. Something dense, soft and smooth. I reach in deep, wrap my fingers around it, and pull out a treasure.

It's a leather jacket. Brown and biker-style, it's more than distressed; the leather has been totally beaten into submission. The elbows are worn thin, the lining is frayed, it smells like a lifetime, and I want it. It's way too big, but the heavy zipper works, and the snaps are all there. I bury my face in it, breathing the smoky remains of good leather, and it's crazy, but I feel like I just found something I didn't even know I had lost.

Mom will be back soon. I need to price these other things and put them out, so I fold my prize carefully and lay it back in the box like a good little employee. A woman comes in and buys a book that promises to *Heal Your Aura In 30 Days* and some sweet-grass soap for the meantime. I start a new pot of coffee and peek into the box every two minutes.

The front door jingles and Mom breezes in, carrying two large drinks. "Whew, it's a scorcher," she announces. "I brought us pomegranate slushees." She sets mine down on the counter and heads for the office. I can't wait even one whole minute.

"Hey, Mom?" She comes out, having dropped off her drink, and darts into the bathroom.

"Yeah?" Water running.

"Una brought some nice things," I inform her through the door. "A bunch of skirts and a small blanket, I guess from the reservation?"

She opens the door. "No, she made that one. It's on commission. Let's see it."

We walk over to the shelves, and she examines the blanket with a practiced eye. There are tricks to knowing if it's a high-quality blanket or not, and I don't know any of them.

"Nice. That's the Ganado pattern. Tag it $450." Mom flips through the skirts and scarves and gets hold of the nightgown. "Oooh, what's this?" She shakes it out and holds it up to her shoulders. The creamy peach gown blends with her skin, and they both glow. "Look at this, Vivian. Bias-cut silk! They just don't make stuff like this anymore."

Inspiration strikes. Déjà Vu policy is that what comes in gets sold, unless it's simply unsellable, which is pretty much never. Maybe if she can make an exception to the house rule for herself, she can make one for me too?

I take a deep breath. "The color is amazing, Mom. It makes you look like a movie star or something. You should try it on."

Well, it's not a lie. It does, and she should.

"You think so?" She holds it closer and steps sideways to see in the mirror. I hold my breath as her sea-green eyes appraise the effect. Then she glances at the antique clock behind the register, and my heart sinks. "My 1:30 will be here any minute." She hangs it back on the rack. Now I will have to go with plan B—simply asking her if I can buy the jacket.

The 1:30 opens the door, and in walks Mr. Helpful. Yep, it's him all right. Same camera-ready clothes, same Ray-Bans, same well-rehearsed smile.

Crap. I really didn't want to tell Mom about the van, but now I guess I'll have to.

"Hello, Mrs. Hawk," he says to Mom and nods at me—then recognition opens his face and the charming smile widens, revealing at least forty-seven of his perfect teeth

"Please, call me Summer," Mom protests. "Vivian, this is Jackson Connor. He's renovating the old gallery next to Noonie's." Of course someone oozing money and flashing a million-dollar smile would have a last name for a first name. I bet all his kids' names start with "J" too.

"We've already met." Jackson Connor nods in my direction again. "I stopped to help after her little accident this morning."

A wrinkle appears between Mom's brows and her eyes lock onto mine with laser precision. *Crap, crap, crap, crap. CRAP.*

"Accident? What accident?"

"Really, Mom, it was no big deal," I babble. "Some van knocked me off the road is all."

"Knocked you *off the road?*" My conscience prickles with guilt at Mom's troubled face. "Are you sure you're all right?"

I show her my scraped elbow. "It barely touched me. See? That's it. I'm fine." If my knees could talk, they'd call me a liar, but I just want this conversation to be over.

"I saw the whole thing," Jackson Connor declares. "Luckily, he just tapped her—but then he drove away. People these days! Nice to meet you *officially.*" He may have a movie-star smile, but his handshake is as cold and smooth as a lizard, sending an uneasy shiver up my arm. When we let go, my skin is crawling.

"Well... thank you for stopping to help my daughter, Jackson. There are some crazy people on the road." Mom's frown smooths out and morphs back into her nurturing customer-smile. "Are you ready?" She ushers Lizard Man Connor to the office, leaving me to my slushee, a sign to paint, and plan B.

After his reading, Jackson Connor buys a sand painting I have admired for a month and two carved turtles for his daughters, Jenna and Jillian (Ha! Knew it.). I wrap them up, making sure I don't touch him when I hand him the bag. Hopefully he isn't going to become a regular.

"I guess I'll be seeing you two around." He smiles at me, then flashes even more teeth at Mom.

"Yes sir, see you around," I echo politely, thinking *Not if I can help it.*

Jackson Connor groans jovially, "*Sir!* Do I look that old?"

I fake-smile. Sometimes it's better to let people answer their own questions.

"Don't answer that!" He chuckles at his own wit as he steps out the front door. Ha. Ha. Ha. Maybe hanging garlic over the door will keep him out.

By the end of the day, the tarot readings, books, and crystals have enriched a lot of lives, and I have finished the Déjà Vu sign with celestial flourishes of purple and silver. While Mom checks on the herb garden in the back, I stand in front of the mirror, holding the jacket. I just *have* to try it on. Maybe it will have scratchy seams or some other fatal flaw, which of course I know it doesn't.

I slip my arms in, and it nearly swallows me whole. I adjust the snaps on the sleeves and the waist and look in the mirror. It's totally huge, but it's *perfect.* It was once an expensive, high-quality jacket, and it still holds wispy ghost smells of its past—a little smoke, a little cologne, and something familiar I can't quite place. Its smooth weight on my neck and shoulders feels like someone's arm around me. I hug it close to my body. I can't leave the shop without it.

"Ready, Vivi?"

I jump. I was so entranced with the jacket, I didn't notice Ninja

Mom in the swinging doorway, purse and keys in hand, ready to go out through the kitchen.

"Umm, yeah." Okay, Plan B, here goes: "Mom, do you think I could have this? I mean, I would buy it, whatever we paid for it. Please?"

Mom crosses her arms, smiling. "That beat-up thing, Vivi? It's huge." She tilts her head a little. "It looks like a jacket your dad had," she observes softly, and then she looks at me with her quiet face, the one I only see when she talks about Dad.

The antique clock ticks three excruciating, century-long seconds.

"Okay, tell you what. You did a great job on the new sign. You can have the jacket as payment for that. A bonus."

"*Yes!* Thanks, Mom, you are awesome!" I was not expecting anything for the sign, so this really *is* a bonus. Mom waves away her awesomeness.

"All right then, let's get out of here. You want to ride with that thing on or put it in the car?"

"Car," I answer promptly and slip my new treasure off. It's brutal outside, even though it's almost 7:00.

"Why don't you grab that nightgown, too, while you're at it?" I look at Mom, and she shrugs, smiling.

Mom turns off the AC and the lights while I carry our reincarnated clothing to the Camry. I hang the gown on the little clothes hook in the back and gently fold my prize.

As I lay it down on the seat, something in the lining pokes me. I slide my hand across the deep inside pocket. Something long, skinny, and flexible is in there. I reach in and draw out a nighthawk feather, almost a foot long and beautiful—light gray near the quill, but darkening to brown, almost black at the tip. The quill is wrapped tightly in deerskin, secured with a turquoise bead. Where did it come from? Mesmerized, I drag the silky, dense edge across my arm, and lightning strikes.

A massive jolt slams through me and knocks me to my knees. A whirlwind of heat and stars envelopes me, roaring in my ears, sucking the breath from my lungs. Icy darkness follows, slamming me to the ground in a crack of thunder. Before I can react, or think, or even be scared, it's over. Gone. No longer on my knees in the dark, I stand in the shimmering heat. The jacket lies folded on the back seat, the feather resting on it as Mom locks the back door.

Mom didn't see it—if there was anything to see. If I didn't hallucinate the whole thing. I take a deep breath. Then another. I slip the feather, *that feather*, back into the lining of the jacket and stand up out of the car, still dizzy. What the hell *was* that?

I break out in a familiar sweat, that same creepy spider-feeling from this morning slithering up the back of my neck. I scan the backs of the other closed stores on our side of the square. Oh, God, did someone see that... seizure? Attack? Whatever it was? Then, as I close the car door, I see him and freeze.

Deep in the shade behind the mulberry tree, an even darker shadow lurks. He—definitely a he—is tall and bulky, but everything else about him is deep in shadow. I squint and lean forward a little, so he knows I see him and I'm not afraid. He is too far away to know that's a total lie, too far to know my head is pounding and my ears are full of buzzing bees. He steps back, dissolving into the shade. In a moment, I'm no longer sure he is still there or how much he saw, but I do know one thing.

Someone is watching me.

By the time I ride over to the Piggly Wiggly for Brian's beef stick cat tails, all I feel is tired and sweaty. The parking lot is practically empty. Just a motorcycle, a couple of cars, and a small red truck—wait, is it Una's? I park my bike and pass through the magic hissing Star Trek doors into the grocery store chill. I look around for Una but don't see her. Then again, she's so short that the store shelves could hide her completely.

I head straight for the essentials: cat tails and cream. I take eight beef sticks and scan the hanging packages of beef jerky. There is really only one good kind. The opposite of a beef stick, Virgil's beef jerky is thin and dry and delicate, not soaked in soy or sugar or preservatives—making it Mom-approved. Just beef, salt, and red or green chile. I pluck every package off the rack and head toward the dairy section.

No sign of Una. Just some grizzled, old biker getting coffee. By the soda machine, a couple of girls I recognize from school peek from behind each other and whisper together. The usual type—Pretty, Entitled, and Popular. Lorena and I call them The Peppers. Meticulous makeup, casually perfect hair that took an hour to style, halter tops, and high-heeled sandals they can barely walk in. The coven of snobs you find in every high school.

I round the corner, wondering why their eyes are sliding in my direction, and run smack into a guy standing in front of the motor oil, sending my load of meat snacks cascading to the floor. Giggles erupt from The Peppers.

"Sorry!" We both say at the same time, and I stoop to retrieve the precious cargo scattered around his cowboy boots. I jam the beef sticks in my back pocket and gather the rest in my arms. As I stand up, my eyes follow the long line of his faded jeans, the tight black T-shirt, his strong arms, and—wow—he is really tall. Then I see his face.

Oh.

The Peppers were peeking at him, not me. I look up into his dark eyes and take in his straight, slender nose, sharp cheekbones, and dark, unruly hair that hangs in his eyes and around his shoulders. My heart jumps sideways, cheeks flaming, before I realize I'm staring. He smiles; I drop half of the jerky again, and now I can't look at him at all.

"S-sorry," I stammer and start retrieving the packages again.

He squats down. "Here, let me help."

At least that's what I think he says, but I'm not sure because the blood rushing to my cheeks has also roared into my ears. He gathers a few packages in strong, capable hands, and when he stacks them in my arms, his hand brushes mine. It's warm and electric and makes my skin jump. Then he looks at me with those eyes and it's like I'm dissolving. I may just faint right here in the Piggly Wiggly.

We both rise to our feet, standing way too close, and I know my face is absolutely crimson, but his eyes shine, and he is smiling that crooked smile, and he smells like clean clothes and the hot sun. Surely he hears my heart give another lurch as he takes a step back, nods, grabs two quarts of oil, and heads for the cash register.

The Peppers grip their sodas, watching like tigers waiting for just the right moment to pounce on their next meal. While I try to recover my power of speech—which, by the way, is not easy while watching him walk away in those perfect-fitting jeans—The Peppers seize their opportunity and get in line behind him at the counter.

"Smooth move," one of them hisses as she slithers past me.

Shiny curls bouncing artfully around their shoulders and sly giggles bubbling from their lips, they circle their prey, practically purring as they move in for the kill. The biker gets in line and I follow, awkwardly clutching the beef jerky. Flames engulf my face while a renegade lock of hair sticks to my sweaty neck.

I peek around the line, feeling the three people between us like three brick walls, and an irresistible urge to shove all of them out of the way just to stand next to him grips me. Hot Guy pays for his oil, and I can't tear my eyes away as he exits through the magic doors, followed quickly by The Peppers.

By the time I get out, the motorcycle is gone, the red truck is gone, and a few more cars have pulled into the lot. No telling where he went. Oh well. He can't possibly be from Zia, anyway—nobody that cute lives around here. He's probably just passing through, trying to leave as soon as possible. I slip the Piggly Wiggly bag into my backpack and coast out of the parking lot. A block down the road, The Peppers roll past a stop sign on a side street in a silver car. Hot Guy is nowhere in sight. Ha! Their prey has escaped.

I can't wait to tell Lorena. A Hot Guy Sighting is rare in this town—especially one who stood three inches away and actually touched me. Replaying that moment in my head, my face flushes again and my heart jumps a little. It's definitely more than just the heat getting to me.

As I power-pedal down Valley Road toward home, it strikes me that one of Una's predictions has come true. I have just met a Mysterious, Handsome Stranger.

[File 201 130614 SANTA FE (15:11)]

Raven: Storefront squared away. Home devices active?

Trigger: Bugs inoperable. Interference on all frequencies.

Raven: Maintain visual surveillance and black bag the tablet ASAP.

Trigger: Roger that.

CHAPTER THREE

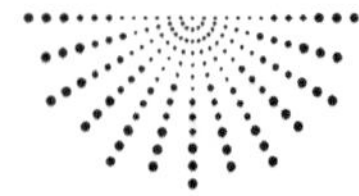

Brian's face is tomato-red from the heat. This is the second day he has walked home from the bus by himself, and I don't like it at all. Normally, I wouldn't give it a second thought, but I did almost get *killed* on the same road this morning. Zia is where you're supposed to die of boredom, not from government vans running innocent people off the road. I put my paranoia on hold, at least until after dinner when I can sort out the day.

Brian chatters about his day, proclaiming the new IMAX show at Space Camp, "Epic!" He feeds his hamster, Ophelia, describing the lunch they served the Space Campers as "bologna on cardboard with mayonnaise and sawdust chips." Sounds like the menu hasn't improved since last year.

From the kitchen, Mom cheerfully threatens us with a healthy dinner. Brian and I exchange a wary glance. The possibilities are endless and all disgusting—salads full of hairy weeds or fish with a mysterious gooey garnish that looks suspiciously like pond scum. We would have died a healthy death by now if it wasn't for the snack stash and the emergency green chile cheeseburgers.

"Did you go to the store? Did they have our stuff?" Brian whispers.

Boy, did they. I nod, remembering the Mysterious Handsome Stranger. "Two kinds of jerky and some cat tails."

"Mmm, a trifecta!" He grins. "That's my word for the week. From horse racing, when someone picks first, second, and third place correctly. Three similarly awesome things. Or similarly awful."

Mom skips the hairy salad and breaks out the whole wheat pizza crust instead. She whips up fresh sauce with tomatoes and herbs from the garden, and we each pile our favorite ingredients on our sections of the pizza. Mom spreads a little sauce on her part, and crumbles bits of good-for-you nasty tofu, some peppers, sliced olives, and a few molecules of cheese. Mine, however, has ground beef, onions, peppers, and a small mountain of mozzarella. Brian, the diplomat, puts a little bit of everything on his section, and Mom slides it into the oven. Soon the seductive smell of fresh pizza winds through the house, chasing away the last echoes of the thunderbolt in my head.

After dinner and a round of dominoes, I hang the nightgown in Mom's room and drape the leather jacket across the back of my desk chair. Somehow it doesn't belong in a closet. It feels even softer and smoother than before. I touch the sleek lining and run my finger along the spine of the hawk feather underneath. It's weird—my heart races, but not from fear. I have to see if it will happen again.

You can do this. I take a deep breath, bracing myself, and slip my hand over the edge of the pocket to run my fingertips down the length of the feather.

Doo nt'e da. Nothing. The Apache word is a wisp of air on my lips.

No lightning, no dizzying darkness, no nausea. So that dizzy spell by the car was just the heat after all. I let out my breath and carefully draw the feather from its nest. It really is beautiful—fragile and strong at the same time. The Déjà Vu dream catchers and other souvenirs use dyed turkey feathers mostly, but this is the real thing.

And from a hawk, which is weird. Wrapped ceremonial feathers like this are usually eagle feathers. A tingle of static tickles my hand as I lay it on my headboard. A nighthawk for a Night Hawk.

I plug my phone into the charger and finish getting ready for bed. I ignore Mom's organic tooth gel and squeeze out a blob of super-strong, nuclear-whitening toothpaste, the kind Brian calls Blisterine. He's blaring Mozart tonight—Mozart for math homework. I set aside the stress-free, happy berry-flavored stuff for him.

At 11:30, my phone buzzes: Lorena. Finally! But as I look at the glowing phone, I decide not to tell her about what happened when I first touched the feather until we can actually talk. It's too complicated for texting, and she will get all New-Agey weird on me and say something that's exactly what I'm already thinking. I *definitely* won't tell her about someone watching me, either. The more I think about it, the dumber it sounds. Why would anyone be spying on me and my so-called life?

I press the inbox button on my stone-age phone.

LORENA

Hey V!! Back from Coronado Island finally, water was freezing. My hair looks like a freak show. We cruised around n went to in/out burg. Double-double and fries yummm

Poor Lori, OMG your life sucks.

Going to Sea World tomorrow. How's work?

Well, I got run over on the way in today, but other than that

WTF? Are you ok?

Yeah, just a scrape.

U need a BF to drive you around. Any hot tourists?

One today at PW. Tall, gorgeous, def not
from around here!!

U never know. Are u going to learn the
cards this year?

Never lol Hey but I got my palm read. One
of Mom's friends, the jewelry lady

FINALLY. What did she say?

The usual. I have adventures and true love
coming. A secret talent.

I bet! Hahaha

My talent is hiding junk food from Mom.
Keeping Brian normal.

Tell Brian to wait for me, no hooking up with
those space camp chicks ;-D

Hooking up? LOL they're not even in 4th
grade. Don't be corrupting my bro!!

U know i <3 Brian. He's my best boyfriend,
my BBF. Anything good come in?

Cool leather jacket Mom let me have

Nice! Girly or biker?

Biker, duh. Sending u a pic. There was a
hawk feather in the lining, how cool is that?

LOVE! Kinda steampunk. A real feather?

yep

Hawk for a Hawk. It's a sign.

(And there it is.)

Yeah right

> Hawks are spirit messengers. Spirits trying to tell you something

> Telling me California has infected your brain AGAIN

> OMG guess what, Dad's gonna let me get my license while I'm here!!!

> Awesome. I prob have to wait til I'm 30.

> Mom calling, gotta go. Ttyl xoxo

> nite xoxo

Lorena is my best friend, but talking to her when she's in California with her dad is depressing. She's all happy and bubbly, and I'm all... alone. She will come home with a tan and beachy highlights in her hair, which is wild and curly like Mom's. She will do all kinds of fun stuff with her dad. She will have new clothes, a new laptop, new jokes and sayings from friends I don't know, the latest iPhone, and now her driver's license. Meanwhile, I will be exactly the same.

Mom says I can't get my license because of the high insurance rates here in New Mexico, and I have to wait until I'm eighteen. I know, it's just another year, but it's not just the license. It's everything technology related. Mom likes to stay off the grid, so the Night Hawks are like the Amish of social media.

My phone is definitely not smart; it's more like a dumb-phone—talk, text, and pics only. Brian has a dumb-phone, too, and even though Duke University gave him a brand-new tablet for his genius-boy classes, it has restricted internet with access to only the Duke server and links to a few sites he uses for school. Mom's one concession to the 21st century is her laptop, which is pretty much for Déjà Vu business only.

I don't know why my basically cool mom insists on living as off-the-grid as possible. I guess after Dad, she likes being able to retreat from the world—which is great for her, but sucks for me. My miniscule online life depends on Lori's smartphone and computer, so without her I'm basically doomed to social oblivion. Not that I actually *have* a social life, but a computer and a driver's license would definitely help.

Dad would have taught me to drive. He always pushed me to try things and not be afraid. When we were stationed in New Jersey, he taught me to ride a real bike, a two-wheeler. I was barely six.

I close my eyes, remembering my kindergarten fingers clutching the handlebars and the dark, gravelly asphalt passing below. His big, warm hand gripped my back, and his smooth, deep voice breathed calm into my terrified ear. "Look up, Vivi. Look where you're going. I won't let you fall, I promise. Look up."

I pedaled as hard as I could and broke free. I was flying! But a patch of sand snatched my bike out from under me, and the next thing I knew, my hands were digging into the asphalt. My front wheel was still spinning as I sat up, a burning trickle of dark blood oozing from where a sharp clam shell had sliced my knee. When Dad got to me seconds later, I looked up at him with a lump in my throat.

"I was flying," I told him, as the lump swallowed me up and disappointment pushed hot tears down my cheeks.

"You sure were!" He crouched and opened my tiny hand in his strong, calloused palm. "Looks like you got a little road rash too." His dark eyes twinkled. "Congratulations! You're not really a bike rider until you get some road rash. Hold it—you have a pretty good cut there." He rolled up his red bandana and tied it around my knee, then tipped up my chin in his hand, examining my face.

"Any broken bones? All your toes still there?" He wiggled the end of my sneaker and held up his hand, waving two fingers. "How many fingers do I have?"

I giggled. "Six?"

Dad laughed, helping me up. "Okay, road warrior, get that bike up. We need to head home."

I wrestled the bike upright. "Hop on," he said cheerfully, but I hesitated. My hands stung, and my knee throbbed. I looked up at him. He waited, his bronze face as patient as a tree. I climbed on again and was relieved to feel his arm around me as I pressed slowly on the pedals. His voice was soft in my ear.

"Vivi, you know what to do. Watch out for the sand traps this time." I pushed out from under his arm and rode home, not quite flying, but by the time I made it down the block to our house, I was smiling again.

I rub my knees, still tender from today's spill on Valley Road. Dad would have taught me to drive as soon as I could see over the dashboard. He would have been patient, but he wouldn't have let me chicken out. He would have taught me to be safe. He would have shown me how to navigate around the sand traps.

Dad was a Navy Corpsman, a career sailor and medic. He used to joke that whenever there's trouble, they send in the Marines—and then they send the corpsmen in to save the Marines. I always wondered what was up with those Marines, and whenever he left, I would cry and think, *Why can't they save themselves?* He missed three of my birthdays and almost didn't get home in time when Brian was born. When his helicopter went down, my world collapsed into a tiny, suffocating tunnel of pain. For years afterward, I tried desperately to find him in Dreamland. Sometimes when I called him I thought I heard his voice, but he was always just out of reach.

I don't miss him every waking minute of the day. Not anymore. At first, I missed him so much I could hardly breathe. I did everything I could think of to keep him near me. He didn't want me to ever cut my hair, so I didn't, even though you're supposed to when someone dies. He stepped outside at dawn to greet every new day, so I began to do it too. His old iPod goes with me everywhere, because the classic rock, vintage heavy metal, and Native American flute somehow feels like it holds his heartbeat. After a while, I slowly got used to him being gone.

I look over at the leather jacket, still hanging across the back of my chair. Mom said he had one like it, and for a moment I pretend it's his, even though I know there's no way. Feather or no feather, letting myself think like this just digs up old pain... but still.

I peel back the covers, turn off the lamp, and slide into my cool sheets. I drift off, spinning lightly into sleep. My room fades completely

Always, the first thing I see in Dreamland is the crystal-clear veil of a million stars. The smell of the pines is clean and sharp. The air is brisk, but the warmth of my blanket curls around my legs and settles across my shoulders as I feel the ground become solid beneath my feet. The sounds of the night mountains wash over me. The wind hisses gently through the towering trees, lifting my hair and sending lavender fireflies skipping down my shoulders, out to the twilight edges of my dream world where a night hawk spirals down from the smiling, silver moon. A broad swoosh of feathers sweeps a tendril of cigar smoke around me as soft footsteps come close, and a gentle voice says,

-I'm so glad I found you. I knew we could do this, Vivi.

-Dad?

The trees shimmer with a new, silvery glow that seems to outline each and every pine needle as his warm, familiar hand envelopes mine.

-Walk with me.

CHAPTER FOUR

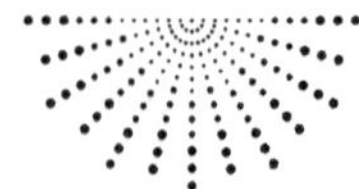

WE WALK. The forest bows low and steps back before us, the twinkling trees and bushes creating an instant path wherever we go. Our feet barely touch the ground, leaving a trail of luminescence over the mountains. Against a lighter sky, the forest gives way to scrub pines and leafy acacia, and the ground is a deep, sandy red. Gigantic spires of blood-and-gold sandstone loom over us.

-Dad, where are we?

-My part of Dreamland, sweetheart.

Huge boulders of white quartz and turquoise dot the landscape, while tiny pieces of glittering, black obsidian pave a faint web of trails across the red sand, as far as the eye can see. I've never been here before, and it's breathtaking.

-We can get into each other's dreams? For real?

Dad squeezes my hand.

-For us, this is as real as when we're awake. Hold onto my hand and watch your footing. It can be tricky when you first step into someone else's dream, but it gets easier. He's right; this place feels odd, as if the gravity here is somehow uneven.

-*But Dad, what* is *this?* This is no ordinary dream, or even a vivid nightmare.

-*It's the next step, honey. It's called dreamwalking. Some of us are born with it, like you and me. Others learn how. Even for us, it takes a lot of time and practice. You were always able to do everything, Vivi. You're very strong, but you're going to have to be even stronger now. Things are happening quickly.*

-*What things?*

-*It's Brian. It's not safe for him anymore. They're looking for him, and they may be there already. We can only walk like this for a short time before they know we're here, so I have to talk fast.* A curly wisp of Baby Brian smell tickles my nose.

- *'They' who? Who is it?*

A high-pitched *beep beep beep* wrenches us apart. I spin out through the stars and crash-land into my bed as the garbage truck outside shifts gears and roars forward from the front of our house to the neighbor's. Sunlight pushes against my blinds. The clock reads 7:50. My brain scrambles for a moment—then I sit straight up in bed.

What *happened?* That dream! The exhilarating, sharp smell of evergreen trees, the cool breeze, and the glittering stars are always part of Dreamland. But that strange silvery glow that outlined every living thing... and Dad. Not the I-miss-you-Dad, the one I feel in my heart every day; this was different. He was listening to me and talking back. He was *breathing.*

So glad I found you. I knew we could do this.

Kitchen noises drift in with the smell of coffee. Mom and Brian are getting ready for work and Space Camp. The blender whirls. The day has begun, but half of my brain lingers deep in the glittering, dark warmth of my dream.

Dad.

I grab some boy shorts and a bra from my drawer and hunt for my cutoffs. I dig out an ancient pink tank top, stick my feet in my favorite pink checkered Vans, and then turn to pull the covers up on my bed. There it is, stretched out delicately across the maple headboard as if nothing happened last night. That feather. My heart jumps and Lorena's words echo in my head. *Hawks are spirit messengers.*

I groan aloud. "Stop!" I am not going to get all freaked out over this one weird dream. But that thunderbolt yesterday, whatever it was, and now this. Are they related?

How can they not *be related?* Lorena counters in my head.

"Shut. Up," I tell her through clenched teeth.

The jacket rests patiently on the chair. I still don't want to hang it up in the closet, so it can live there for a few more days. As I put the feather back in its pocket-nest, Dad's voice whispers in my head. We can do *this* again—*this.* What did he call it?

Dreamwalking.

I close my bedroom door and head for the kitchen, the strong coffee fumes already clearing the fog from my head.

Brian. Something about Brian.

"Rise and shine," Mom greets me cheerfully from the table. A magazine lies open in front of her, next to her phone. The morning sun streams in, tinting her cloud of light brown hair Irish-princess-red, and coffee steams in one of her favorite handmade mugs.

Brian is already dressed for Space Camp in a neon green New Mexico International Spaceport shirt and cargo pants. His wavy hair has been braided and gelled into temporary submission, and his backpack lies by the door, the jagged edge of a cat tail wrapper sticking out by the zipper's end.

"Hey, V."

"Hey, B."

Mom swirls a tall glass of... something. Pale green froth with little specks of some darker stuff, possibly seaweed. Ugh. Brian's got some wheat toast and is shoveling scrambled eggs into his mouth, so all is not lost. But a small glass of the green slime sits ominously in front of him.

"What's that?" I ask, as neutrally as possible. Too curious, and she might make me try it. Too suspicious, and she might make me try it.

"A Noni-juice cleanse I'm doing for a few days. It has kelp and yogurt, some protein powder, aloe, honey, chia seeds, and a few blueberries. Want some?" I look at Brian. His glass has the telltale slime track of one swallow. He shrugs almost imperceptibly. Translation: it's pretty bad but didn't make him gag outright.

"I'll taste some of Brian's." I pop bread in the toaster and grab the jar of peanut butter and a handful of blueberries. "What's on the list for today?"

"Weed the chile garden and get some water on the flowers before they die, please." She flips a page, and the cover catches my eye—it's not a magazine, but the catalogue from Cottonwood Springs Community College. "Summer Continuing Education." Mom catches me looking and smiles her enchanting You-Are-Going-To-Love-This smile.

Uh-oh.

"Vivi, you did such a wonderful job on the sign. People commented on it all day long. It gave me an idea."

Oh, no. Last summer's "idea" was going to Las Cruces for a class on auras: seeing them, interpreting them, healing them, photographing them. Mom and I went every week to the Karma Collision, a bigger version of Déjà Vu, where a dozen earnest people studied everything about auras. Well, a dozen minus me, the aura infidel. I gave it an honest try anyway, for Mom's sake, but I never saw a single one. Mom practiced relentlessly and declared that Brian's aura is mostly yellow with streaks of bright green. According to her, my aura is purple and gold—a deeper version of her lavender and yellow—and such a vibrant color combination shows strong intuition. Right now, that purple and gold intuition wants me to jump on my bike and ride like the wind.

"You have such a strong sense of color, honey. I'm thinking you could paint a mural for the front wall. Something people could see from all around the square."

Cautious, I pause my urge to flee. "What kind of mural?"

"Whatever you want. Something celestial, like the sign. Something with a welcoming energy, you know?"

My toast pops up. I slather peanut butter on both pieces and take a bite. "Hmmm."

"I know you've never done anything that big, but what do you think?"

The peanut butter glues my mouth together, and I grab Brian's glass, swallowing a shot of Mom's concoction. Contrary to what his shrug indicated, this stuff is *hideous*. Sour and grassy, with a bitter aftertaste. Didn't she say there was honey in this? My "bleccch" face begins forming, but Brian shoots me a criminally innocent look, so I shift gears and give him the "I'll get-you-later" squint instead. Gah, this stuff is so gross! But I swallow and shake my head.

"Mom, you have outdone yourself there." I put down Brian's glass and pick up a coffee mug, hoping to scald out the taste of the fungus juice. "But, yeah, I could do that. I could make a few sketches and see what you think, but I'm not exactly sure about how to paint them on a stone wall."

"Yes, I was thinking about that too. I think a little professional advice would help, don't you?

More peanut butter toast, so I just nod. "Mmm-hmm." Then I freeze. Too late. Ninja Mom has struck again.

"I'm so glad you agree. I signed you up for this painting class at Community College." Mom smiles, pointing to a spot in the catalogue. "I just reserved your spot and paid them. You'll need to go online later today and finish the registration part."

"But Mom, what about work?" I protest feebly through the peanut butter, even though it's a lost cause.

Mom waves away my protest. "The class is Monday, Wednesday, and Friday, starting next week. You can work Tuesday, Thursday, and Saturday, just like we planned. It's perfect!" She beams triumphantly and finishes her Noni Fungus Ninja Slime. "I'll leave the laptop here, so you can finish registering today." She tilts her head toward Brian and says, "Go brush your teeth, and let's go." Standing up, she adds, "You guys also need to clean the patio when Brian gets home."

Brian turns to me. Our eyes lock and widen, and we both chime merrily, "Yes, Mother!" like the subservient little patio-cleaners we are.

A few minutes later, they are out the door, and I have the whole day ahead of me with a very short to-do list. Lots of time to think about the mural and the art class. I'm not against taking the class. I just hate it when someone else decides what I need to do and hooks me into doing it. It's the principle of the thing. I like making my own decisions, the way I do in my dreams. But lately, even Dreamland has been as slippery as New Mexico magic—until Dad showed up.

I have lots of time today to think about that, too.

I feed Ophelia a corner of my peanut butter toast and a blueberry. She gobbles the toast and noses the berry suspiciously before hiding it under her hamster wheel. I refill my coffee and slip out into the backyard. The air is still cool and fresh, with only a hint of the blistering heat to come. The neighbor's enormous cottonwood tree shades half of the yard, while their also- enormous orange tomcat lolls in a sunny spot, blinking his slanted green eyes at me.

"Hey, Rufus."

"Meh." He acknowledges me languidly and closes his eyes.

I water the jalapenos, the marigolds, and the hot-pink zinnias. As I pull weeds, I retrace my steps through last night's dream. This dream—this "dreamwalk," as Dad called it—was rich and three-dimensional, clearer than any lucid dream and stronger than any nightmare I've ever had. His warm hand molded around mine as if he was awake and alive. *I felt it.*

I roll up the hose and brush the dirt from my knees. There's a faint bruise from yesterday alongside a thin, pale permanent question mark from that New Jersey bike lesson. As I look at the dirt on my palms, the garden shimmers and dissolves as the sun goes dim. My hands turn clean and small, wrinkly from my bath and holding on to warm covers. I'm in my old bedroom, and the only light filters in from the soft golden night-light in the hall. The scent of lavender bubbles lingers in the bathroom, and the tang of the ocean drifts through the window.

Dad leans over my bed and kisses my forehead. He smells faintly of dark, scratchy cigar smoke.

"Ready for Dreamland?" he asks as he always does. I yawn and nod. Sleep is creeping up on me, soft and fuzzy.

"Where are you going tonight?"

"Six Flags!" Mom and Dad took me there for my birthday, before Baby Brian came. Ferris wheel, funnel cake, and fireworks. The Six Flags in Dreamland is almost as fun.

Even in the dark, Dad's smile breaks through. "Will you try again tonight, Vivi?"

"It's hard," I tell him. He wants me to stop in the middle of a dream and look at my hand. I thought it would be easy, but it's not. Most of the time, I can't remember to do it, and when I do, it feels like I'm pushing a heavy chair across the living room with my forehead. Then I wake up.

"You can do it, Vivi, I know you can. When you reach for the cotton candy, look right at your hand."

"Funnel cake," I correct him sleepily, as I nod off.

Startled, I open my eyes to the bright sunlight and cobalt sky, and there are my hands, just as they are, dirty and pale against the background of green grass. The vision departs as quickly as it came.

This is what I always knew you could do.

Dad always had ideas about where to go and what to do in dreams, not just how to change the bad ones. He told me how to fly to Grandma Lily's in Arizona, and how to go to Six Flags. Be a hawk, he would say. Float up to the sky. Keep your eyes open, look at where you want to go, and push like crazy. It took me months before I could find my hand, though—find it and still stay in the dream. But I finally got it, and after I did it a few more times, I realized I could do more than just go places, more than just sculpt and paint the layers of Dreamland. The wild animals that live in Dreamland, the strays who wander in from somewhere—I can make them do things. Come. Go.

Find this, show me that. Every command produces specks of radiant color and pulses of light.

Nobody knows this, but sometimes if I push very carefully, smoothly—like slipping a heavy deadbolt into its slot—I can push people too. Not Mom. Not Brian. But kids from school, the guy at the Dreamland Six Flags Ferris Wheel—sometimes even Lorena—I can make them say and do things.

In Dreamland, I make things happen.

I wash my hands in the kitchen sink and grab a hat from a peg inside the garage. Before I register for Mom's art class, I'm going to need fortification from Blake's Lotaburger—home of the world's best take-out green chile cheeseburgers.

As I sail down Valley Road on my bike, the sun simmers in the sky, burning away the last wisps of my dreams and memories. I fly past the turn to Brian's bus stop and enter the pecan orchard. It's been irrigated, and the black trunks spangled with luminous green leaves are reflected upside down in a green, gold, and black mirror of still water, creating a parallel world. By tomorrow, that second world will have sunk into the dirt, but today it's the Magic Forest.

When I pass the Piggly Wiggly, I scan the parking lot for the Mysterious Handsome Stranger. His eyes. His smile. His hands... well okay, *everything* about him is totally hot, and I can't help hoping he wasn't just passing through.

Like I told Una yesterday, I don't have admirers. I did have a boyfriend last year for a few months. Rick's dad was in the Air Force, and we had a bond that all military kids have— "gone" means something different for us than it does for civilian kids, and the TV news from far away matters. We made out a little and texted nonstop. Being clueless, I had to have Lori coach me on everything. She is a fearless flirt, while I'm pretty much tongue-tied after, "Hi," if I really like a guy.

Rick asked me to homecoming and bought me a mum the size of a war drum, strung with teddy bears, feathers, and bells. When he hung it around my neck, I felt uneasily like the prize cow at the county fair, but at least everyone knew I had a boyfriend.

Halfway through the homecoming dance, we went out to the car where Rick flashed his cute smile and produced a flask from under the seat.

"Look what I got for us," he said, waving it proudly. "Fireball." A few swallows later—I had one, he had four—we had a difference of opinion about where his hands belonged. Things went downhill pretty fast after that, but Lori and her date gave me a ride home, the World's Biggest Mum went into the trash, and my love life was over before it had even begun. Mom declared she knew Rick was up to no good all along, because matching a Taurus (me) with a Capricorn (him) was just asking for trouble.

I haven't gone out with anyone since, but some astrological drama might be worth the risk with the Mysterious Handsome Stranger. For a brief, deranged moment, I *will* him to simply appear on the road. Better yet, he should just *show up at my house*.

My stomach growls me back to reality and I push MHS out of my mind. Pedaling quickly to Blake's, I wish for the millionth time that I had that Dreamland power in real life—the power to make people do what I want. But right now, I'll settle for a cheeseburger.

CHAPTER FIVE

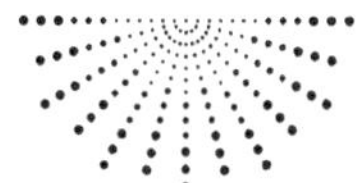

AFTER POLISHING off my burger and a peach milkshake, I clean the kitchen and do a load of laundry. I'm feeling pretty virtuous as I sit down at the table with Mom's laptop and the college catalogue to finish registering for the art class. Our Neanderthal Wi-Fi only works at the southeast corner of the house, which usually means the kitchen table or Brian's room.

I log in and click on the bookmarked college website. Name, birthdate, a few more assorted crucial numbers, and poof—I have officially beaten Brian into college. I check out Lorena's pictures of Coronado Island and yesterday's In-n-Out lunch on Instagram. I already know the drill. Selfies will morph from Lori and her dad to Lori and a bunch of surfer types—her summer BFFs.

I Google "lucid dreaming" for the thousandth time, but there's nothing new. Same with "astral traveling." That seems closer, but still not exactly right. I research dream sites a lot, but they're all New Age supernatural woo, generic dream interpretation or pervy Freudian stuff. I guess I'm hoping there might miraculously be something to explain last night. The dreamwalk.

I Google "dream walking" and get that Toby Keith song on

YouTube. Country music isn't really my thing, but I play it anyway. It fits my mood today, but I doubt Toby Keith ever went dreamwalking with someone who's been dead for seven years.

There's another site where nothing ever changes. I click on Mom's bookmark, and the Navy Corpsmen Memorial site blooms on the screen.

There's Dad in full dress uniform, smiling in front of a flag. Ian Night Hawk, 1972-2007. Beloved husband of Summer, father of Vivian and Brian, son of Liluye. *Do not think of me as gone. I am with you still, in each new dawn.* Prayers offered up from fellow corpsmen and family friends in Eastern and Western Apache, also some in Navajo, along with the same pictures of him with his units from Desert Storm, Bosnia, and Iraq. The Desert Storm pictures look bleached out, but his lively smile makes him stand out from the other young, short-haired guys in fatigues—at least to me. The Bosnia picture is darker, with a few of the same guys from Desert Storm. But it's cold. Everyone sports pale faces and pink noses, bundled up in jackets, huddled together, but smiling—and Dad stands at the end near a campfire, his black hair covered with a watch cap and his hands shoved into the pockets of his brown leather jacket.

Wait, *wait, what?*

Trembling, I click on the picture, which doubles its size, but makes it grainy. I squint, and I swear it looks like the jacket. *My* jacket. The diagonal snaps, the straps around the wrists. The deep collar. My heart leaps. I feel a little dizzy as a shiver snakes its way down my spine. *Is it?* No, no, no. It is not even possible.

Remember, Mom told you Dad had a jacket like that. She told you.

I scrutinize it, marching my eyes across every pixel of that grainy picture until I'm cross-eyed. Everything *seems* the same, but I'm feeling extremely weirded out. And then a closer look at the collar—there's something on it. Something small and shiny. Another snap? My jacket doesn't have a snap on the collar. Or does it?

The indecision paralyzes me. *Don't just sit there, Vivian, go look.* I leap from the chair, grabbing the laptop, and head for my room.

Flinging my door open, I set the computer down on my desk, and open the blinds.

On the screen, the Chrome Tyrannosaurus growls, "Sorry, no connection." Gaaaah, I lost the Wi-Fi! I run back to the kitchen, clutching the laptop, but it's gone. I log in and click *Refresh*, but all I get is that maddening spinning wheel.

"Dammit!" I collapse on the kitchen chair, fuming, as the front door pops open.

"Home," Brian sings out. "Hungry!" Door closes.

"In here," I grumble. I look at the clock, which smugly informs me it's almost 5:00. I have spent all afternoon online with nothing to show for it. I snap the evil laptop closed.

Brian traipses into the kitchen, drops his backpack by the door to the garage, and then flops into the chair opposite from me, announcing, "Must. Have. Food." He tilts his head back, rolls his eyes, and in his best Homer Simpson voice, moans, "Me so HUN-GEE." He spies the laptop, becomes Brian again, and asks, "Did you register for that class? Mom sure ninja'd you good."

I am still mad. Mad at my dumb phone, the laptop—technology in general. And I'm still mad at the Peppers for getting between me and Mysterious Handsome Stranger, who seems to be setting up a permanent spot in my brain. And then here comes Brian, stomping into the middle of it all, reminding me of Mom's art class ambush and demanding to be fed.

Thank God, some things never change.

"Yeah, she did." I sigh loudly. "How about a PB and J?" Slathering the sandwich together, I turn and shoot him a menacing glare. "Oh, yeah. Thanks for warning me about Mom's fungus juice this morning."

His brown eyes are smug. "Knew you'd appreciate that."

"Dude. Let's get the patio done before the sun hits it. We can finish those Macaroonies before Mom comes home." A little incentive never hurts.

Brian smiles sheepishly. "Too late. I had differential equations to do last night. I needed fuel." Oh, right. Differential equations. I nod like I know what those are.

"I thought this was supposed to be Space Camp, not Math Torture."

"Nah, it was for Duke. I had assignments that had to be posted by midnight."

I pop Dad's iPod into the dock on the kitchen windowsill, hunt for some vintage AC/DC, and open the window. We lug the furniture off of the patio and then sweep quickly, screeching along with *Back in Black* and making up our own words.

Grab a broom, gonna clean, gotta scream 'cause we just can't sing!

The late afternoon sun seeks us out, pressing down on the patio roof. And even though we speed up, sweeping furiously to try and beat the heat, we fail. By the time we drag the patio furniture back into place, rivers of sweat have glued our clothes to our skin. Red-faced, we collapse on a pair of iron chairs and survey our work, gulping down cold sodas.

"You know, Vivi, this still isn't right." He burps loud and long, raking his hands through his sweat-darkened hair and making it stand on end.

"What are you talking about? It's fine." I burp right back, beating him by at least two seconds. Having a prodigy for a brother can be exasperating. Things can be perfect, but Brian's head for details means they are never quite perfect *enough*.

"Hold on." Brian leaps out of his chair and walks over to the side of the house. I close my eyes, annoyed, wondering what the brainiac is up to. It's hot and I'm tired, and he wants to clean some more?

A blast of water hits the wall above my head and cascades down, drenching me completely. My eyes fly open. He crouches on the edge of the patio, hose in hand, squirt nozzle set to "stun."

"Oops, I missed!" He giggles and then turns the hose directly onto my stomach.

"You are so *dead!*" I leap from my chair and chase him into the yard. He bolts ahead of me, turning around to squirt me every few steps, but I step on the hose, causing it to yank out of his hand. He shrieks and zigzags all over the yard while I pursue him relentlessly, finally grabbing the back of his T-shirt.

"Now, you die," I proclaim grimly and shove the end of the hose down the neck of his shirt, soaking him completely. "Revenge for the fungus juice!"

My hair hangs in my eyes, so I don't see the back gate open, and the blasting water mingled with our laughter muffles the sound.

"Hellooo!" Una walks toward us, carrying a brown paper bag. I drop the hose and Brian simultaneously, then shove the hair out of my eyes. Her wide face is smiling.

"Oh, hi!" Awkward. Yes, this is normal. We drench each other in the backyard all the time. "If you're looking for Mom, she's still at work."

Brian stands up and wrings out the edge of his dripping shirt. "Hi!" He waves, unfazed.

"Hi, Brian. Nice day for a water fight, huh? I brought some cantaloupe. Your mom said to drop it off here since you guys are home." Una wiggles the bag. "I knocked at the front door, but we heard you out here, so we came around. My nephew and I are headed up to Santa Fe for a couple of days, and I wanted to get these to you."

Nephew? The orphan? I look behind her and see a guy leaning against the rock wall, in the shade by the gate. Tall, in faded jeans, boots, and a maroon T-shirt. This is no scrawny waif, no pitiful Wimpy Kid.

Oh. My. God.

"Vivian, Brian, this is Lucas."

His eyes crinkle at the corners like his aunt's, as the Mysterious Handsome Stranger steps forward and uncrosses his arms to shake my hand. I am suddenly and acutely aware of the fact I look like a drowned rat with stringy hair plastered to my head and clothes stuck to me like wet paint. My face burns for the second time in two days as he takes my hand and stops my heart completely.

"Nice to meet you."

His fingers linger on mine, his warm hand calloused and strong. *Say something cool, Vivian.* I open my mouth, but nothing comes out. *Okay then, just say* something. I manage a squeaky, breathless, idiotic, "Umm, yeah. Hi," before Brian takes Una's bag and drags her toward the patio.

"Did Mom tell you I'm going to Space Camp?"

Lucas and I drop our hands. The late afternoon sun shines on his hair, raven-black, thick and straight like mine. "You look familiar," he says.

My heart flutters under his gaze. I know my wet tank top is showing everything, but his eyes are holding steady on my face, so I take a breath, push the dripping strands behind my ears and venture, "I think we ran into each other yesterday. Literally."

A smile spreads across his face. "The Piggly Wiggly."

"Yeah, I was on a jerky run. It's one of the basic food groups around here." My breath is trapped in my throat, but at least my voice is not betraying me.

Una and Brian are heading our way. Brian waves his hands around, explaining how the space station zero-gravity toilet works.

"Gotta run, guys. Santa Fe awaits," Una announces.

Already? My brain races for something interesting to say as we walk through the gate to the front yard. The red truck is out on the street, the bed sitting low with something heavy in it, covered with a tarp. What kind of load could they be hauling to Santa Fe?

As if reading my thoughts, Lucas says, "Metal sculpture for the Sunday artist market."

The Santa Fe Sunday Market is one of my ultimate artist fantasies. Besides the crafts and jewelry from a dozen Nations, the sidewalks around the square are crowded with local art for sale. Someday, maybe even mine.

"You're an artist?" I peek at his profile. It's easier to look at him if he isn't looking right at me.

"Sort of. Aspiring?" His voice is deep and smooth. "I signed up for a metalworking class at Community this summer. My aunt has a weird schedule, but I think I can work it in."

"Me too." Another brilliant reply. "I mean, I'm taking a painting class. And working at Mom's shop."

We reach the back of the truck, where a small bumper sticker announces, "IT'S A NATIVE THING." Lucas turns as he approaches the driver door and says, "Cool. When's your class?"

I'm finally able to look him in the eye and say, "Monday, Wednesday, and Friday mornings." No hint of the wobbly pudding that my knees have become.

"Mine too. Maybe we'll run into each other again." He smiles and looks at me a little longer than he really needs to. His eyes are warm, and I almost fall into them, but then he nods and gets into the truck.

I'm not sure he hears me say, "I hope so."

Wait until I tell Lorena.

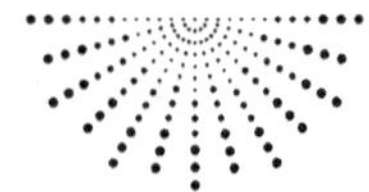

CHAPTER SIX

It's Brian's trifecta. Life sucks—times three.

Suckage Number One: When I call Lorena and tell her about MHS Lucas, she says, "Oh, cool!" then immediately bubbles over about some twenty-two-year-old surfer guy she met on the beach, and how they are going to go on the Universal Studios Tour together, and he's soooo smart ("He's graduating from *college*"). What kind of freakazoid college graduate would be going out with a high school girl? I listen to her gush on 'til it's time to go and tell her I'll text her after art class.

Suckage Number Two: There is definitely no snap on the jacket collar. But there is a little hole where a pin might have been. It looks so much like Dad's that even though I know it's impossible, my stubborn heart hopes maybe it's really his. I put it on a lot, and it just *feels* like him. I still can't put it in the closet. He said he'd be back and we would dreamwalk again, but it's been almost a week, and nothing. Was it really him or just a crazier-than-usual dream after all? Either way, it's definitely better than the thunderstorm nightmare.

How to find out about the jacket, I'm not sure, other than to just ask Mom, but I don't want to see that faraway look she gets when I mention Dad. Besides, we are crazy-busy at work. Apparently, word has gotten out, and Summer Hawk, Psychic Life Coach, is booked solid.

That helpful preppy-lizard, Jackson Connor, has been in three more times in the last two weeks. Once for another reading, and another to talk to Mom about the perils of doing renovations in an historic district. He buys something every time, including Una's rug—but last time, he also brought Mom her favorite acai-pomegranate slushee. It just seemed too... personal. There's something I don't like about him, besides his chilly handshake. To be honest, though, would I like him better if he brought us some Macaroonies instead?

Whatever. I wouldn't.

And now, here I am zooming down Valley Road again, heading for art class. I balance a big new sketchbook under one arm, which brings me to Suckage Number Three: I have no idea what to paint for the Déjà Vu mural, and I have no idea if Lucas will be there.

I spent way too much time getting ready this morning, digging for something to wear that makes me look awesome yet also shows I don't care about superficial stuff like clothes. Looking casually perfect requires a lot of work. I finally settle on a purple hippie-looking smock with a V-neck and flutter sleeves that Mom gave me. Instead of my usual thick ponytail, I make a loose French braid, pulling out a few strategically messy strands. I tint my eyelids the lightest wash of lavender and flick on a coat of mascara. My green eyes look huge, and I make a face at the mirror, smooching my glossy lips. I like what I see, but I'm not good at this, and just for a second, I envy the loathsome Peppers, who are experts in all things glamour. When I come out of the bathroom, Brian takes one look at me and raises an eyebrow.

"It's a *college* class, Brian," I explain unnecessarily. "There are *professionals* there."

"Professionals like *Lucas*." Brian grins as he singsongs the name.

I narrow my eyes and shoot him my best withering look. "Well he *is*. He sells his work, and that makes him a professional."

"Uh-huh." Brian is not fazed in the least. "I didn't say he wasn't."

I punch him on the arm on my way out of the bathroom. He snorts with laughter.

"Hey, V!"

I turn. "What!"

"You look nice."

"Oh, shut up."

"Get some Macaroonies, okay?" The mocking tone has disappeared.

"If I go there," I reply grudgingly. Our stash *is* dangerously low.

"See ya, Vivipara."

"Laters, Briarpatch."

Sigh. My 620 on the SAT reading section is a respectable score. However, Brian made a perfect 800—at the age of *nine*. Now I have to go look up what a vivipara is before he has to explain it to me.

I swing my bike into Community College and scan the parking lot for Lucas's red truck. A ball of uncertainty coils in my stomach when I don't see it anywhere. Lucas *has* to be here. I want to know I didn't waste a half-hour in the bathroom for nothing. I want to know if he really was looking at me the way I thought he was. Most of all, I want to see his smile again, the one that lit up the Piggly Wiggly and my back yard. The one that made my heart jump sideways.

That would totally make up for the "Life Sucks" trifecta.

Two hours later, I'm no better off than I was when I went in. There are fifteen people in my class, all of them way older than me. I have a list of supplies I need to buy, but still not even one idea for the mural, and no sign of Lucas. I peek into every one of the classrooms in the Fine Arts wing on my way out, and he isn't in any of them. A helpful Community College employee calls down the hall, asking if I need help finding something. *Ugh, only my dignity.* I shake my head.

I unlock my bike, prop my sketchbook under my arm, and decide to circle around the parking lot, over to the back side of the building, and see if his truck is there. This is *not* stalking. Something has to be in your sight in order to stalk it. This is just, um, checking thoroughly.

I swerve around the speed bumps, scanning the parking lot, and I almost ride right past his truck. It's parked, engine running, in front of a loading dock outside of Automotive and Welding. *Well duh, Vivi,* I scold myself. *Welding.* Where else would you be working on metal sculpture? I shade my eyes and peer into the deep shade of the platform.

"Hey, thanks man. See you later!"

He backs out of a double door, wrestling with a large twisted piece of steel. It looks like a truck fender that got caught in a wringer. But at least until Lucas turns around, I can look at him without having a heart attack. His navy-blue T-shirt, branded with "HEA-THEN" in red letters, stretches across his muscled back, and his legs look just as long as they did in the Piggly Wiggly. The wreckage slips out of his grip, and he swears as one corner of it hits the deck.

"Need some help?" I call out, hopping off my bike. He looks up quickly and sets the rest of the steel down, balancing the heavy load with one hand and pushing dark shocks of hair out of his face with the other. And then there it is, that smile. Oh!

"Hey, Vivian. How was your class?"

The flush rises from the back of my knees. "Not terrible. How was Santa Fe?"

"It was great. Actually, I *could* use some help. Can you back the truck up a little closer to the edge here while I hold this?"

I hesitate, then decide honesty is the best policy. "Lucas, umm, I can't drive...a stick shift." Okay, I didn't say *total* honesty.

He shakes his head. "It's not a stick. Just back it up another foot, okay?"

"Okay."

It's true I don't have a license, but I have moved the Camry for Mom a few times. A truck can't be all *that* different. I lean my bike and my sketchbook against the concrete loading dock and walk toward the truck. That familiar electricity slides up my spine, and I know he's watching, but this time it's nice and I'm glad I wore my best jeans. I hop into the truck and look in the rearview mirror to see Lucas gripping the hunk of metal again, twisting it to the edge of the loading dock.

"Okay, ready."

You can do this, Vivi. I shift into reverse, but the truck doesn't move. I tap the gas pedal, and the truck leaps back instantly. *Crap!* I slam on the brakes just as the tailgate bumps the loading dock, and Lucas yells, "Whoa!"

Oh my God, I am such an idiot. I slide against the back of the seat. My face is on fire and embarrassment wells up, threatening to submerge me. I peek in the rearview mirror, and he is standing there, straining to balance the hunk of metal with one hand, looking at the tailgate with his head tilted down so I can't see his face.

"Sorry, *sorry.*" I groan loudly at the mirror, but as he looks up he smiles. Okay, not like grinning wildly or anything, but a smile just the same.

"Vivi! Put it inPpark," he calls.

Duh. Is it possible to feel any dumber? I shift into Park, then he rolls the metal into the bed of the truck, laying it down gently. I open the door and slide out, wishing I could just sink into the parking lot, when Lucas hops over the side of the bed and lands in front of me.

"Hey." His eyes are kind. "Truck's okay. Are you?"

"Sorry. Yeah," I stammer. He is so close; the warmth of his body is like a force field as it touches my skin. "Lucas, I—"

I can't finish. All I can do is stare at him.

"You haven't driven very much, have you?" Now he is smiling again, though he's trying not to. Total humiliation.

"No. Not really." I look down. I can't look in his eyes. I can't think straight with him standing so close, much less talk like a normal person. Then I realize I'm looking at his belt buckle. I yank my gaze back up before he thinks... but where to look? That lean, wiry body or those strong shoulders? Jeez, even his collarbone is cute. I settle on his mouth, which is still smiling.

"Mom won't let me until I'm eighteen," I explain faintly.

His face turns mischievous. "Maybe you can't get your license, but you can still get some practice, right? I could give you a few lessons. I mean, if you want to?"

I look back up into his eyes, take a breath, and before I can change my mind, I pop my head up out of my pool of embarrassment and firmly say, "Yes. That would be awesome."

He holds my gaze for another fraction of a second. "Okay, then. How about now?"

Now? A driving lesson right *now?* I nod, shaking off the last drops of awkwardness. Lucas walks over to my bike and sketchbook, lifts them both into the truck, and then slams the tailgate closed. I hop back into the driver's seat again. This is going to be amazing.

"Hold on, Vivian." Lucas laughs as he comes back over. "I better drive 'til we get somewhere, umm, safe."

"Ha, ha, very funny. You volunteered for this," I remind him as I scoot over to the passenger seat. My cheeks burn, but I can't stop smiling. As we roll through the parking lot and jolt over the speed bumps, I stealth-glance at his profile. Those angular cheekbones, the long straight nose over that curvy mouth, and those strong hands on the wheel all make my heart beat faster. But I'll be okay—if I don't look at him for too long.

CHAPTER SEVEN

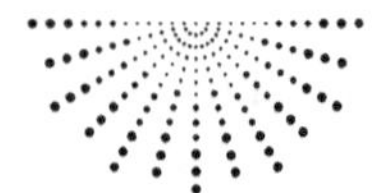

I PUT on my seatbelt and survey the alien landscape of Lucas's domain. There are a few spiral notebooks, a library book, and a Community College catalogue on the floor by my feet—the same one Mom ninja'd me with this morning. A tiny dreamcatcher sways from the rearview mirror, and a phone charger dangles from the dashboard. A backpack and a rolled sleeping bag sit behind his seat, along with some empty Piggly Wiggly cups, a quart of oil, a bag of trash from Blake's, and a roll of those blue paper towels mechanics use.

As if reading my mind, he comments, "Sorry, the truck's a mess. I haven't cleaned it since I got back from Santa Fe." His eyes gleam in triumph. "But I sold that sculpture."

"Hey, that's great! Are you taking this one up next weekend?"

He laughs out loud and looks over at me. "No, I haven't even started this one. I get the metal from the auto shop here, but I do most of the work at home. Then I bring it back here for the finish. They have tools I need."

"Wow, that's a relief. I was kind of wondering, but I didn't want to say anything, because what if it's like, your greatest piece ever, and to me it just looks like a hunk of metal?"

He laughs again. As we drive down Valley Road, the mangled fender makes scrapey clunking noises whenever we stop or start. The entrance to Zia Square is ahead on the right, but Lucas turns left.

"So, where are we going?"

"Out to the levee, but I want to drop this stuff off at home first."

"Home" turns out to be a small stucco house about a mile west of the square. Black-eyed Susans and purple coneflowers cluster around the mailbox, which reads "WOLFSONG" in faded letters. A short wrought-iron fence surrounds the yard, and two metal wolves guard the gate, their heads tilted to the sky. These are not stamped-metal roadside tourist wolves, but battered ribbons, twists and knots of metal transformed into fur and throats and ears and tails.

"Did you make those?" I can't stop looking at them. "They're beautiful."

Lucas nods. "Thanks. I make all kinds of animals."

Within a few minutes, his tools, a welding tank, and the future work of art are out of the truck, and we head to the levee. My mind races, searching for something to say.

"So, how long have you and Una lived here? You didn't go to Zia High, did you? "

Zia High has about 500 students total. He is a couple of years older than me, but if Lucas Wolfsong went to my school, I would definitely remember. So would Lorena, and all the Peppers too.

"No, we lived here when I was in elementary school, when my dad was stationed at White Sands. When he was deployed to Iraq, we moved to the reservation for a while. Then, California. After my mom, I went to live with Una in Albuquerque." His eyes watch the road, but for a split second they wander a thousand miles away.

"We lived in Whiteriver for a summer with my grandmother," I say, remembering the reservation's cool mountain pines and Grandma Lily's tiny, tidy home. "She still lives there, but we hardly ever go. Don't you miss it?"

"My parents grew up there, but we moved around a lot, so it's not really my home. You know how it is."

I know exactly how it is. The time we lived in Wildwood, not quite three years, was the longest we ever lived anywhere. For military kids, "home" is wherever you are.

"We came back here to my grandfather's house a few months ago. This place never changes—just as quiet as ever." He glances over at me and smiles. "But things are definitely looking up."

Things are looking up? What things? Just when I can almost relax around him, my heart ignites with pleasure, setting my cheeks on another slow burn.

We arrive at the long straight road that runs along the levee. Since it's not technically a "road," you don't technically need a license to drive on it. The river is low, but large, soggy-looking clouds are stacked up on the horizon, gathering behind the mountains. Lucas gets out of the truck, and I follow. When we meet in the front, Lucas nods his approval at the clouds.

"*Nagóltįįh.* It's going to rain."

I almost never hear Apache unless we go up to the Mescalero Reservation or to Grandma Lily's. I only know a little bit, but it always makes me homesick for a place I never really lived.

"I hope."

"If you stand still and watch, you can almost see the clouds grow," he observes. "You can smell it even before you see the clouds. The trees, all the cactus—everything alive—it's like they know for *hours.* Even before the clouds come, they open up all their pores, waiting. Like the whole valley is holding her breath." He breathes in. "Can you smell it?"

I take a deep, even breath. It smells like the desert, of sage and mesquite. But under the scorched desert smell, something else lurks. Anticipation? Something the slightest bit... wet.

"You're right, Lucas, I *can* smell it."

"Not everyone can. Just us—the desert people." He turns toward me. "You ready?"

"For rain? Always." I nod, watching the clouds. He's right—

they're rolling upward, blooming thick and pulsing even as we stand here. Slippery magic.

"Driving. Remember?"

"Oh, *driving*. Yes. Ready!"

While he explains how to adjust the mirrors, my brain spins cartwheels. He loosens his seatbelt a little and sits close to me, his arm behind me on the seat as he leans in and slowly coaxes me down the levee road. He smells like warm skin and clean clothes, and I can hardly keep my mind on the road. I clutch the steering wheel, white-knuckling it at first, but his voice relaxes me as he keeps talking low in my ear.

"You're doing great. You're a natural. Whoops, careful. Don't look at me. Look where you're going. That's it. You've got this."

Almost an hour later, I decide Lucas is right: things are definitely looking up. I have driven seven whole miles with his arm practically around me. I park in a spot by the bridge, and I park straight, too. Well, almost. The clouds in the west have turned dark, bruised-looking—and they're a lot closer. A cold breeze, the ancient signal that we have about ten minutes before all hell breaks loose, stirs the dust in the parking lot. We switch seats and decide to go back to Zia Square for slushees. Thunder rumbles in the distance.

I eyeball the books on the floor and nudge them with my toe. "Are you taking other classes?"

"Nah, not right now. Those are my dream books."

"Your what?"

"Dream books." He hesitates like he's not sure he should keep talking, then takes a breath. "I write down my dreams whenever I can remember them. There's a book there about what they mean. Well, one of them. I have a few." He sighs. "They aren't much help. They're compiled by anthropologists and come from all around the Nations, so they're pretty generic."

I pick up *The Native American Dreambook,* and it falls open to a dog-eared page: "Eagles, Hawks, Birds of Prey."

Lucas glances over at the page. "'Birds are considered spirit messengers,'" he quotes, echoing Lorena in an exaggerated, careful tone, like he's narrating a documentary for kindergartners.

I tear my eyes away from the pen-and-ink drawings of birds and feathers—long, silky, familiar-looking feathers—and ask, "Do you know what other people's dreams mean? You can interpret dreams?"

He laughs. "No, I totally suck at it, but Una can. My dad used to call her The Dreamcatcher."

My gaze jumps to the one hanging from the mirror, and his meets mine in the reflection.

"He said sometimes a dreamcatcher is a person. Una doesn't need books. She just knows." This doesn't surprise me at all. Sometimes people do. I never *just know* anything, but it certainly fits Una.

"So, you're having weird dreams?"

Lucas doesn't answer. He doesn't even seem to be breathing, and an odd, tingly feeling works its way up my neck.

Finally, he clears his throat. "Yeah. It's hard to explain, but I've been dreaming about my dad. You know he's MIA, right?"

The tingly feeling reaches into my hair like sharp fingernails. "Mom told me, yeah."

"Well, he was kind of like Una, but different. Do you know what lucid dreaming is?"

My mouth goes dry and my throat closes up, but I manage to whisper, "Yes. When you can control some things in your dreams."

Is he a lucid dreamer too? And he's dreaming about—

"My dad could do that. He taught me some before he left, but I'm not very good at it. Not like him. He could go places and do things in his dreams."

"My dad could do that too." I stare at him, my heart hammering almost as loud as the approaching thunder.

Lucas doesn't say anything as we pull into the gravel alley behind Déjà Vu. Fat drops splat on the windshield. I can't breathe; it feels like my heart might leap out of my chest. Lucas stops the truck, his face completely still. He looks straight ahead, exhales slowly, then turns to look at me. His eyes are two dark wells of confusion. "I know this sounds crazy, but sometimes I think he's still alive."

My breath's trapped in my throat. Trying not to panic, I finally strangle, "Why do you think that? I know he's MIA, but it's been—"

"Seven years. I know. Like *your* dad, Vivian. They went missing the same week."

I shake my head. Mom and Una have known each other for a couple of months, but somehow he must have gotten the story wrong.

I hate even saying the words. "My dad's not missing, Lucas. He was killed in action." The raindrops pelt the truck in earnest now, and my racing pulse matches the staccato taps on the roof.

He nods, and his mouth briefly forms a grim, twisted line. "That's what they told us too. He broke his leg, and after they put on his cast, Joseph Wolfsong somehow supposedly wandered out of Bagdad Hospital without anyone seeing him. Yeah, right—you know how many people he'd have to go through to get out of there?" He grips the steering wheel. "Then a car with an IED explodes a few blocks outside the zone, and his tags are found at the scene. Nothing else. So officially he's MIA—missing, presumed dead."

Hearing his father's name jolts me. Apaches don't usually say the names of the dead—but he looks so bitter, so lost. Loss and bitterness have regular battles in my heart. I swallow, hoping the hard ball in my throat doesn't get any bigger.

"But Lucas, why do you think he's alive? After they told us about Dad, there were times I was sure they were wrong, and he would come back. I just *knew* it would all be a terrible mistake. But he didn't. It wasn't." I close my eyes, and for a moment the grainy video replays in my head the way it played over and over on every TV channel: the chopper spiraling down wildly through the dark, greasy smoke, sinking behind some trees, and the huge ball of fire blazing afterward. My thoughts race as thunder blows open the sky above us, and the splattering drops become a roaring downpour.

What if it *was* a mistake? What if he's really out there? The dream. *That dreamwalk.*

Determination pushes the pain and confusion out of his eyes as Lucas shakes his head.

"Because it's different. It's like he's really *there*. He even said it was a different kind of dream. He called it dreamwalking."

The hair on the back of my neck stands up. The prickly feeling curls around my shoulders and the top of my head. I clutch the seat on either side of my knees with icy hands and try to control my jagged breathing. I look over at him, and his eyes meet mine, soft and concerned in his angular face. Some of the dizziness recedes, and I can breathe again, so I ask, wobbly, "Why... why are you telling *me* about this?" I keep my eyes glued to him. Now, instead of not being able to look at him, I can't look away.

His hand is strong and warm as he lays it on top of mine and intertwines our fingers. Our hands fit like locking puzzle pieces, and for a split second, I can't tell where each of our hands begin and end. "Because—"

BAM!

The back door to Déjà Vu flies open, and the wind slams it into the wall. My gaze darts from Lucas to the porch. Mom is framed in the doorway, and through the downpour, she waves for us to come in.

"Come on, get in here, you two! It's raining cats and dogs, and it's not stopping for a while," she calls out, just barely audible over the roar of the storm. A shadow moves behind her, and Jackson Connor's face appears in the doorframe over Mom's shoulder. I groan softly. Him again?

Our hands slip apart, but I grab his wrist. "You better tell me," I whisper fiercely.

"I will, I swear. As soon as we can get out of here."

Lightning crackles through the sky and thunder explodes like a cannon. I take a deep breath. Our eyes lock, as he counts, "One, two, three—go!" We bolt out of the truck and up the porch steps, through a barrage of cold, stinging rain-bullets. Soaked, we spill through the doorway into the Déjà Vu kitchen.

CHAPTER EIGHT

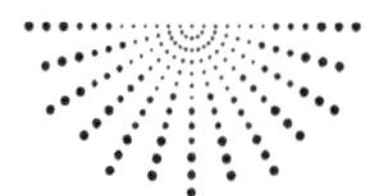

THE KITCHEN IS warm and fragrant with coffee and melon. Jackson Connor peers at a weather website on Mom's laptop. I try to camouflage my agitation by babbling about the rain, while Mom hands us a couple of next-to-useless dish towels.

"Here you go. Whew, it's bad out there! I saw the truck and thought it was Una, but I'm really glad to see you two." She smiles her kind Mom smile and extends her hand. The sudden humidity has spun her curly hair into a halo, and her soft, rosy dress makes her look like Glinda, The Good Witch of the North.

"You must be Lucas. I'm Vivian's mother. It's nice to finally meet you."

Lucas shakes her hand, rubbing the towel through his dripping hair with the other one. "Nice to meet you, Mrs. Hawk," he says, sounding completely normal—as if the universe had not just threatened to unravel out in the truck.

"No, no, please call me Summer," Mom protests, and turns toward her guest. "Jack, this is Una's nephew, Lucas Wolfsong."

"Hello, Lucas. Heckuva a storm here—we were just tracking it on the radar." He gestures toward the laptop. There are mugs and plates on the counter, with the remnants of Una's cantaloupe, feta crumbs, crackers, and a sliver of prosciutto on one of them. So, Jackson Connor has bumped it up from slushees to lunch. Irritation needles me. *I do not like green fruit and ham,* I think childishly, *I do not like you, Jack-I-Am!*

I scold myself: *Act normal.* He hasn't done anything but be nice to us, and plus, he buys stuff. He's only here for a while, anyway.

"Hi, Mr. Connor." See? That didn't even hurt.

Mr. Connor flashes his professionally whitened smile and shakes Lucas's hand. "That makes me sound like some old guy. *Jack,*" he corrects, then displays all seventy-two of those shiny shark teeth again. "Your Aunt Una is very gifted with the loom. She really captures the spirit of your people so *well.*"

No. Way. "The spirit of your people"?

My gaze flies to Lucas's face as he drops his eyes and Connor's hand at the same time. "Thanks, Mr. Connor," he says neutrally, "I'll tell her you said that."

I admire his grace under pressure, because I am barely able to control the sudden urge to smack Jackson Connor's clueless face.

"So, you two ended up having class at the same time after all?" Mom asks, peering out the window over the sink, where the rain has settled into a steady shower. She seems to have not heard the patronizing remark, but her back is stiff, and her voice is a little too bright. Mom's not likely to call out a customer for what he thinks is a compliment. She says there is a time and place for helping people understand. She clears her throat. "I'm glad you were there, Lucas. I don't like Vivi riding her bike in the rain."

She's good at picking her battles, but I'm not.

"Come on, I'll show you around." I squeeze one last bit of rain out of my braid, drop the towel by the offending dishes, and push through the heavy swinging door. I don't want to look at Jackson Connor's face another moment, and I have to get Lucas alone. He can't just drop a bomb on me about *dreamwalking* and get away without explaining.

The store is deserted. Horn and Nakai's flute notes patter through the air, mingling with the percussion of the raindrops on the roof and the smell of herbal tea. The spotlights over the shelves announce every crystal and carving and illuminate the paintings. Outside, Zia Square is empty; everyone has ducked inside to escape the storm.

"Well, here it is, my home away from home," I offer with a quick wave of my hand. I want us to keep moving, keep talking, and get out of here as soon as we can.

Lucas stares at a painting, and I stop. My stomach flips over. My one and only attempt to capture Dreamland on canvas, with its deep piney shadows, jagged mountains, and a swirl of cobalt, violet, and gold stars winding through the twilight sky.

He tilts his head a little. "I like this one."

My knot of impatience eases a little. "Thanks." I hear them talking in the kitchen, and I make a beeline for the front door. "Come on out front."

He tears his gaze away from the painting and follows me past the counter, saying, "That's *yours*? It's really good." Then, in a low voice, "Where are we going?"

I open the front door to the sound of rushing rain. I turn in the doorway, determined. No more distractions. I grab his arm firmly. "We are going out here, and *you* are telling me what's going on."

Out under the front porch, the sound of the rain will keep us from being overheard. We sit on the long, low bench below the window. I can see the whole square and also keep tabs on Mom in case she comes out of the kitchen. Facing him, I force myself to look into those endless dark eyes. My heart pounds, and the lump in my throat is making a comeback. I say it quickly before I lose my nerve or start crying—or both.

"I know how it is about your dad, I really do." Grief and confusion well up behind my throat, spilling into my eyes, but I plunge ahead. "I've been having weird dreams too, about *my* dad. And they're getting weirder. And that word, *dreamwalking...* what's happening? Why are you telling *me*?"

Miserable tears roll down my face. The scar that holds my grief is raw, threatening to rip open again and flood me with pain. And there's the reason for it, right in front of me, irresistibly drawing me to him like a magnet. I scrub the tears away, determined to keep that pain locked up tight.

Lucas takes my left hand and tucks my arm in close to his. From elbow to fingertip, I'm nestled in his warm grip, and our shoulders touch as he leans close. My swirling emotions steady a bit, and his voice is low and fierce.

"Why you? Because you and I—we have a connection. It's not just our dads, Vivian. It's the *dreams.* It's because you're a dreamwalker."

"What do you mean?" I whisper. "What *is* that? How do you know?"

"Una told me."

"*What?* What does she have to do with this?" The rain slows down, no longer covering our voices completely. I'm clutching his hand like a vise, so I relax a microscopic amount. He does not let go but keeps looking at me steadily.

"She knew when she touched your palm."

"I've seen those palm charts, and I've never seen any dreamwalker line. What are you talking about?"

"She didn't exactly see it. It's more like a feeling. Like I said, she just knows things sometimes."

I let this sink in, remembering the look on her face when she was poring over my palm. Like she had found something she was looking for. She didn't seem scared. In fact, she had seemed almost glad.

"What else did she say? What does a dreamwalker *do*?"

Across from us, Noonie's door opens, and a few customers step out cautiously. The sky is still dripping, but movement around the square has begun again, and I can hear Mom talking. Time is running out.

"It means you can get into other people's dreams. Like you can really be there," he explains quietly. His radar is up too, and his solemn profile watches the square. He's still holding my hand, and the sweet hum weaving through my fingers competes with the confusion in my head. "You can talk to them, and they'll hear you. My dad said some dreamwalkers can even make people do things."

"Like what?" Now I'm getting nervous again, thinking about the people and animals in Dreamland, the ones that do what I say.

"I don't know exactly. I can't really do that." Lucas sighs, and his voice drops even lower. "I can control my own dreams mostly, but Dad made it sound like a dreamwalker can control someone *else's*—wait—"

The front door opens, and Mom sticks her head out. I hadn't heard or seen her coming, but Lucas had. Impressive—not many can detect Mom when she's in stealth mode.

"It's stopped," I say, amazed my voice sounds normal.

"For now," she decides. I'm sure Mom can tell I've been crying, and even though she doesn't look directly, I also know her ninja-vision can see us holding hands. "Someone needs to go get Brian. The bus will be there in a few minutes, and I'm not sure this is over."

"There's a big red spot on the radar," Jackson Connor announces, stepping up behind her and annoying me for the fourth time today. This must be some kind of record. "I'd be happy to pick him up in the Escalade." The shiny, black SUV lurks in the small lot at the end of Zia Square.

"No, we'll go, if that's okay," Lucas says suddenly, standing up. He runs his hands through his damp hair, making it stick out in random, choppy spikes. He looks at me. "Vivian's bike's in my truck, and we're going that way anyway."

My hand feels lonely without his. I stand up too. "Yeah, we'll go."

"Are you sure? It's no trouble." Jackson Connor's smile is so charming. Too charming. I don't care if he's just here for a while, and I don't care that he buys stuff. I'll just save time and start hating him now.

"Brian wouldn't know your car," I say abruptly. "He only met you like once, right? He won't get in a car with a stranger."

Mom looks at me with an almost imperceptible frown. I don't want to be completely rude, so I laugh a little to take the edge off. "Mom, you know even if you call him, he probably doesn't have his phone on."

She sighs. "This is true. Okay, see you at home."

We slip back into Déjà Vu, leaving them on the front porch, and don't say anything until we are out the back door and back in Lucas's truck. A whoosh of air escapes from my lungs. It feels like I've been holding my breath for a half an hour. I sink back in the seat, twisting the ends of my damp, disheveled French braid.

"Thanks. That was quick thinking," I say. "I couldn't wait to get out of there."

"Yeah, me neither. Who is that guy, anyway?" Lucas maneuvers the truck out of the driveway into the narrow alley.

"Some customer. He came in a couple of weeks ago and turned into The Thing That Wouldn't Leave. He's remodeling the old gallery. Mom likes him, I guess." Above us, the gloomy clouds are skittering away, and shades of aquamarine and gold streak the late afternoon sky. "But he's practically a stranger. Maybe I'm being over-protective, but I don't want him picking up my little brother." The idea of Brian riding in Jackson Connor's Escalade makes my blood run cold.

"Well, I don't like it either," Lucas frowns. "I don't trust that guy. There's something about him." He shakes his head, lost in thought for a moment.

"Lucas. Oh my God. *The spirit of your people?*" We look at each other, and our faces dissolve into laughter.

He rolls his eyes. "*Which* of my people, exactly? Apache? Cheyenne? My mom's French grandfather?"

"You know. *Indians.* What does he know, anyway—something he read in a book? He moved here like last month."

"I'm sure it was his idea of a compliment." His mouth twists into a sarcastic grimace.

"Are you going to tell Una what he said?"

"Hell yeah," he laughs. "We've been getting back-handed compliments like that for a long time, so *our people* are used to it."

We stop at the traffic light that will let us out onto Valley Road. Relaxing by microscopic intervals, I direct Lucas to the bus stop. The painful heart laceration that is my Dad seals up again, and I realize the idea that someone else knows about dreamwalking is actually pretty cool. I want to ask some more about Una, but before I can, Lucas looks at me and smiles.

"So, tell me about that painting. It reminds me of *Starry Night*, but with mountains."

A jolt of pleasure flushes my face. My painting reminds him of a Van Gogh? I peek to see if he's kidding. His eyes are warm and not kidding, and for once, I don't have to look away. In fact, at this moment, I could look at Lucas Wolfsong for a really long time.

"Where is that place? Is it Whiteriver?" he continues. I snap out of my momentary trance and look at the road. The light turns green, and I point out the turn for Brian's bus stop.

"Well, I thought it was imaginary. But I don't know anymore. Not after today."

He considers this for a moment, then asks, "What's it called?"

"*Naa tsaałe yu*. Dreamland."

"Wow." He looks thoughtful but says nothing else.

"So," I venture, "what exactly did Una say? I've never heard of this until a few days ago. I've always had lucid dreams, and my dad used to have me do things in them. Stuff like flying. He never called it anything." Until now, that is. I spy the dream book peeking out from under the seat. "Is it in there? I looked online, but there's really nothing. Lots of dream interpretation sites, but not dreamwalking."

"No, nothing. I looked online too, but there wasn't anything specific. The closest I found was astral traveling, out-of-body stuff.

There are lots of books about that, so I guess it's something that people from all over can do." Lucas shrugs slightly. "It started with a lot of weird dreams. Canyons and hawks, someone calling me. Then last month, there was this one that was different. *Really* different. Usually I remember my dreams, but when I woke up, all I could remember was it was beautiful, with billions of stars—and Vivian, he was *there*. And when I woke up, there was that word in my head. *Dreamwalking*."

Boy, does this sound familiar. "Me too," I breathe, "almost exactly."

"I looked in my dad's stuff—you know, like there'd be a file labeled 'Dreamwalking 101'—but it's all just clothes, pictures, and his service file. So, I finally asked Una, because she always knows. All she said was it sounded like there was a dreamwalker trying to tell me something. It might not actually be my dad; it could just be *about* him. She wasn't sure."

"So, the dreams could mean anything."

"I know, right? But then last week she said if I was still having the dreams, I should meet you. She thought you might be a dreamwalker, and maybe you could help. So I went with her to your house, and there you were—that same cute girl from the store with those green eyes." He looked over at me, his own eyes gleaming. "I was hoping you remembered me."

He thought I was cute? He hoped I remembered him?

I swallow. "I remembered you right away."

"Anyway," Lucas continued, his eyes returning to the road, "that's it. I know it sounds crazy. But the only dreamwalker I've ever known was my dad. And now, you."

"Same here. I think my grandmother is one too." My head spins. Our fathers, the dreams, our research turning up the same things— maybe he is right. Maybe we really *are* connected.

"Can you ask her about it?"

"I would, but she doesn't have a phone, and it's not something I want to leave a message about with the neighbors."

At the end of the block, the small gold and white Alamogordo

Space Museum bus pulls to the curb, and Lucas slides in neatly behind it. I roll down the window and wave, calling, "Hey!" to Brian as he steps out onto the sidewalk. As he heads toward us, swinging his backpack, Lucas turns to look directly at me.

"I don't know much about dreamwalking yet, but I don't think you can do it when you're dead."

"So, this is why you think your dad—"

My eyes widen as the sudden possibility stops me cold.

"*Both* of our dads, Vivi. I think they might be alive."

CHAPTER NINE

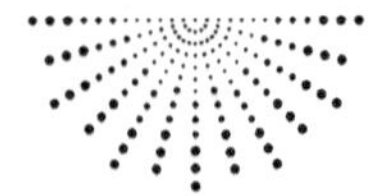

"Hi, Lucas!" Brian's noisy little-brotherness spills into the back of the truck and takes up the remaining space behind the seats. As I push my seat back into place, he spies Lucas's trash. "Oh man, you guys went to Blake's? I'm starving!"

My brain struggles to shift gears. *Alive. Our fathers could be alive.*

Lucas shakes his head. "No, sorry dude, that's just trash from the weekend. How was Space Camp?"

"Cool! We saw this video of lightning filmed from the space station and watched the storm come. Did you know there are over a million lightning strikes every day? What did you guys do?" Brian catches my eye as I climb back into the truck. His brown eyes flicker with approval instead of this morning's mockery.

"Art class and rain," I shrug. "No Macaroonies. Sorry, B. But there's jerky."

"Don't forget the driving," Lucas reminds me.

"You were driving?" Brian's eyes grow round with awe. "I thought Mom said you can't 'til next year."

"Mom wasn't there," I explain pleasantly.

"I won't say anything. I'm no squealer." He laughs at his own gangster-movie lingo, then asks Lucas, "How was it? Did she almost kill you?"

"No, she did pretty good." He nudges me. "Want to show him?"

There is no traffic. A car and a van are parked down the block, but the street is otherwise deserted, as usual. I hesitate for a second, then shrug and say, "Okay." After all, they say when you are learning something new, you're supposed to repeat it until you get it right. Right?

Lucas gets out to switch sides, and I slide over to the driver's seat. As I roll the window down to adjust the side mirror, Brian moans, "Our lives are in her hands," and collapses back into the seat, immediately springing forward again to watch.

The sky is almost completely clear now. The sun has gone behind the mountain, but there are still another two hours of light. The only remnants of this afternoon's storm are the wet street and the heady scent of drenched sage and mesquite that has settled sweetly across the valley. I shift into drive and roll down the street, staying in my lane and holding the wheel in a slightly-less-than-death grip. I'm almost going the speed limit of 30 mph when I see the parked van.

"I can't look." Brian moans. I glance in the rearview mirror. He holds his hand over his eyes, peeking out between his fingers.

Lucas leans toward me—not as close as he did on the levee, but still. "Go down to the tire place, and we'll switch back."

I nod, wondering again if he always smells this good. I peek at him for a nanosecond. His hair is dry now, sticking out all over. A sudden urge to smooth it back with my hand seizes me. Then it happens.

I swear it's not my fault.

The parked white van pulls out directly in front of me. I slam on the brakes and steer to the left a little, thinking I will either stop or go around him, but the wet street causes me to skid. As if in slow motion, the truck slides closer and closer, slowly but inexorably. *Nonononono!*

Helplessly glued to the view, I brace for the crunch. The right front fender glides into the back of the van, but there is no crunch—

just a sharp tap as we come to a halt. It sounds just like the tap on the loading dock at Community College. No one says anything, and then we all start talking at once.

"Sorry, oh my God, *sorry*—"

"It's okay, Vivian, it's—"

"Whiplash! I have whiplash!"

Lucas pops open the glove box. "Vivian, it's okay. Don't freak out. I don't think it did anything. You barely touched it. Wait here." He grabs a white envelope with an insurance company logo on it, gets out of the truck, and walks around to the front.

"Oh, man," Brian breathes, and I can tell he's impressed. "Your first wreck."

"Shut up, Brian." I am absolutely mortified. Shaking, I do not inform him this is my *second* wreck in one day. "Don't say anything. At all."

He sits back and digs through my backpack until he finds the pack of beef jerky, which he holds up silently. I nod once, and he settles in, chewing loudly.

Lucas calls, "Back up a little," and I carefully, perfectly, shift into reverse and back up a couple of feet. I turn off the ignition. He takes his phone out of his pocket and takes a picture of the van's rear bumper. I can see the government plates... then it hits me. What if it's the same van that sideswiped me last week? I sink further into my seat. Is this cosmic justice, or am I in even more trouble than I thought?

The van's driver hasn't gotten out yet. Lucas walks over to side of the van, holding his wallet, phone, and the envelope. All I can see besides him is a large, muscular forearm resting on the open window. Government muscle. Lucas shows him the phone, and the arm gestures calmly, briefly. No one gets out. Lucas heads for the truck, and as I climb into the passenger seat, the van drives away.

"Wow, that was weird," he puzzles as he gets in. "He didn't even want to get out and look at it." He shrugs. "Don't worry, we just traded a little paint. There's barely a tiny dent."

"Are you sure?" I can hardly look at him in my humiliation. "Let me see."

"Yeah. He didn't want my name or number or anything." Lucas shakes his head and hands me the phone. A short, vivid red streak, like a brush stroke, underlines the license plate. I hand the phone back, silent.

He looks at me. I can't read his expression at all. "Vivian."

Here it comes. I guess there won't be any more driving lessons. I brace myself for the inevitable.

"You're gonna need some more lessons." He shakes his head, trying not to smile.

"Can I talk now?" Brian bursts out.

"Yeah," Lucas cautions. "But remember, Brian, this is a need-to-know situation. And no one else needs to know." He winks at me, and I can breathe once again.

"I know that. I told you, I'm no squealer," Brian says, indignant. "But what about *that?* What's that thing?" He points at the open glove compartment.

I look where Brian is pointing. There is the insurance envelope, the phone charger, a battered map—normal glove compartment debris. But resting under the map is a small flexible red tube, its translucent ends hooked together in a ring. Some other small, unidentifiable items are inside it, including a piece of paper with tiny writing.

Lucas leans over. "That? It's a snakebite kit. It's for sucking out the venom if you get bit. There's a little blade in there and directions."

Brian exclaims, "A blade? Like, a razor? Cool! Why do you have it? Do you go camping where there are snakes? Did you ever get bit?" His eyes widen with curiosity.

"Nah, but a friend of mine did. We were up in the mountains, two hours from nowhere with no cell coverage. I was glad we had one, and so was he." He laughs and starts the truck. "Una has one in her first-aid kit too. She volunteers at the wolf preserve near

Santa Fe, and sometimes there are rattlers. Better safe than sorry, right?"

Brian's eyes are big as golf balls as he nods and lets out an admiring whoosh of breath. "Yeah."

I do not whoosh, but I, too, am impressed. "I don't think I could just cut into someone."

"You could if you had to," Lucas replies as he turns the truck around in the street and we head back toward home.

Five minutes later, we park in front of our house. Mom's car is here, and—thank God—there's no sign of Jackson Connor. Lucas takes my bike out of the truck bed, setting it on the driveway. Brian lifts up my soggy, ruined sketchbook with a questioning look, but I shake my head and tell him to toss it in the trash. When he disappears behind the back gate, I turn to him.

"Lucas, I am *so* sorry about the truck. Twice in one day!" I groan.

"It's no big deal. Really. We'll go again." He glances at the house, rubbing the toe of his boot in the gravel. "But I need to ask you something."

"Sure, what?" I'm so relieved he doesn't hate me for banging up his truck, I would tell him anything.

"Does anyone else know about the dreamwalking? Your mom?"

"Mom and Brian both know I have lucid dreams. I tell Brian about them sometimes, but he can't do it."

Lucas's eyes are black, earnest pools. "Can you help me do it? Can you tell me what you know?"

"I-I guess so." I consider the possibilities. "If you can teach me to drive, I guess I can teach you dreamwalking. I can try, anyway. At least there's nothing to crash."

He nods solemnly. "Good thing."

I laugh. This has been an amazing-scary-annoying-awesome day.

"You could text me," I hear myself suggesting, "and I can give you something to try. Later tonight, like after ten?" I totally don't know how to do this. Is this the same as asking him for a date? We get out our phones and exchange numbers. Lucas looks at my flip phone, amused.

"Don't even say it," I warn, "I'm lucky to even have *this* one." It's getting darker, and Mom's and Brian's voices float through the open window. "Do you want to come in?"

"I do, but I need to go. Una's on her way from Albuquerque, and I still have stuff to do." He says that, but he doesn't move. We stand, looking at each other without speaking. *What happens now?* We couldn't stop talking all day, and now... silence. But it's not awkward. An energy hums around us. *From* us. That sounds like something Mom would say, but sometimes Mom knows.

He takes my hand gently, and our fingers meld together. "Okay then. Ten o'clock?"

I nod, and he steps closer, then hesitates, glancing at the house again. My heart does a cartwheel as he leans in to hug me. He is warm and smells like soap and rain. It's a quick hug. His arms and back are smooth and strong, and I could stand here for a hundred years breathing him in, but something big and furry rubs my leg and then winds its way between us as we break apart.

"Hello, Rufus," I sigh.

"Meh." The cat eyes Lucas speculatively, then strolls away.

[FILE 201 190614 SANTA FE (17:30)]

Trigger: Unable to acquire target. Contact with Unknown Subject, male. Black Sky traced the vehicle, and the truck belongs to—get this—the Wolfsong boy.

Raven: (pause). This complicates things, but I'll handle it. Add him to your surveillance.

Trigger: Complicates things? You know what will happen if—

Raven: I know what's at stake here more than anyone. I said I'll handle it!

Trigger: (low whistle) You'd better.

DINNER IS PEACEFUL AND FUNGUS-FREE, except for the mushrooms in the spaghetti sauce. Brian eats three bowls and chatters about Space Camp and Lucas's snakebite kit. True to his word, my little brother doesn't squeal about my driving—or my wrecking. As he heads to the shower, I clear the table and make a mental note to get extra lemon Macaroonies for him tomorrow.

"How was the painting class?" Mom asks. She loads the dishwasher while I feed Ophelia half of an olive and a bit of crust from the organic whole-wheat Italian bread. "Did you get any ideas for the mural?"

"It was okay," I admit. "The rain drowned my new sketchbook. But yeah, I do have an idea." It has been brewing in my mind since we left Déjà Vu. "I think I want to use 'Dreamland.'"

Mom smiles. "I think that would be lovely." She dries her hands on a towel. "You seem to be getting along very well with Lucas." It's a statement, but it sounds an awful lot like a question.

"We have a lot in common." Boy, do we—like possibly-alive fathers who talk to us in our sleep.

She nods thoughtfully. "Yes, I suppose you do. Come here." She hugs me and kisses my forehead. "I'm going to bed. Don't stay up too late, okay? Early day tomorrow."

"Okay."

At 10:00, we are all in our rooms. The sound of Brian's radio, tuned to Riverwalk Jazz, drifts out from under his door. Mom is running water in her bathtub. The jacket sits patiently on the back of my chair. I pick it up and slip its smooth weight across my shoulders, then reach inside the liner pocket and carefully draw the feather out of its nest. Sitting cross-legged on my bed with my phone in front of me, I will it to buzz.

While I wait, I add up the scores for the day, starting with the Life Sucks Trifecta.

1. I found Lucas: Plus!
2. I now have a plan for the mural: Plus!
3. I got to drive three times, but I crashed twice. I decide to call it even.
4. Jackson Connor created a new Annoyance Trifecta all by himself, with a bonus. Minus, minus, minus.
5. Lucas held my hand three times. *Three times—and we hugged.* Trifecta Plus! I'm ahead for sure, and I vow to ask Mom about the jacket tomorrow. I want it to be Dad's, but I'm afraid to want it too much. Of course it isn't, but I need to hear it from her.

My phone buzzes. Lucas!

LUCAS

Hey there.

> Hi. Is your truck mad at me? Ugh, the lameness continues.

Haha, no.

> I was hoping my driving didn't scare you away.

Nope. I was actually hoping my life didn't scare you away.

> Our People don't scare easily

:-D

So what do you want to know about
dreaming?

Everything?

How about flying. Can you go places? Can
you go where you want?

Sometimes. I picture a place or a person,
and I kind of end up there for a few minutes

It helps if you can picture the way there.
Float up high, and kind of push your way
there. Once you start moving it's easier

Like swimming?

Kind of. I imagine I'm a hawk. Oh. You have
to keep your eyes open

While you're sleeping? How?

Not your real eyes. I just know that in the
dream, I need to do that to go where I want

OK, I'll try it. Does it matter where I go?

Someplace easy. The Piggly Wiggly? :-P

Hahaha! How about your painting? Can I go
to Dreamland?

I guess? I'll go there, and you see if you can
find me

OK. If I see a hawk, I guess that will be you

Lucas. Today was one of the craziest days
of my life. Our dads, what if they're alive?

I don't know. I'm thinking we can figure it
out though. You working tmrw?

All day

OK, I'll txt you. See you in Dreamland

OK. Remember, push hard and keep your
eyes open!

We text good night, and I sit there, enveloped in the safety of my jacket for a few minutes. The hawk feather is smooth and lustrous. I close my eyes and brush it across my face. I feel the same electric energy I felt with Lucas this evening. It hums gently in my hand and seems to leave an invisible trail across my eyelids, my nose, along my chin. The hum grows stronger and brighter. My eyes fly open, because suddenly, *I know.*

I can't just keep waiting for Dad to come back. Maybe he can't. Maybe something's wrong. I have no idea, but I do know this: Dad is somewhere in Dreamland and I have to go find him myself.

CHAPTER TEN

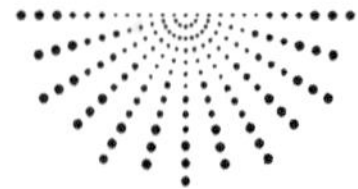

Rising through the hills is effortless, like riding ocean waves over the dark forest. I breathe deeply, inhaling the clean aroma of pine trees. Nestled in the shadows, other smells stir and awaken deep memories of new crayons and old books, fresh ciabatta bread, Dad's cigars, and Baby Brian after his bath. Wherever I walk, whatever I think, an infinity of scent and memory awaits.

Tonight, splashes of wet desert and fresh gardenia infuse my lungs, bringing Dreamland more into focus with every breath, and with every weightless step into the mountains, my body becomes more solid. It's always cool in the mountains of Dreamland, but tonight, I brought my jacket, and its smoky, honeyed warmth cocoons my body as I materialize completely.

The last streaks of purple-gold twilight rim the horizon in all directions, casting a luminous reflection in the far-away sapphire ocean. A large sunset-moon glows silver over the forest, and every living thing greets me with vibrations of color and clarity I can never quite capture in my paintings. The familiar stillness and beauty of this place settles into me like stepping into a warm bath. I'm tempted to relax and enjoy the view, but I have a mission.

I will not wait for Dad. I will scour this place, my own creation—at least, I thought it was my own until last week. I'll find him, and he'll tell me why he came to me this way.

I'll find out if he is alive.

"Dad," I say clearly. I don't have to call out; this is my world, and I can be heard everywhere. The name leaves my mouth the way a pebble hits a pond, sending violet sparks rippling across the mountains, canyons, forest, and ocean. Every tree, every leaf, and every flower shimmers and nods. Then all goes still, waiting.

"Dad," I say again, and again the violet filigree rolls out to the horizon. The greenery stirs around me, offering up the scent of chocolate Macaroonies, and the creatures of the forest pause in their Dreamland wanderings, glowing faintly in shades of russet, fawn, and pewter.

"Where is Dad?"

The deer, the squirrels, the owls, and the nighthawks all face me, puzzled. Questions are rare around here. They cock their heads as I repeat, "Where is Dad?"

The web turns pink, coral, and crimson as each animal ponders, and their colors mingle as they consult each other. I hear the rustle of night wings in the trees, the leaves shivering in their pale violet outlines, and suddenly the sharp, savory smell of bacon and coffee descends around me. A low hum conjures the wavering translucent image of Dad laughing in our Wildwood kitchen. It is the Dad of photographs and Sunday morning memories, the Dad that lives in my heart—not the Dad I'm looking for.

I sigh in frustration. The image retreats, the animals dim, and the forest reverts to vibrant shades of celadon and sienna outlined with tiny, glittering amethysts. When he was here, there were diamonds. Suddenly I freeze.

Could it be that simple?

Seized with inspiration, I stare at a cluster of azaleas, willing the sparkling purple outline around it to change color, to become a silvery crystal prism. I frown and concentrate as hard as I can on just one thing.

Dad.

The bush quivers a little, and its outline seems to... blink.

I zero in on one tiny pink blossom, determined to find the alchemy that changes amethyst to diamond. The blossom pulses, as if it's turning itself inside out. It shudders and goes still—lush and gleaming proudly, embroidered with silver.

Yes.

Dad.

My head throbs as the surrounding leaves and flowers slowly bubble and turn, clothing themselves in the silvery web. Then the nearby bushes and trees—faster now, the clear, crystal glow spreading across the infinite boundaries of Dreamland until every last glint of purple is gone. The horizon is dark; the twilight has transformed into midnight. I can barely tell where the diamonds end and the stars begin. The wind hisses gently through the trees, and the cool breeze lifts my hair.

Soft footsteps come close and then... a voice. *His* voice, gentle and triumphant.

-I knew you could do this, Vivi!

A warm hand clasps mine.

-Dad!

-Walk with me, Vivian.

My head still pulses, but the pain is receding quickly as we soar up over the jagged mountains into Dad's high desert. Only a few stars are visible in the indigo sky, and the towering formations of sandstone and quartz glow amber in the coming dawn. The moon here is as full and large as mine, but translucent, like a milky opal. His profile is no longer deep in shadow, and I can see the creases around his eyes, his strong brow and white smile. The sharp scent of an expensive cigar drifts by my nose.

-Dad, what happened? I waited for you all week!

-I know. I'm sorry. I had to make sure you could get here on your

own before you find Brian. This isn't going to be easy, and they're very close.

-Who?

-The Stargate Project. A government program I was part of. We did everything we could to hide you two when you were little.

-But why do they want Brian? He's not even ten.

-They know how smart he is. They want to control his thoughts and use him as a weapon in people's dreams. They think he's a dreamwalker.

-But he isn't, Dad. He's just an ordinary genius. Can't we just tell them?

-They know this runs in our family. Grandma Lily, me, and now—

He breaks off sharply, listening to something I can't hear. My heart jolts as I finish his sentence silently... and now, you.

-What do I have to do? Fear gathers into a cold knot, deep in my stomach.

-You will have to walk into Brian's dreams, like you did with me tonight, but it's going to take every bit of strength you've got. He won't be able to help you. You have to take him back into your dreams, and make him stay there, to shield his thoughts from them. And be careful. They may follow you.

-They can follow me in my own dreams?

-Some of them can. These are very dangerous men, Vivi. And you'll have to work fast, because when you're in someone's dreams, they start to wake up. You'll only have a few minutes before you get pulled out.

The rich tang of the ocean circles around us, followed by an acrid, oily smell that is gone almost as soon as it arrives.

-What about Mom? Can't she do anything?

-Your mother's not a dreamwalker. I can visit in her dreams sometimes, but for her, it'll always be just a dream. You're the only one that can do this. The oily, burnt smell doubles back, as if it forgot something.

-I have to take you back now, honey, but we'll walk again.

A thousand questions are whirling in my head, but there's one I have to ask.

-Dad, where are you? I'm so confused right now. Are you—are you alive?

-I'm in a safe place. Don't worry about me, just focus on Brian.

-But there's something else. My friend Lucas knows about dreamwalking. His dad—

-We have to go. Now!

He turns abruptly away from the approaching dawn, and we face the mountains that circle my corner of Dreamland. The sky is still dark there, dusted with the scattered glitter of stars. I feel a strong tug deep in my chest, urging me home.

He holds my hand tightly, and together we skim quickly over the red sand, like a pair of pebbles skipping across a pond, until we are up in the cool pines again. Shards of crystal and amethyst swirl around us when we stop. Dad is transparent now, and the silvery web is almost gone, replaced by gossamer strands of lavender.

He smiles at me, tilting his head.

-Nice jacket. I used to have one just like it.

Far below us on the side of the mountain, a tiny cloud of cobalt blue fireflies drifts slowly, uncertainly, toward us. Alarmed, I point to them mutely, wondering if "they" have found us already. The dangerous men. I can no longer see Dad, but his voice is still close.

-Don't worry, it's not them. They don't know about you. But you can always tell when they're near—it smells like an oil fire. See you soon, Vivi. Be strong.

-Wait!

But he's gone.

-I love you, Dad. Fuchsia sparks shoot a whispered trail over the horizon and return as silvery flashes dusted with the faintest whiff of cigar.

-I love you too.

I breathe deeply, but all I smell now is the honey-butter leather of my jacket.

The stars in my violet-amber sky begin to spin. My body feels fizzy and weightless once more as I leave Dreamland. My eyes touch upon the brilliant blue fireflies receding below, and just as a molecule of Downy darts past my nose, I realize maybe Lucas made it here after all. But it is too late. I am gone.

Always, the last thing I see in Dreamland is the crystal-clear web of a million stars.

CHAPTER ELEVEN

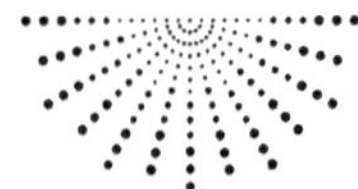

It's waiting for me as soon as I step out through the front door of Déjà Vu. Like a coiled snake slithering up my spine. That feeling of being watched. *Again.*

At first, I ignore it, because there is a low-level humming in my head that won't go away and just about *everything* feels off. I'm out here at the crack of dawn, trying to feel normal—or at least act normal—but there is no normal anymore. Not now, and maybe not ever again.

I told Mom I was going in early to work on enlarging the "Dreamland" painting to fit the front wall. She looked at me, and her clear green eyes registered both everything and nothing before she said, "Okay, I'll see you in a bit."

I'm hoping that going through some artistic motions might give me a handhold on the planet. I clutch my small sketchbook and some pencils in a death grip, battling the feeling that if I let go, I am going to fly right off and spin out into space or back into Dreamland.

Dreamland.

The place that is not just about my dreams, but everybody's. The place where a poisonous knot of dread has embedded itself in my gut because my brother is in danger, and I'm supposed to be able to save him—from I-don't-know-exactly-what—by jumping into *his* dreams. The place where Dad is—alive?

In a safe place, he said. As scared as I am about Brian, I'm also insanely happy because no matter what happens, that place is where my father walks.

Brian knows right away that something's up. He looks at me quizzically as we pass in the hallway this morning.

"Whatcha been dreaming about, Vivi?"

OMG. Does he know?

"Your new *boyfriend*?"

I glare at him and punch him in the arm, relieved as he smirks and dances away from my empty threats.

Never have I been so glad to see his annoying, smartass-little-brother grin. But I can't tell him anything. What would I say? Be careful bro, some ruthless government thugs are trying to get into your head and use your non-existent powers to turn you into some kind of dream-warrior? Oddly enough, Brian would probably believe *that*. He doesn't believe me when I tell him purple and yellow make brown. He demands proof. But something crazy like dreamwalking and evil government conspiracies, he would turn over in his head, chewing on it in his mind like a lemon Macaroonie, then nod and say, "Okay." I can't do this alone, but Brian isn't the one I have to tell about this.

Not yet.

Whatever "this" is.

I ignore the slimy feeling of surveillance as it slithers up past my neck and into my scalp. I need to talk to Mom. Dad said they tried to hide us, so that means Mom knows *something*. Maybe that's why she keeps us living so far off the grid. Maybe that's why she uses the name Hawk professionally, instead of our full name, Night Hawk. I always thought it was so she wouldn't have to explain her last name and her dead husband to every curious customer, but maybe it's because Hawk is so generic. Easier to hide.

Maybe Dad can't talk directly to her, but I can—and I have a feeling I need some Ninja Mom skills on my side.

Lucas. I need Lucas too, and not just for the obvious reason of him being totally hot or the fact that he turns my heart into a sweet, warm ache that leaves me speechless and turns my brain into a puddle. Not just that. I need him because when he took my hand, it was impossible to tell where his ended and mine began; as corny as it sounds, they fit perfectly, as if our hands belong together.

I need him because when he didn't even know me, he was looking for me. Because he trusted me enough to ask me to help open the door to a miracle—a miracle that feels like it may be true but might escape if I think about it too much. You can't hold a miracle hostage.

I need him because he texted this morning, and when I asked him to find out about the Stargate Project, he said he would. I know I can trust him to do whatever he says he will do.

I need Lucas because, even though right now the dread-knot in my stomach is small, I think being really terrified really soon is a distinct possibility, and for all of my bravado, I don't know if I can do this alone. Lucas is brave. And when I'm with him, I feel brave too.

Well, brav*er*.

Who is looking at me? I whirl around, my heart thumping, but I don't see anyone out in the square. The souvenir shop and the fudge place are still closed. Noonie's is open though, and I need to replenish our stash. I glance up and down the walkway, and there's no one.

Wait.

Something twitches in the parking lot, the tiniest ripple of movement. Sandwiched between a couple of trucks, a large shiny black roof catches my eye, just like the roof of Jackson Connor's Escalade. Why would he be lurking over there, staring at me? I wouldn't put anything past Mr. Jackass-Spirit-of-Your-People-Douchebag Connor. I put on my "I see you" face and narrow my gaze, then wait for any trace of movement. Nothing.

Sigh. Okay, Vivi, quit being so paranoid.

The dread-knot reminds me that it's not paranoia if they really are out to get you.

I cut across the square to Noonie's before the day gets away from me and I forget to buy the Macaroonies. Tiny dream-sparks of turquoise and diamond seem to dance just outside my line of sight. I pretend to peek nonchalantly at the parking lot as I go by, but there's no one there, in the lot or the cars. The Escalade turns out to be some other black SUV thing I don't recognize, and I feel both stupid and relieved. *See?* I scold myself. It was probably just one of those heat shimmers that ripple up from the road when it's really hot. One of those.

Hmmmph! says The Knot, unconvinced.

When I get back to Déjà Vu, it's almost time to open, and Mom is in the kitchen, setting up the customer coffee tray. Her sky-blue peasant blouse is edged at the neck and sleeves with those little crystals that look like rainbows; tiny, glittering echoes of my jewel-edged dreamwalk.

I position the cookies around the plate, creating a perfect galaxy of chocolate and orange planets surrounding butter-lemon suns, not looking at her. The Knot pokes at me, *Tell her!* so I take a breath and ask, "So, what's it looking like today? Is Una coming?"

"She's still in Albuquerque until tomorrow. Maybe Thursday." Mom sips her coffee and delicately selects a chocolate planet from my galaxy, declaring, "These are the best ones," and bites it in half. Every now and then, Mom indulges in what she calls 'mental health food,' usually involving chocolate or something with butter and salt, if not all three. Her relaxed, cheery smile is encouraging.

"Mom, can I talk to you about something? If you don't have a reading right away?"

"There's nobody until ten. I was going to work on the books, but they can wait a few minutes. What's up?" Her face is kind and expectant, and I feel super guilty for what I'm about to dump on her. I'd better be careful. There's no easy way to say all of this, and I don't want to sound like a mental case right off the bat.

"Do you ever dream about Dad?"

"Of course, honey," she says, setting down her cup. She pauses wistfully. "All the time."

"Mom... ever since I got the jacket, there've been weird things happening. A lot of weird things."

"What kind of things?"

Where to start? A feather made of lightning? An amazing artist who fits my hands and my heart, who knows about my dreams? Dreams where I can talk to my not-so-sure-he's-dead father? I hesitate because it sounds crazy and she will never believe me.

If she believes stuff about auras, this won't be too hard, argues The Knot. *She believes in dreams.*

This is true, I concede. I better start talking before I lose my mind completely.

"Things about Dad. Dreams. First, though, I need to know something about the jacket. What happened to the one he had?"

"His jacket? He lost it." She rests her chin on her slim hand and reconsiders. "Well, he didn't exactly lose it. You know how he was; he'd help anyone who needed something. He was up at Fort Apache, visiting Grandma Lily before he went back to Iraq. He lent it to his friend one night and never got it back." Mom looks at me closely. "Are you thinking it's your dad's actual jacket?"

I nod. "I know it sounds crazy. But it's the same one in the picture on his web page. It looks exactly like it, except for this one thing on the collar. There's a snap or a pin or something in the picture, and on mine there's a pin hole. Did Dad have a pin there?"

Her face softens. "I can see why this has got you wondering. But you know they probably made thousands of jackets like that."

"I know, but *Mom.*" My throat is suddenly a painful ball, and tears are threatening. "It just feels like him. It—it even smells like him. And there's more, but I have to know. Was there a pin?"

She looks close to tears herself as she slips her cool hand across the counter to mine. "He wore his caduceus."

"Cadu—what?"

"Caduceus." She pronounces it *ca-doo-see-us*. "That medical symbol of a snake winding around a pole with wings at the top. Medics and doctors wear them in the field. I'm sure you remember it —it's in my jewelry box." She's right. I *have* seen it: small and gold, a sharp masculine bird gleaming in her feminine nest of silver. How can I have forgotten?

Mom shrugs, smiling gently. "Maybe the jacket *is* his and it found its way back to you. Stranger things have happened." She pauses, in no hurry. "You said there was more."

"Okay, but you have to promise you'll listen to the whole thing before you say anything." I glance at the clock over the sink. Can I explain this in twenty minutes? There's so much, and I haven't sorted it all out yet—the feather, how Lucas fits into all of this, and Lucas's dad. The Knot elbows me hard.

Brian.

"Mom, it's about Brian. I think he's in trouble. Or, might be—" Words spill out crooked and fast, an avalanche of speech. "You know how my dreams are, right? I had a dream about Dad—no, a dream *with* Dad. He called it a dreamwalk, but it was really him, not a dream. He was really there with me—and he said they are trying to get Brian."

"Hold on, slow down!" Concern flickers across her face. "Now, what about Brian? Did you dream he was in trouble?"

"Yes. No. Dad told me it's some project where they get into your dreams and make you do stuff, you know, like I can do some-times? Like Dad and Grandma Lily? It's called dreamwalking, and Lucas knows about it. They think Brian can do it." It's coming out all wrong, and an odd little shadow of doubt touches her eyes.

"They? Who are they?"

"What do you mean, Dad *told you?"*

"What is it exactly you can do?"

All these possible responses, and what does she say as she lets go of my hand?

"Lucas? Is he the one giving you these ideas?" Mom tilts her head uncertainly, a slight furrow appearing between her brows.

The Knot groans. *You're blowing it.*

"No, Mom, it's Dad. Lucas just knows about dreamwalking." My thoughts are drowning, flailing desperately for something to grab onto to keep her with me.

Get a grip, Vivian, warns The Knot.

Panic bursts out of my heart, and I'm almost shouting. "I know you know something about this. Dad said you guys tried to hide us when we were little. He said it's that project. The Stargate Project."

Her face wavers, and she goes very still. "Stargate?" she whispers, and her ashen face belies her calm voice. She takes a deep, ragged breath. "You had a dream about *Stargate?*"

This is exactly what I was dreading. This stunned look, as if someone has just slapped her in the face. Her mask of serenity and patience crumples completely, and she closes her eyes, clutching the edge of the kitchen counter, swaying a little. I'm horrified at the power that word has over my mother, but I could also weep with relief because *finally* she's going to listen.

Jing-a-ling. The silver bells on the front door.

"Hellooo, anyone home?"

A furious cross between a groan and a growl escapes from The Knot. Every murderous cussword known to mankind floods my head as the cheerful, hearty voice of Jackson Connor rings out in the front room.

"Mom!" I glance desperately at the clock. It's five minutes until opening time. Can't he ever leave us alone?

"Vivian." Mom's voice is quiet and deadly serious. Her normal, serene face has mostly reassembled; only her bright pink cheeks give her away. "We'll talk about this later. I don't know what you think, but—

"What I *know* is that Brian's not safe. Dad told me," I whisper fiercely. I can barely speak, and I can't *even* deal with that pest out in the store. I turn toward the back door, hoping to escape, when Mom grips my arm and leans in close.

Her voice is calm, but her eyes are urgent as she warns me, "You are not to say anything to anyone about this. Not to Lucas, and especially not Brian."

"I won't tell Brian." I fume. She must think I'm an idiot. "But if it wasn't for Lucas—"

"Knock-knock!" The ice-cream door taps and swings open as a manicured hand waves a lumpy brown paper bag filled with what smells like bagels, followed by J.C. Douchebag's grinning face.

"Good morning, ladies!" He steps through the doorway, then hesitates, his smile fading as he glances from my mother to me, then back to her. "Everything okay? The door was open... I hope I'm not interrupting."

I can't help it. My eyes fling daggers at him while I bite the inside of my cheek to keep from telling his stupid, pompous face that *I* hope he drives that Escalade of his right off a cliff.

"No, it's fine," Mom says smoothly, picking up the customer tray of Macaroonies. "It's time to open anyway."

I can't stand this for another minute. I am not Mom, and I can't just take a few breaths and act normal when my whole world is splintering and rearranging itself like some kind of terrible kaleidoscope

"It is *not* fine!" I snap, whirling to face him, and the word avalanche roars out before I can stop it. "This is a private conversation, and you *are* interrupting. *Why are you always here?* Don't you have a life somewhere? You're supposedly here on business, so why don't you take care of your business and stay the hell out of ours!"

"*Vivian.*" My mother's stern face and sharp tone tell me what I already know, that I'm way out of line.

But I don't give a rat's ass. I'm out of line? He's out of line! My whole stupid life is out of line!

"*Just leave!*" I yell wildly. "Stay away from my mom, stay away from my brother, and stay away from *me!*"

Jackson Connor's snobby mask of a face is blooming thirteen

shades of crimson. Awesome. Seeing Mom's eyes blazing at me is definitely not awesome. I have never seen her this angry with me.

Oh, way to go! sneers The Knot, kicking me hard in the gut, scattering shame and fear like shards of glass from my ribs to my knees. *Just when you need her the most.*

I freeze, stunned at what I have done—even though this is all Jackson Connor's fault—and ugly words seethe in my head, ready to explode in a war of brains versus mouth. A wave of nausea rolls over me, threatening to erupt with more than words, and I need to get out of here before I vomit all over his Top Siders, which, come to think of it, would give me enormous satisfaction right about now.

Vivian, warns The Knot, echoing my mother.

Screw you, too, I spit at The Knot. I stomp out the back door, slamming the screen so hard the hinges rattle. I hop on my bike and pedal savagely up the alley, away from Déjà Vu, away from Mom and that worm, Jackson Connor. Angry tears blur my vision as I jump off and drop my bike under the deep shade of the enormous mulberry tree behind the Slushee Stop. My side hurts, my lungs are on fire, and I can go no further. I collapse under the tree, drawing my knees up to my chest. Tears scald my cheeks as I rock back and forth, ignoring my ringing phone, while fear and frustration roar over me in deep, shuddering waves.

CHAPTER TWELVE

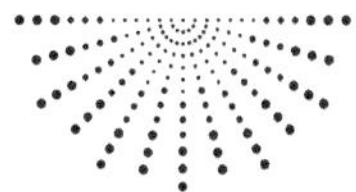

THE WORST PART about making a dramatic exit is that eventually you have to go back. You feel like an idiot, you're all awkward and say you're sorry, and even though everyone's still kind of mad, there's this uncomfortable understanding that everyone has to chill and at least try to act like everything's okay. You know, fake it 'til you make it.

I can't sit here crying miserably under a tree forever. Sooner or later, I'm going to have to look at my phone, which hasn't stopped buzzing for ten minutes. Sooner or later, I'll have to face Mom and try to get her back on my side again, which will mean apologizing to Jackson Connor. Sooner *than* later, actually, because her first reading is in fifteen minutes. Reluctantly, I peek at my phone, and I'm not surprised to see I have missed three calls and a text—but they're not from Mom.

"Call me right away!" Lorena's message insists. I haven't talked to her in a couple of days, which seems like a lifetime ago. I suddenly need to hear her confetti-like laughter and her uncomplicated view of life. I press *call sender*.

She answers before the first ring stops, urgent. "What's going on?"

"What? Nothing," I blurt out. "I'm okay."

It's true, *I'm* fine—it's just that the universe is imploding.

She sighs impatiently. "Yeah, right. What's *wrong?* Just tell me."

She gets these clairvoyant flashes now and then, like Mom. I've given up trying to explain them. Just because people don't know why or how this happens doesn't mean it's supernatural or magic. They are a lot alike, Mom and Lori. They even look alike, enough to be a mother-daughter team. Right now, I'm sure my mom wishes this was the case—that her daughter was the friendly, open, bubbly one, and this stubborn, angry Vivian-girl was the friend in California.

"I had a fight with my mom." How much can I tell her? The Knot, silent until now, nudges me. *Tell her. Maybe she can help somehow.*

"It's a long story, and I can't really talk now, but there's a chance my dad might be alive." I'm too wrung out to do anything but just blurt out the bottom line.

"Who-o-o-o-oa." Lorena pauses. I can feel her digesting this, and then puzzling. "But this is *good* news."

"It—it's a secret right now. I'm not even sure about it, and it's dangerous. Brian—all of us—it's not safe." My voice wavers. "I might be able to do something, but I don't know what, yet, and I'm scared." This is totally incoherent, I know. How can she make any sense of what I'm saying?

She takes a breath, activating her BFF Translator. "Hmm. Well. What I think is that if you don't know what to do, don't do anything yet. See what's happening first? You know, be still."

"I don't know how much time I have. And I just made her really mad at the worst possible time," I groan. "I yelled at this guy. A client, her friend—I don't know *what* he is—but I totally hate him, and I was really rude. Then I walked out." Just telling her is embarrassing.

She brushes that aside. "Been there, done that. She'll get over it. Especially if it's true about your dad." She laughs a little. "Hmmm. What sucks right now is you have to walk back *in*. But you better own it, you know? Cuz you *are* sorry for the rudeness. And don't be all quiet and sulky, like you get sometimes."

I do not sulk. What I do is retreat and regroup. But I suppose it could look like sulking to the untrained observer.

"Okay, I'll try. I gotta go, but thanks for the phone-a-friend therapy. I feel a little better about this now." And I do. She's right, and she's on my side, even though she doesn't know half of what's going on.

"Good. And you better call me. I want to hear the whole thing. And this Lucas guy too. I want a picture. How can you have this hot boyfriend, and I don't even know what he looks like?"

"We aren't at the selfie stage just yet. He's amazing. It's... hard to explain. But I'll call you tonight, I swear." I pick up my bike and swing my leg over, getting ready to go back to Déjà Vu.

"You better! And, Vivi?"

"Yeah?"

"Be safe."

Two minutes later, I hitch my bike to the post in the back. As a warm-up, I apologize silently to the screen door I slammed, and then slip into the kitchen. Mom murmurs pleasantly to the customers out front. I stop at the sink and splash cold water on my face, then tuck a few errant strands back into my braid. There is no mirror to check, and I hope my face doesn't look as ravaged as my heart feels. I open the ice cream door a few inches and peek out. Two women stand at the register with Mom, and I'm relieved there's no sign of Jackson Connor. Yeah, I'm a total coward, but I have to make things right with her first.

She looks over when the door opens, nods to me slightly, then turns back to finish ringing up the sale. I step through the door and nonchalantly rearrange a few large crystals until the women leave.

"Mom, I—" That's all that comes out before my throat dries up and closes.

She sweeps out from behind the counter and looks at me with

neutral, unreadable eyes. I wonder what she sees in mine, before I drop my gaze to the floor. The Knot twitches deep in my stomach.

"I'm glad you're back. My ten o'clock will be here any minute." Smooth and cool. Waiting.

I take a deep breath. "Mom, I'm really sorry for what I said. I didn't mean it. I don't know why I was so rude to Mr. Connor. I guess I'm just really worried about Brian." Is there a certain percentage of an apology that has to be pure and true, like sterling silver, in order for it to count? Because even though I totally meant what I said to him, I really *am* sorry I said it.

Her eyes are two chilly, green oceans. "I certainly hope you are, Vivian. That man is not just a client. He's trying to bring some business to this town, trying to make friends and get this renovation off the ground, and you made him feel like an unwelcome intruder."

I open my mouth to defend myself, but she holds up her hand to silence me. "I know what you're going to say, how it's about Brian and your dream, but we'll talk about that later. It's no excuse. He's a nice man, and he didn't know what he was walking in on. You had no reason to do what you did."

Jackson Connor is not a nice man.

I know this is unreasonable—as in, I have no actual, concrete reason to believe this—but I feel it from my head to my toes, and I have since he first walked in the door. No, even before that, out on Valley Road. I also know I've hurt and embarrassed my mother for that exact same lack of a reason. Opposing forces of shame and hostility struggle with each other briefly in my head, but I close my mouth without saying anything. Like Lori said, *Be still.*

"I'll apologize to Mr. Connor," I offer, subdued. *You'd better,* hums The Knot, *or we're getting nowhere.*

"You'd better," Mom says, completing the You'd Better Trifecta, just as an eager-looking, hipster couple comes through the door. The ten o'clock. "But it will have to wait 'til lunch."

Crap. I was hoping to talk to Lucas at lunch. "Okay, Mom. I'll make it good, I swear."

"I know you will, Vivi." She gives me a thoughtful look. Do I detect a slight defrosting around the edges? I hope so.

HIGH NOON ARRIVES, the hour of my penance. I stride quickly across the grass, heading for the vacant store that is Jackson Connor's latest project. The square bustles with tourists, and a road crew is repairing the asphalt in the parking lot. Construction noises reverberate from across the way, pulsing though the noon heat, and I'm glad our store is away from all the racket. I may love loud, heavy music, but *noise* is something else.

The smell of freshly cut boards, oily power tools, and old coffee greet my nose when I knock on the half-open door. I push it open and see no one.

"Hello?"

The former gallery is smaller than Déjà Vu and much brighter. There's no covered porch or even an awning to block the sunlight, and I know this place will be roasting by mid-afternoon. An old air conditioner cranks valiantly in one window, but there's no way that fossil can defeat the New Mexico sun in June. The wood floors are bleached from sun and neglect, and a fresh layer of sawdust covers everything, including the blueprints spread on the ancient desk and the plastic yard chairs serving as office furniture. An old milk crate acts as a Styrofoam coffee-cup graveyard, and a few Riverbend Construction business cards are scattered on the floor.

"Hello? Mr. Connor?"

Masculine voices in the back room, then the high–pitched "*REE-AARR-RRR*" of a circular saw assaults my ears as Jackson Connor steps in, closes the door on the din, then turns and sees me. Surprise flickers across his face but evaporates immediately. He smiles pleasantly, only displaying about thirty teeth this time. His crisp white shirt is rolled up at the sleeves, an expensive watch gleaming on his tanned wrist.

"Well, hello there, Vivian. I was hoping to see you. Would you like some water?" He waves his hand toward a water cooler in the corner.

"No thank you, Mr. Connor. I know you're busy and all, and I have to get back soon. It's about this morning."

He runs the watch-hand through his hair and nods thoughtfully. "Yes. This morning. I think an apology is in order, don't you?"

Really? I shouldn't be surprised by anything about this guy, but *really?* How pompous can he *get?* Resentment ignites in my stomach but is extinguished quickly and smoothly by The Knot. *He'll get his. Karma is a bitch, remember? This is for Brian, not him.*

I take a deep breath and nod in agreement. "Yeah. I really—"

"I know, Vivian. You and your mother were having a private talk this morning, and I just barged in. I should have waited out front. I didn't mean to intrude, and I'm sorry I upset you." His blue eyes are earnest, his smile kind, and I am completely dumbfounded.

I have been struck dumb with anger. I have been tongue-tied with embarrassment and stupefied by Lucas's magnetic warmth and easy smile. But I have never been made speechless by someone's politeness. This is a new one. Even The Knot is silent.

My cheeks are hot, but I recover quickly. "It's okay, Mr. Connor. I came to apologize to *you.* I was totally rude, and you didn't deserve it."

"Apology accepted." He perches easily on the corner of the desk, resting his hands on his knees. "I really like this town, Vivian. I like the history and the people here. Your mother has been very gracious about helping me get started, and I really enjoy her company."

"Everyone does."

Mom is really good at making you feel like you can do whatever you set your mind to, whether she's reading your cards or signing you up for a surprise painting class. I feel another twinge of guilt for being such a pain-in-the-butt Drama Daughter.

"Well, I plan on being here a little longer. I'm even buying a summer cabin up in Pacheco Canyon. I'd like for you and me to start over, if we can?" He stands up and extends his hand.

"Ummm, sure, Mr. Connor." I hold out my hand almost automatically.

"Please. Call me Jack. Or, J.C. Some of my friends call me that."

I don't think we're quite at the initials-only stage in our new relationship, but I can at least concede his first name. I'm pretty sure it won't kill me, and if it will make Mom happy, I'm willing to call a truce.

"Okay, Jack."

His grasp is warm and firm this time, with no trace of the cold lizard grip.

"I'm glad we're back on track." He beams.

"Me too." This is not actually a lie. I need to focus on Brian and dreamwalking, and I need Mom's help. I can't let my temper get in the way again.

The power saw in back grinds and screeches up and down the scale. Jackson—er, Jack—stands up, tips his head toward the racket and shouts over the noise, "Well, back to work."

I nod pleasantly, and shout back, "See you!" Satisfied, I head out the door, thinking about a sandwich from Noonie's and a Coke.

As I step out the door and stroll down the sidewalk, the burning, oily smell of power tools follows me. I can only imagine what kind of overblown castle Jackson Connor would call a "cabin," but who cares? Pacheco Canyon is over three hours away—an acceptable distance.

Once inside the bakery, I breathe deeply, happily replacing the construction smells with fragrant muffins and Macaroonies. I order sandwiches for both me and Mom. She eats very little meat, but she loves Noonie's chicken salad as much as I do. It has a ton of celery, plus grapes and pecans. Drinks and homemade organic potato chips complete the order.

I dig in my pocket, looking for more change for the tip jar on the counter. All I have is one of those two-dollar bills no one ever wants. I drop it in the jar and hurry back to Déjà Vu. The apology went well, and I'm bringing Mom an excellent peace offering.

Smooth sailing, I text Lorena. *Call u tonight.*

My phone buzzes back immediately, but it's not Lorena. It's Lucas. A dart of happiness spears through my chest.

LUCAS

When are you off? You gotta see this
Stargate stuff ASAP.

V: Hopefully early. Can you come over?

LW: Yep, txt me when you're out.

V: I have a lot to tell you. Last night was
crazy. I saw my dad again, and I think I
saw you.

I definitely saw something. Hope it was you.

"My heart skipped a beat" sounds so lame, but that's exactly how it feels. I guess some clichés are true, which is why they are clichés. I scour my brain for the perfect response and get... crickets.

be there or be square. Yup, if you can't say
something lame, say something even lamer.

TUESDAY AFTERNOONS ARE ALWAYS SLOW, so Mom and I are usually able to eat lunch at the same time. I'm hoping for the right moment to bring up Dad and Brian again, but by the time I put our plates on the counter, I'm not sure exactly how much I want to tell her about Lucas. I want to see what he found out today, and I want to talk to Mom when there's no chance of us being interrupted. So maybe Connor's not the total douchebag I thought he was, but I still don't like him—and Mr. Clueless has a way of showing up just at the wrong time.

We sit at the counter with the ice cream door propped open, listening for customers, but no one comes in. While we exclaim over the luscious sandwiches and crispy chips, I give Mom a play-by-play of my apology, including Connor's new place in the canyon near Santa Fe. She is still a little stiff, but when I get to the part about him apologizing to me, her face thaws completely and she says, "See?"

Washing the last bit of pride down with my Coke, I admit, "You're right, Mom, he's... not that bad. I guess I'm a little too protective of us. You know how I hate new people." I'm joking, but as they say, many a truth is spoken in jest. My whole life, I've trusted only a few people outside of our tiny family.

"You are fierce. Just like your dad." Mom smiles as she wraps up half of her sandwich for Brian. "But you have to let people in sometimes." She raises one eyebrow in a speculative Mom Look and adds, "Like Lucas."

The Knot sits up immediately. Yes! The perfect segue.

"He's different," I begin cautiously. I don't want to just blurt out that Una thinks I can get into people's dreams, and Lucas came looking for me to tell me our dads are alive and they're sending us dream messages. Even though that's exactly what's happening, saying it like that makes him sound like some kind of psycho freak. Besides, what Lucas told me is about *his* dad. I don't know exactly how this all fits together with mine.

Or with Brian, nudges The Knot. *That's what she needs to know about, not Lucas.*

"Mom, he has the same kind of dreams. He calls it dreamwalking, just like Dad."

"You mean lucid dreaming?" she ventures. "Like when your father used to coach you when you were little? That was so you could move yourself out of nightmares. You've always been good at that."

"It was way more than that, Mom. He taught me how to go places and do things. Talk to people, even. But these dreams are *different*.

It's because of the jacket—and there was this feather in it. A hawk feather. It was like Dad *found* me. I felt him with me. I could hear him breathing." And for just a moment, I feel him again, warm and solid, surrounded by the smoky turquoise-gold of his dream desert.

She has stopped cleaning up lunch. She stands completely still, looking at me intently, wheels turning. "Really? It sounds like astral traveling. Tell me the part about Brian. Do you remember it clearly?" This is the Mom I know and love, the Mom I need so badly. I need her steady, calm voice. I need her listening carefully and thoughtfully. I close my eyes briefly, determined not to screw this up.

"Everything, Mom. I remember everything. He said men from the Stargate Project are looking for Brian. They want to use him because they think he's a dreamwalker." Like me, I add silently. And possibly, like Lucas.

Mom takes a deep, even breath. "Did he say anything else?"

"No. But he said I can protect Brian's thoughts somehow, by getting into his dreams."

A group of women come down the sidewalk, chattering as they pass by the kitchen window and head toward the front door. Another interruption, but unlike this morning, my emotions and temper are under control. Smooth sailing.

Mom notes the arrival of customers with a quick nod. She stretches her hands above her head, sending her bracelets twinkling down her arms. She smooths her hair thoughtfully, puts her arm around my shoulder, and kisses my forehead gently. Her eyes are troubled for only a moment before clearing to their usual smooth jade.

"Okay, honey. We'll talk more tonight."

"Will you tell me about Stargate?"

She nods, and pauses before replying, "I was hoping I'd never have to."

[FILE 201 200614 SANTA FE (15:13)]
    Black Sky: Raven, what's your status?
    Raven: SNAFU with sister and mother.
    Black Sky: Were you made?
    Raven: Negative. Mission secure. Diplomacy prevailed.

CHAPTER THIRTEEN

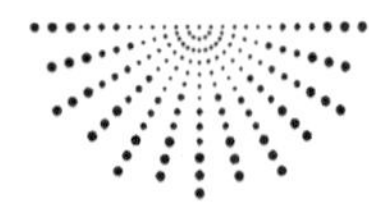

By 3:00, Zia Square is practically deserted. Mom has no more readings scheduled, so I get to leave early. I nest Brian's bag of Macaroonies carefully in my backpack, using the sketchbook to shield them from being crushed. Lucas is going to meet me at home with whatever he found out about Stargate. Mom will only tell me what she thinks I need to know, but maybe Lucas and I can figure out how it fits with our dads and last night's dreamwalk.

Was it only last night? It feels like a lifetime ago.

Stepping out on the back porch feels like walking into a fiery kiln, and the thermometer reads 107 degrees. In a few minutes, I'm out on Valley Road, where even the World's Largest Pecan looks thirsty and exhausted, but I'm heading into the cool relief of the Magic Forest. The speckled sunlight dances through the trees, reminding me of the gossamer sparks in Dreamland, and for a few precious minutes I push my worry aside, ignore The Knot, and enjoy the impossible: Dad may not be just "somewhere safe," but alive. His luminous smile and low, gentle voice were not the flash photography of memory, but real and solid.

Alive.

The cruise through the canopy of shade and miracles ends too soon. The sun slams into me as I come out the other side, and with it, my mission returns: find out everything I can about the Stargate Project and keep Brian safe. I pedal home with a vengeance.

I park my bike in the garage and stash the Macaroonies. Sticky from the hot ride, I head for my room, peeling off my shirt. I stop in the living room to flip the A/C switch to high and poke the radio on. Smash Mouth's *Walkin' On The Sun* blares out. I love it when the universe agrees with me, and sometimes even old Top 40 songs get it right. I crank up the volume all the way and dance down the hall in my bra, shaking out my braid and singing along.

No one's supposed to know, but I do know how to dance. Well, a little. Last year Lorena declared that there was no way I could go to homecoming and not be able to dance, so along with flirting and texting, she taught me the Electric Slide and a few salsa moves to save me from crippling embarrassment. I didn't get to dance much that night, but I still practice sometimes because:

A. You never know, and

B. I only do it when I'm alone. No witnesses.

The song buzzes and chimes, and as I step, turn, and slide along with it, I realize the chiming is not just coming from the song but from the front door. The front door with a narrow window running down the wall right next to it. The window with a tall, dark shadow in it. A shadow with a bronze, muscular arm, thumb hooked on the belt loop of those lean, perfect jeans. He's not peeking in right this second, but OMG. How much did Lucas see?

A hot wave of embarrassment rolls over me as I switch the radio off and shout, "Be right there!" I run down the hallway to my room and scramble into a clean shirt.

"Hi." Lucas smiles at me as I open the door. The hand not hooked in the belt loop is holding a few printouts. I pray to the universe he was reading them and didn't see anything.

I'm now faced with a conundrum. That's one of Brian's favorite words. It means a difficult problem. A dilemma. On the one hand, I must watch closely and try to determine how much dancing around Lucas actually witnessed. On the other hand, if I look at him too long, there is the distinct possibility of a heart attack, ending with me melting into the ground like a happy Wicked Witch of the West. Yeah, a conundrum.

"Hey, come in. Sorry I didn't hear you. Want some iced tea?" I decide that since every time he sees me I embarrass myself, if he saw me dancing without a shirt, at least I got today's clumsy awkwardness out of the way.

"Sure. You okay?" He looks at me closely, still smiling. I nod, but my flushed cheeks give me away.

"Yeah. It's just... hot. Come in?"

Lucas follows me into the kitchen, stopping to admire Ophelia on the way. She stands on her hind legs staring at him, preening her creamy fur and quivering. He digs in one of his pockets, produces three sunflower seeds, and drops them in her cage. She squeals with fright and delight, stuffing them into her cheeks immediately.

"She'll love you forever now," I comment and dig some glasses out of the cabinet. He brushes by me, sending a spark of lightning from my arm right into my heart. He smells like soap and seems to take up the whole kitchen. *Make tea, Vivian*, I admonish myself.

"So, what happened last night?" He sits in a kitchen chair, drops the printouts on the round table, and stretches out his long legs, crossing one boot over the other. I drop ice into our glasses, hoping he can't see my hands shaking.

"A lot, actually. I found my dad. But first, tell me what *you* saw." The ice cubes make crackling sounds as the tea splashes into the glasses. "Want limes?"

"Please, yes, I love limes. Okay, I was trying to do what you said. Float, swim, keep my eyes open. That's a lot of stuff to do when you're falling asleep. I was trying to imagine that painting of yours. It felt like I was sinking down, not floating—which is pretty much how I fall asleep anyway—but then I started spinning and saw this curtain of stars."

"That's how I know I'm almost there," I observe, placing the glasses carefully on the table and sitting next to him. "Did you go through them? The stars?"

"Not through them. More like inside them. They were everywhere. Then I could see mountains, like the mountains in my dreams, but different. Huge pine trees. Flowers. A lot of colors in the sky too, like a sunset. Purple and gold." He pauses for a huge swallow of tea. "It was weird. I couldn't seem to get my footing. I wasn't exactly touching the ground all the way. It was like walking through water, but with a lot of rocks underneath. I was looking for you, but I didn't see anyone." Then Lucas laughed. "For a second or two, I thought I smelled breakfast. Bacon, coffee, and bread. Is that crazy?"

He was there. Lucas was in my dream

"No." I shake my head, heart pounding. "Not crazy. Then what?"

"Well, I looked around to see where it was coming from, and I saw a hawk circling around, way up near the top of the mountain. I thought maybe it was you, so I headed up there. But then these lights —really small, like sparks—rolled down, across the whole place. It's hard to describe. Like a wave breaking, kind of purple and pink, swirling past me. Then they pulled back up again, but they changed from purple to white. Clear. So, I just stood there watching, and then everything was outlined, like a million Christmas lights. I looked back up to where the hawk was, and there were *two* of them, flying over to the other side of the mountain."

He looks at me eagerly. "Was that it? Did I make it into Dreamland?"

"I think so." I can't help but grin. "Everything you saw matches up. I think those hawks were me and my dad."

I gulp down some tea. "We went to his—his corner of Dreamland, he called it. I always thought Dreamland was just mine, but it seems to be a whole universe, where everyone can make their own world. His is beautiful and huge, like Monument Valley."

"What did he say? Did you ask him about my dad?" Lucas shifts in his chair, his dark eyes anxious.

I shake my head, and the disappointment on his face makes my heart ache. "I tried to, but the whole thing didn't last very long. He was telling me about Brian and Stargate. That's why I wanted to see if there was anything about *that*—if it's a real thing."

He taps the printouts with his index finger. "Oh, it's a real thing, all right! Wait 'til you read this. It's like something out of a movie. There actually *was* a movie about some of it—and I'm positive both of our dads were involved in this. *Are* involved," he corrects himself. "Vivian, did your dad seem... did it feel like he's... okay?"

"He felt real. He felt solid. I could hear him breathing. So, I asked him."

"You asked if he's alive?" His eyes widen in surprise. "What did he say?"

"He said he's in a safe place."

"Which could mean anything," Lucas says cautiously. "But it doesn't sound like greetings from the grave."

"Yeah, but where? Where could they even *be*?" We sit in silence for a moment, thinking.

"God, I have no idea." He sighs. "Some secret CIA spot. Area 51, maybe?"

"That's for aliens," I say, but— "Wait. Isn't the code name for Area 51—"

He looks at me, and we both say it at the same time:

"Dreamland."

Goosebumps prickle up my spine and across my arms.

"Okay, *now* I'm freaked out." I crunch on an ice cube and reach for the printouts. "He was warning me about Brian, how the Stargate people want to use him somehow. And he said my mom knows about it too. I tried to talk to her this morning, but it turned into a meltdown."

"Your mom had a meltdown? I can't even picture that. She's so calm."

"No, I did. Jackson Connor showed up, and I was rude to him. Really rude. It was... bad. I ended up having to apologize to him."

"Ouch. How did that go? He's not exactly our favorite person."

Our favorite person? My hand starts shaking again. There's an "us"?

"That part wasn't completely terrible. He actually apologized to *me*. But I didn't get much out of Mom. She said she'd tell me more about it tonight, but I don't know how much. Okay, let me read this. I'm glad you printed it out, since our Wi-Fi is so lame."

"I went to the library. I was going to send it to you, but I wasn't sure your phone could get any files. I saved the most important parts and the links to the sites."

Lucas scoots his chair close to mine and puts his arm around the back of my chair. How am I supposed to concentrate? His face is so close, his hair almost brushing my cheek...

We bend forward and read together. It's a series of copy/pasted paragraphs:

MKUltra was a U S Govt project that spanned three decades and experimented with mind control, most notably through the use of hallucinogenic drugs. The program also explored attempts by the U.S. military to employ psychic powers as a weapon.

In 1979, the Peoples' Republic of China publicly reported that several thousand of its children aged 8-14 were capable of telepathy, clairvoyance, or psychokinesis. Sparked by this program, the Central Intelligence Agency (CIA), National Security Agency (NSA), Defense Intelligence Agency (DIA), and the US Army simultaneously poured millions of dollars into their own similar research at Fort Meade.

Mind control research continued through the Gulf War, via the Stargate Project, made famous by the novel and movie The Men Who Stare at Goats. The primary focus was remote viewing, with the goal of training an elite force of psychic warriors—some with the power to influence the enemy through dreams

There are several more paragraphs, and then:

The CIA insists these programs officially ended after the Gulf War, but CIA veterans say the program was active well into the late '90s. There is little reason to believe it does not continue today under a different name.

"Holy guacamole," I whisper, and slump back in my chair against Lucas's arm. It's warm and strong, and he doesn't move except to drop his hand lightly onto my shoulder. "This *is* crazy. You think our dads were in this? They were... *goat-starers?*"

He smiles. "Well, maybe not goat-starers." He points to one of the sentences, leaning forward. "But this part about getting into people's dreams. Our dads can both do that."

"My dad said these people—the CIA, I guess? —think *Brian* can dreamwalk. They know about my grandmother too. He said they are going after Brian, to get into his mind somehow, and that I can protect him. I have to go into his dreams and hide him. How the hell am I supposed to do that?"

There aren't a lot of details in that printout, which isn't a surprise when you're looking for a secret government program. But most of this isn't very secret. I remember seeing a video in Psychology class about MK-Ultra when the CIA gave prisoners and even their own agents LSD. And then there's that goat-staring movie, which I didn't see, but now I guess I have to.

Lucas's arm is still around me, and I don't know which is making me more nervous: the warm closeness of him or the sci-fi insanity I'm seeing on this paper—*psychic warriors, remote viewing, influencing the enemy through dreams.*

I look at the second page with a list of links where Lucas searched for information. Pages from Wikipedia. The CIA website. Some site called "Cosmic Army." Fort Meade. A university academic database with papers about psychic research from the 1970s—but the source makes me gasp and sit up straight.

"Lucas! All of these research papers are from *Duke University*."

He looks at me, not comprehending. "I didn't read any of those. But they did psychic research for a while, so I was hoping there might be something about dreamwalking."

Panic rises in my throat. "Lucas, that's where Brian is taking all his classes."

He frowns. "Hmm. It's probably not related. That Duke program for gifted kids is pretty famous. Didn't you have to take the PSAT in middle school to see if there were any geniuses?"

Actually, Brian and I both took it one Saturday in October. I was twelve, and he was in kindergarten. The seventh graders took it on big tables in the cafeteria, but he took it alone in the counselors' office. I could have saved everyone a lot of time if they'd just asked me. Not a single one of my classmates was a genius—least of all me— but I knew he was.

"But what if it's really screening for... for this?" I wave the papers around, trembling.

Lucas wraps his free hand around mine, intertwining our fingers —and there it is again, that feeling of rightness, of *fitting*. "That test was all math and reading, remember? Nothing I saw shows any connection between Duke's research and the CIA. We'll figure it out, Vivi. They may think they know about my family and probably yours. What they don't know about is *us*—but after last night, I do. I'm sure of it." He smiles triumphantly. "*We* are dreamwalkers."

"I want to look at those research papers. I want to see what kind of creepy experiments they were doing at Duke." Lucas is probably right. Maybe there's no direct connection between Duke's research and the Stargate Project, but it seems like the CIA had its own thing going on.

"Is your laptop here?"

"No. But Brian's tablet is." I stand up, but I don't let go of Lucas's hand. Looking at him makes me weak and shaky, but holding onto him makes me feel strong—another conundrum. I tuck the papers under my arm, grab my tea, and lead him through the back hall to

Brian's room, trying to ignore the fact I'm kind of dragging him into a bedroom. I remind myself to focus on getting the tablet.

Lucas seems even taller in here. He gazes at the posters of scientists and superheroes and nods appreciatively at the spacecraft models hanging from the ceiling. Two space shuttles, a couple of moon landers, one Mars Rover, and three kinds of rockets wobble gently under the A/C, threatening to land on unsuspecting visitors.

"These are really cool. Did he build them?"

"Yeah. All of them. He's a total space freak. If you want to know anything about any space mission ever, Brian's your man." Behind the door, a poster of Neil DeGrasse Tyson smiles in cool astrophysicist agreement.

Lucas ducks his head under the Apollo 11 Lunar Module and sets his glass down on Brian's desk. On the shelf above, there is a long, narrow diorama of a moonscape. Plaster craters and boulders dot the lunar terrain, while a half-dozen space landers form a semicircle around a tiny NASA dune buggy. Astronaut action figures are positioned strategically around Brian's moon village, but on a small hill a miniature red and blue Spider-Man triumphantly plants the American flag. On the desk, another Spider-Man—full-sized—stands menacingly on top of Brian's tablet, warding off intruders. He may be a boy genius, but the genius is still a little boy.

I move the sentinel, grab the computer, and we sit side by side on Brian's bed. Reluctantly, I let go of Lucas's hand, but it's okay because our shoulders are only inches apart and his leg is touching mine. How can I feel weak in the knees when I'm sitting?

The tablet is on, and Brian's wallpaper is that Escher drawing of all the staircases twisting into each other, going nowhere. His playlist is open, full of jazz songs, but I only recognize a few names.

"He's an unusual kid," Lucas observes. "Not too many nine-year-olds listen to Thelonious Monk or Bill Evans."

"It started when he saw the Charlie Brown Christmas show when he was two. He loved the music, ran around singing it, so Mom got him a CD of the soundtrack. He turned into a total jazz freak." A tiny lump gathers in the back of my throat. The idea of some CIA goons trying to infiltrate and use his mind—

I look at Lucas, tears blurring the angles of his face "If anything happens to him…"

"Nothing will happen. We'll make sure of it."

I tap the Duke icon, and their in-house search engine opens. "I don't know what we can find, but there should be something. These links are from their own database."

I type in one of them. Lots of numbers, dot-edu, slashes, more numbers, and "clairvoyance." The screen blinks and then fills with words and charts, all in about size-two font. Ugh. I scroll down through dozens of pages from the Duke University Department of Psychic Woo. If I find anything important, how will I even recognize it?

"Words… words… chart. More words. Looks like a huge file. How can someone write a hundred pages about ESP and make it look so *boring?*"

He leans over the tablet. "Search for the Stargate Project," he suggests. "If there's any connection, it could be buried anywhere. But probably not in"—he peers at the title and grins— "Human-Canine Clairvoyance Protocols."

"How to read your dog's mind—be a dog whisperer? Well, that's definitely not it!"

I abandon the list of links on the bedspread and type "Stargate Project." Wheels turn. The screen blinks. *Sorry, no items match your search.* Okay, "Dreamwalking," even though I know it's futile. This time we get two screen blinks, but the same indifferent message. The Wi-Fi drops from three bars to just one.

"Wi-Fi's done," I announce and close the server, sighing. "Epic fail."

"This is not failure," he protests. He stands up, ducking his head to avoid a large rocket, and drains the last bit of amber liquid from his glass. "We found out what the project was, at least. And we were able to dreamwalk. I've never gone into someone else's dreams before."

His eyes gleam with mischief as he looks down at me. "You were dreaming about me when you weren't even there."

I roll my eyes as if that didn't make my heart race. Not one bit. "So, what happened while I was gone?"

Really, what does a dream look like when the dreamer isn't around?

Lucas leans back, perching on the edge of the desk. "It was dark. I kept going up the mountain, but it was even harder after the hawks— you guys—were gone. I could barely see the path, like wearing sunglasses at night. There were animals around, kind of glowing? So I sort of knew which way to go." He tips his glass and crunches on a piece of ice. "But I thought I saw you again, right before I woke up. Even after I woke up, I kept seeing purple sparks for a few minutes."

"I thought I saw you too." I pause, remembering the blue glow and the passing scent of Downy. "You were way down below. But it wasn't you exactly. I was looking for you, or maybe a wolf, but what I saw was a swirl of bright blue fireflies. It just... felt like it was you." I don't mention that I could smell him. Dreamwalking, webs of fireflies and hawks are okay, but "I smelled you in my dream" is just too weird.

He nods as if this makes sense. "Cobalt blue, my favorite color."

He sits on the bed again and chomps down on another ice cube. "Okay, so what do we actually know? A government program that is supposedly over, but really probably isn't. Our dads are part of it or at least know about it. Your mom knows about it too. Your dad says they want Brian because they think he's a dreamwalker, but he's not—and we are. My dad? I don't know what he wants. He wasn't around last night, and I don't know how to find him." He tilts his head at me speculatively. "How did you find yours?"

"I couldn't, at first. I was calling him and concentrating on him. That's probably why you smelled breakfast. Sometimes smells come with the memories. But nothing was really happening, until... okay, you know how you saw the purple lights? Those are usually all around Dreamland whenever I'm there. I guess it's some kind of energy that's part of me, like the blue ones I saw coming from you. Well, when my dad was there before, that whole web of light changed to silver. Bright white, like diamonds. So, I thought if I could change the colors, maybe it would bring him."

"And you did it. I saw them change. But how do you do that?" He shakes his head. "It can't be as easy as just thinking about it."

"No, actually it's really hard. I concentrated on just one small bit of the web. I... pushed it. I can't explain it any other way. I pushed really hard on one spot, and it hardly moved. Then it kind of gave way and... I don't know, it turned over."

"You push with what—your thoughts?

"Yes. From right here." Impulsively, I reach out and brush his thick hair aside, touching the center of his forehead with two fingers. "It's hard, but that's all it is..." My words fall away as I look from that spot to his eyes, and they are locked on mine, and the lightning between us jolts my whole body.

"Oh!"

Embarrassed, I pull my hand away, but he takes it gently, his gaze never leaving mine. A heat wave spirals up from somewhere around my knees and floods my whole body, but I can't move or look away. His eyes are soft and dark as he says quietly, "There's more to this, Vivian."

My heart is pounding—surely he can hear it?—and suddenly I can hardly breathe. He softly runs one finger down the side of my cheek and up under my chin, leaving a trail of dizzying warmth. I sway toward him and close my eyes as he leans closer. His breath is shaky as his lips brush across my cheek, whispering, "Way more." His mouth presses gently into mine, and I pull him in deeper as the floor falls away, taking my spinning heart with it.

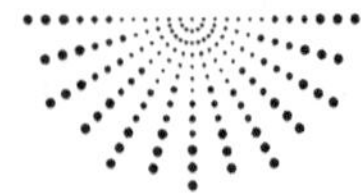

CHAPTER FOURTEEN

"EEEEEEEW!"

The piercing shriek of a banshee slices between us, slamming my heart back into my body, and we leap apart, up and off of the bed. Covering his face with his hands, Brian staggers through the doorway, screeching, "My eyes! *My eyes!*"

"Shut up, Brian! Stop yelling!"

Eyes still covered, Brian groans, "Gross! How could you do that *in my room?*" He drops his arms and glares at me, then Lucas, then back at me, and demands, "What are you doing in here, anyway?"

The clock by Brian's bed says 4:37. "Where's Mom? Did she pick you up?"

"I don't know. No, I walked from the bus. Why are you in here?"

"Sorry, Bri," Lucas jumps in smoothly, "We needed to look something up on your tablet. We only came in for a few minutes."

"Yeah, right. What were you looking up, kissing lessons? Yuck!" He stomps over to his desk and carefully places Spider-Man back on duty.

"No, it was some stuff from Duke. I thought we could find it using their server," I explain. Our gazes lock over Brian's indignant head, and I wonder if Lucas is as dizzy and dazed from that kiss as I am. I can still feel his lips against mine, taste the limes, taste *him*.

"Mom says you can't have boys in your room."

"Well, as you can see, this isn't my room," I remind him primly.

"Brian, these models are amazing," Lucas jumps in again, looking up at the dangling spacecraft. "How long have you been making them?"

"Since I was four." Brian points to one of the rockets. "That one, the Redstone Rocket, was the first one I made. It was pretty easy. The Mars Rover was the hardest." I think we are out of the woods, maybe, but he crosses his arms, not quite ready to be detoured. "So. What were you guys looking for?"

I have to tell him something. Something he will believe.

"Some stuff about dreams," I venture. Lucas watches me, his face cautious. "You know those weird dreams I have sometimes."

Brian's eyes narrow, still suspicious but interested. "Yeah... the lucid dreams."

"Well, Duke did a bunch of mind experiments in the '70s, and some of them were about dreams. I was thinking there might be something about them. But there wasn't—and then the Wi-Fi went out, as usual."

He rolls his eyes, sighing. "You have to keep the tablet on the desk, or you'll lose the signal."

"Yeah, I figured that out. But we did find this one thing about how to read your dog's mind."

Brian snorts. "That's easy. 'Feed me! Take me for a walk! Whose butt am I smelling?'"

Lucas laughs out loud at Brian's doggy wit, and I find myself actually giggling. He is finally appeased. "Well, okay. But stay out of my room."

We solemnly promise, and then I hear the garage door opening. Mom's home. I snatch the printouts off the bed, fold them quickly, then stuff them in my back pocket. I motion Lucas toward the kitchen, grab the tea glasses, and almost trip over a small, yellow plastic box on the floor in the hall. It has pea-sized holes in the top and sides and a Space Camp logo on it.

"What's this?"

"Hey, be careful!" Brian steps into the hall, picks up the box, and peers into one of the holes. It's not empty. There's a small shadow inside, and it's... moving. He offers the box to me. "It's a tarantula for my experiment. Wanna see it?"

I hold my hands up in front of me and step back. "No hairy Jurassic spiders for me."

"He can't hurt you," he reminds me. "He's not one of those South American ones."

I don't care what continent he's from, but Lucas accepts the box, peers in, and pronounces it, "Cool."

Experiment? As in, let a tarantula loose in the house and see what happens?

"What kind of experiment?" I demand.

"The effects of zero gravity on an exoskeleton," Brian explains. "They have a zero-gravity chamber, and we get to use it Friday. We went out in the desert today to gather our subjects. Everyone caught crickets, and I caught some too, but I used mine to lure Hamlet into a paper bag."

"Hamlet?" Lucas looks at me and raises an eyebrow, which tugs on a spot deep in my chest.

"Hamlet and Ophelia." A tarantula-hamster couple is probably just as doomed as Shakespeare's tragic prince and princess.

"Well yeah, but also because Prince Hamlet wonders about life and his existence. Nothing is as it seems," Brian warns the unsuspecting arachnid through the holes. He snickers and adds, "Especially in zero gravity."

"I'm sure this guy will be wondering about the same things." Lucas nods his approval. Brian moves Hamlet to a secure location in his room while we head into the kitchen.

The kitchen door pops open. Mom comes in carrying several

brightly-colored raffia grocery bags—no planet-killing plastic *or* paper for her—and plops them on the table with her purse.

"Whew, it's a scorcher! Hi, Lucas." Her face is radiant with perspiration. She's the only person I know who looks good while sweating. But, remembering the sheen on Lucas's arms and face when he wrestled that hunk of car accident into the truck, I think maybe there are two of them now.

"Hello, Mrs.—" Cut short by a meaningful look from Mom, he amends, "I mean, Summer."

"Hi, Mom. Want some tea?" I volunteer.

"Definitely. Would you put this stuff away while I change?" She disappears down the hall, stopping to say hello to Brian, and closes her door.

We unpack the bags full of the usual fruits and veggies, salad stuff, and a pound of grass-fed organic hamburger from happy cows— at least, happy when they were still alive and blissfully unaware of their impending doom—plus jasmine rice, hummus, a slice from a wheel of Brie, and some whole wheat crackers. Healthy but minimal, and I'm glad I brought home those Macaroonies.

I refill our glasses with ice, plus one for Mom, and squeeze fresh lime over the ice. As the tangy smell reaches my nose, a bullet of pleasure ricochets through my whole body. Am I going to relive that kiss every time I smell limes? I sure hope so. I also wonder if it's the *first* one, as in the first of many?

I peek at Lucas, who has wandered over to Ophelia's cage with one final sunflower seed. The moment my gaze lands on him, he looks up at me quickly, as if I'd touched him, and he doesn't look away. A slow smile lights his eyes, softening his sharp cheekbones, and something in that smile says there will definitely be more kisses. *Way more.*

Our gazes break apart when Mom breezes back into the kitchen, wearing something gauzy and cool. She is smiling too, not a soft, contented smile like Lucas, but that familiar, cat-who-found-the-cream smile.

"Mom, can Lucas stay for dinner?" I know, you aren't supposed to ask in front of the guest, but my Ninja Mom Early Warning System is on red alert. That smile means art classes and aura workshops. My only defense is to get her talking, especially now that he is here. He did all the research this morning, and he deserves to hear about Stargate too.

"Certainly." She takes a long drink of her tea. "Is your aunt back yet? Do you have plans for dinner?"

"She texted she'd be back later tonight," Lucas says. "So no, I don't have any actual plans."

"Well, you do now," Mom quips cheerfully. "We need to move Ophelia out of the dining room, though. We are celebrating tonight, and company is on the way."

"*Mom!* Celebrating what? What company?"

I don't believe this. What about the dreamwalk? Stargate? Brian? Did today even happen?

"Now Vivi, I haven't forgotten about our talk, but there's plenty of time for that later." Her voice is reassuring, but she swooshes by me into the dining room and doesn't look at me. Lucas does though, and he looks as perplexed as I feel. "Brian, come out here and set the table. Lucas, would you please move Ophelia into Brian's room?"

"Not my room. I have an experimental subject in there, and he can't be disturbed," Brian announces, and I have this flash of him all grown up, in a lab coat and safety glasses, surrounded by test tubes, shadowy machines, and laser thingies, dissecting the secrets of existence.

"Okay, my room." I lead the way with Lucas behind me, carefully carrying Ophelia's cage. He sets Ophelia down on the long, low dresser, then straightens up and looks around.

"It's nice in here," he says. "It's like your painting."

I guess it does because my room is all deep shades of blue and green with bits of purple and gold. There are a few paintings on my walls, mostly of mountains, and a few sketches of fractal patterns, which look like lightning or tree branches.

Lucas checks out my desk and my pictures of the family—Mom and Dad on the beach, another one of Brian and me building a sandcastle covered with dribbles. There's one Mom took before Dad left for the last time, with me, Brian, and Dad in the narrow shafts of sunlight of the Pine Barrens. There's a big one from the summer we lived in Whiteriver with Grandma Lily and the cousins.

"There we are, the whole Night Hawk nest," I say, but it's not the pictures that have his attention.

"Where did you get this jacket?" He steps over to where the jacket rests gently on my chair and rubs his thumb on a worn shoulder seam.

"It was in that box Una brought last week." I haven't told him about the jacket or the hawk feather that lives in the lining, but I can't explain that now—not with Mom and Brian here and "company" on the way. Or maybe I should, and we can all join together in a happy truth fest about dreamwalking, hawk feathers, and the Stargate Project. "This sounds crazy, but I think it was my dad's. It feels like him."

Lucas is frowning, sorting through memories but coming up empty. "I've seen it before. I know I have."

"Did you help her pack that box of clothes? It was in there."

"Nope." He shakes his head. "But I'll probably remember at two in the morning."

The doorbell chimes. Brian yells that he'll get it.

"Oh, yay. *Company*," I sigh.

We face each other, and he smiles that lopsided smile, and my heart starts thrumming (WAYmoreWAYmoreWAYmore), and he is so close, looking at me with those dark eyes, and to hell with the rule of no-boys-in-my-room. I want to kiss him again, right here right now *yes*—

"Hellooooo!" The rattle of multiple bags shakes the moment apart. That voice. Déjà vu. I mean *Déjà Vu* all over again. It can't be, but it is. This time in my *house*.

The "company" is Jackson Connor. Aghast, I swear under my breath.

"Tacos!" Brian announces gleefully from the living room. "Tacos from Tacos Del Fuego! Awesome!"

"Can you stand it?" I sputter. "She'll never talk about Stargate with him around."

"I can stand it if you can. For our people." He winks. "You know, us dreamwalkers."

I nod and groan. "Let's get this over with." I head for the door, but Lucas takes hold of my hand, stopping me in my tracks.

"Wait." He pulls me back gently to him. "Thank you for the dreamwalk. It was amazing. I owe you about twenty driving lessons. Can you go after class tomorrow?"

I nod and close the door on my way out—better to trap that moment for reliving later. We head for the kitchen, dropping hands to pick up plates and load them with food: tacos, rice, beans, tostadas, and the nuclear salsa that is Del Fuego's specialty. But I can't eat. I still taste that kiss, and I don't want to taste anything else. I sit at the dining room table, poke a few grains of rice into the beans, and nibble the edge of a taco.

"Okay, everybody, I told you we are celebrating," Mom begins cheerily. "Today is a landmark in the career of our future famous artist—that would be you, Vivian—because today, Vivian sold her first painting."

"I did?" I sit up straight. "Which one?" Mom's right. This *is* big. I've sold a few sketches and a watercolor, but never one of the bigger ones. They've been hanging in Déjà Vu for months.

"Jack came in this afternoon after you left and bought *Dreamland*." Mom smiles at me, and a beaming Jackson Connor reaches across the table to hand me an envelope.

What is the word for simultaneously happy, stunned, and horrified? Is there one? Uneasy, I look in the envelope, and inside are three crisp $100 bills.

"No, no, this isn't right." I stare at Mom, confused. "That's the smallest one. It's only $150."

"It's the *best* one," Jackson Connor assures everyone, "and I think it's worth much more. I want to hang it in my new office as soon as the dust settles."

He smiles at me, all seventy-two teeth gleaming in the dining room light. A layer of expectation settles around the perfect, yacht-club wrinkles in the corners of his eyes. He's waiting for me to say something grateful, and despite the envelope of cash in my hand, that smile makes me feel like somehow he's won and I've lost, when I don't even know what the contest was.

A sour bubble of distrust percolates under my rib cage. Beneath the table, Lucas takes my left hand and squeezes it, as if he can feel that bubble threatening to rise and pop. Okay, okay... But *Dreamland?*

Deep breath. *He's not that bad. Remember the apology?*

"Umm, wow. Thank you, Mr. Con—I mean, *Jack*. This is very nice of you."

The satisfied glint in his eyes tells me I'm right.

Jackass Connor: 1, Vivian Night Hawk: 0.

I know from past experience that these tacos are delicious, but the next bite is nothing more than a thin, crispy cardboard shell filled with ground and shredded wet newspaper. The beans are just warmer, goopier newspaper with cheese on top. I finally quit forcing myself and marvel at Brian and Lucas, who scarf down their food while cheerful non-conversation ping-pongs around the dining room, bouncing off my defensive force field.

Jackass Connor exclaims over the salsa and makes jovial, clichéd threats about moving here permanently just for the Mexican food, and Brian chatters excitedly about Hamlet the Space Spider, but I notice Mom is not eating either. She is talking and smiling, her fork activity is fluid, and a molecule of rice or bean passes her lips from time to time, but her net calorie intake is probably in the single digits.

Brian wants to show Jackson Connor his experimental spider and leads him happily to his room, while Lucas and I clear the table. Mom shoos us away from the mess, and as she loads the dishwasher, he and I sit at the kitchen table. My head whirls with all of the things competing for my attention: Stargate, Brian, Dreamland, Dad, and Lucas's right foot being an inch from my left.

The foot wins, at least for now, and I slide my left sneaker over just enough to touch the edge of his boot. He nudges back just the littlest bit, and I peek at his face, golden in the warm light of the lamp, and then look away to keep from melting right out of my chair.

"So, Vivian, how does it feel? Your first big sale!" Mom looks over, smiling.

"I don't know. Pretty good, but also kind of weird," I answer honestly.

"I felt weird when I sold my first sculpture," Lucas remembers. "It was the idea that something of mine was living at someone else's house—not as a gift or even with somebody I knew. Just a little piece of me, somewhere else. I got over that pretty quick, though."

"Because of the money?" I push my shoe forward again so our feet are touching, matched up from heel to toe. Even through shoes, I feel him.

He smiles and pushes his foot gently against mine. "The money helps. But also, I decided it wasn't about a piece of me being gone; it was about me being out there a little farther. It was adding to me, not subtracting. Does that make sense?"

Mom pauses in her counter wipe-down to nod approvingly. "Absolutely. Sharing your gift is empowering, whether there's money involved or not."

"I guess," is my lame response. Well, I was distracted. I had no idea playing footsie was so mentally challenging. How is it possible that our two feet—not even actual feet, but *shoes*—barely touching can completely disrupt my brain circuitry?

Brian laughs, and Jackson Connor exclaims something as they step into the hall, returning to the dining room. *Finally*. I'd better get my scrambled thoughts together because as soon as he leaves, we are having that talk. Me, Mom, and Lucas.

Then I hear the distinctive, solid click-clack of bones being dumped on the table.

"Dominoes! Who's in?" Brian calls happily. Uh-oh.

He learned regular, double-six dominoes before he was three, and when he was five, Mom got him a double-nine set. He mastered that in a week. Sometimes Mom will play him, but I gave up trying to win long ago. Now he has a new, unsuspecting player. Fresh meat.

Lucas looks at me, and I shrug. This could go one of two ways. Most likely, Brian will find every possible multiple of five before Jackson Connor even finishes looking at his dominoes and sweep every game. Or, if the man is actually good at this, it will take a little longer, but Brian will prevail. Either way, Jackson Connor isn't leaving for a while.

A sigh escapes me, and Mom gives me a pointed look. "I'll play." She hangs up the dish towel and goes into the dining room. Irritation buzzes through me.

Well, goody for you.

Lucas's phone buzzes with a text. "Una's back," he says quietly. "Want to go to my house?"

"Yes!"

Good. Maybe Una will have some answers. And if I don't get out of here pretty quick, I'm going to scream.

CHAPTER FIFTEEN

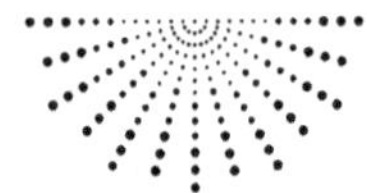

LIKE GREEN CHILE CHEESEBURGERS, New Mexico sunsets are the best in the world, and tonight, the Land of Enchantment lives up to its name. The clouds are rich, bubbling pink pillows lined with coral and molten gold where the sun has dissolved behind the mountains, as if grateful for a billowy refuge after a grueling day. I can definitely relate. Bits of turquoise sky peek through, while smoky gray cloud-feathers curl their way up from the mountains to the deep indigo directly above. For a few moments, I let everything go, allowing the light and color to saturate me.

Since I'm getting nowhere with Mom, I better find out whatever I can from Una. She definitely knows something. She knows I can dreamwalk and sent Lucas to me. Maybe she can even give me some dreamwalking pointers. Even though it did get easier, navigating the surface of Dad's dream was like walking out onto a jetty at the beach —solid, but uneven and slippery, demanding one eye on the shifting path below, and the other on the unfamiliar landscape above.

We stop at the Piggly Wiggly to pick up ice cream. As we walk through the magic Star Trek doors, Lucas grabs my hand, and the feel of his strong hand around mine almost makes me stumble. I am impossibly happy. We round the corner of the aisle by the slushee machine, and I half-wish the Peppers were here to see us. All right, I admit it. I totally, completely, 100 percent wish they were here.

We peer through the freezer doors. "Una likes pistachio." He retrieves a quart and asks, "What kind do you like?"

I like every kind of ice cream, especially coffee or double chocolate. Before I can answer, he appraises me and decides. "Coffee. You want coffee ice cream." His eyebrow flies up, waiting for confirmation of his mind-reading abilities. As soon as I nod, he hands me the pistachio, dives back into the freezer fog, and emerges triumphant. "I knew it! You like it strong and sweet. Like me." As we walk to the register, my heart bubbles and my brain frantically tries to decipher whether he's talking about strong, sweet ice cream—or something else.

"You're pretty quiet," he says as we pull out of the parking lot. "You okay? Is it the painting?"

The painting, and the kissing, and the ice cream, and the dreamwalks... and the way he looks at me. Strong and sweet.

"Yeah," I sigh. "I'm not sure I want Jackson Connor having *Dreamland*. Even though the money is great, and he apologized and all. He has been nothing but nice, but I still don't trust him. Maybe *because* he's been so nice. I just wish he'd picked a different painting."

"I know how that is. I always think too much nice is a warning that something's gonna bite me in the ass, you know? I don't trust him either. But that *is* the best painting." He turns into the driveway on the side of the house. A dark green Jeep Cherokee is in the carport, and a light glows in the kitchen.

"Besides, you still have the original." He turns off the truck and faces me, placing his fist over his heart. "Right here."

He reaches over and touches my forehead, mirroring my touch back in Brian's room. "And here," Lucas says, smoothing back a stray lock of my hair. The glowing dusk has deepened his eyes to black velvet. He leans closer, but the front porch light comes on, and there's

Una in the doorway, so he reaches past me instead and snatches the bag with the ice cream off the floor.

"Better go in before everything melts," he whispers on the way back up. His hair has fallen over one eye, so I don't exactly know if that was a blink or a wink, but I am definitely already melted.

She ushers us in, beams at me, and gives me a brief, cantaloupe-scented hug. She peeks in the bag as she disappears into the kitchen. "Mmm, pistachio! The nephew knows what I like. I guess you guys will be sharing this other stuff?"

She hums around the kitchen. The cheerful clatter of dishes and spoons, the melodious scraping of jars, the mysterious rattling of cellophane—and suddenly I'm starving, the newspaper tacos a distant memory. My stomach growls loudly, and I occupy the next few hungry minutes checking out Lucas's house.

The living room has a large, sand-colored couch and loveseat with overstuffed cushions. Several of Una's weavings hang on the walls, and a twisted metal wolf, similar to the ones guarding the front gate, lurks above the door to the backyard.

"Yours?"

"Yup, eighth grade. My primitive stage."

"It's really good. I can't do anything with three dimensions. Are there more?"

"The ones at the gate and some in my room."

The large wall hanging over the couch grabs my attention. It's not Una's usual style of traditional weaves and pattern combinations. Suspended from a strip of twisted copper, deep greens, blues, and violets swirl around the edges, with a gold silken spiral working toward the center. It's like the traditional Man in the Maze, but there is no one at the top of the maze. Instead, a series of small carved animals tied with silk and woven into the spiral make their way to the center where a crouching wolf of mottled marble with turquoise eyes waits. A smaller wolf of red jasper tips his head to the sky with a green jasper turtle close behind. My gaze sweep along a trail of tiny turquoise beads circling the golden trail to another wolf, a black bear, and a white onyx eagle.

"This is amazing," I breathe, stepping closer. "Where did it come from?"

"My mom started it when my dad left and we were in California. She wanted to incorporate his fetish animals and make something special for him."

"Did he carve all of those?" They are impressively detailed, from the fur on the wolves to the faceted shell of the turtle.

"My grandfather made the center wolf, but his father did the red one. *His* father made the eagle, and my dad made the bear. When my mom—after we came here—we decided to finish it. Una made the turtle."

"Wow. You guys are really talented. Five generations."

Lucas shakes his head. "Not me. I just made the hanger. I can't do carving. It's too small, and I don't have the patience. My mom and I used to make dreamcatchers to sell to tourists—like the one in my truck—but that's the extent of my fine motor skills."

"Ice cream," Una announces. All three bowls are piled high, drizzled with fudge sauce and sprinkled liberally with chopped pecans.

I may survive this day after all.

We take our bowls outside to the back patio. There is still a fading glow on the horizon, and the stars are peeking out one at a time. The air is hot and twilight-still. She lifts her loaded spoon in a toast. "Congratulations, Vivian. I hear you sold a painting today."

"Thank you." I take a huge bite of ice cream, hoping I sound more enthusiastic than I feel.

"You don't seem very happy about it," Una observes.

"Jackson Connor bought it," Lucas tells her. "That same guy who bought your rug."

"Oh, *that* guy." She smiles, no doubt remembering his "compliment."

"Yeah. And he paid way too much for it, which I guess should make me happy? But I don't like him."

With her sympathetic nod, my trickle of resentment opens into a stream.

"He keeps hanging around the store, and now he's been to our *house*. He was even in Brian's room. And I don't get Mom at *all*. How can she not see it? She can usually spot a poser a mile away, and that's what he is—a total poser."

"What makes you think she doesn't see that?" Una asks calmly.

I open my mouth to keep trashing Jackson Connor, but her question stops me mid-rant. Mom makes her living reading people, not just cards. She *has* to see what a phony he is.

"Because. Because she's too nice to him." I know that's a stupid reason, but it's all I can come up with. "And she let him buy *Dreamland,* which I was using for the mural," I add, the explanation sounding weak even to my ears.

"Mmm-hmmm." Una takes a big bite of ice cream and lets me think about it for a moment. I follow her lead and pause to enjoy a bittersweet, fudgy, crunchy bite of heaven while considering the idea that Mom may know more than it appears.

"So," I venture, "you think maybe Mom doesn't like him as much as she seems to."

"What I think is that your mom knows exactly what she's doing, even if you don't."

That certainly fits the Ninja Mom profile.

"I guess I don't like him having the painting because of everything else that's been going on." I glance at Lucas, who has already polished off his ice cream and is leaning back in the patio chair, long legs stretched out in front of him, listening. "I keep trying to tell her about the dreamwalk, but *he* keeps getting in the way. It's almost like he's trying to be in on it. And except for the first time I said the word 'Stargate,' Mom just seems to be humoring me, like she doesn't really want to even hear about it."

"I'm sure she will. But maybe I can help you a little in the meantime. Lucas told me he thought he got into your dream, that he saw you. Was he there? Did you see him?"

I nod. "I saw lights. Blue ones, like fireflies. I knew it was Lucas." If she asks how I knew, I have no logical answer, but nothing about any of this is logical.

In the dim light from the house, I see her smile, and for just a split second, that same flicker of satisfaction in her eyes I saw in the kitchen at Déjà Vu.

"That's him," she confirms. "His energy is blue. I suspected this—he's a dreamwalker like you. He's just a late bloomer."

"Hey, I'm sitting right here," the late bloomer reminds us.

"Of course you are, *shibéhé*" Una turns to her nephew and waves an exaggerated acknowledgement with her spoon, then swats at a mosquito.

"I don't know what I'm supposed to do," I confess. "My dad said these guys from the CIA are trying to make Brian be in their dream-weapon project. Stargate. My dad was in it, that much I do know. Brian isn't a dreamwalker, but I guess we can't just tell them that and hope they'll leave us alone. Dad seemed pretty sure about that."

"They won't leave your family alone," Lucas interjects. His voice is tight. "I *knew* Dad was in this Stargate thing as soon as I read about it this morning. And now, Vivian's dad. How do they even know about people like us? We hardly even know about *ourselves*." He waves his hand in my direction. "They've probably been tracked and followed, just like we were."

Wait, *what*?

Una sighs as if she's had this conversation a dozen times. "I think they followed you and your mother until they decided you weren't a dreamwalker."

Followed. My gaze latches onto Lucas.

"They tracked us everywhere we went," Lucas informs me as he paces the patio. "No matter where we moved, they found us, and it started again. People calling and hanging up, strange cars parked on our street. I was just a little kid. I didn't know what was going on—just that we had to move again." His fists are clenched. "They harassed her until they killed her."

I clap my hand over my mouth quickly, but a small gasp escapes. They killed her? His mother was *murdered*? I never even considered that Mom might be in danger. I don't remember any weird phone calls or mysterious cars hanging around—but I wasn't ever looking for any either. Maybe I was right about the dumb phones and the spotty Wi-Fi. My non-existent driver's license—even Mom's name—were they all intended to keep us off the CIA radar?

Horrified, I look from Lucas to Una. Her face is as still as a tomb. "Wh-what do you mean, they killed her?"

"She drowned," Una says quietly. "Lucas. We can't go back. We can only go forward. Maybe we can use what we *do* know to set things right."

"Set things right? We can't set things right for my mom." His brows are dark slashes across his face, and his curvy mouth is a flat, bitter line. He stands next to my chair, his breathing ragged, agitation pulsing off his body in waves.

"We might help Vivian's mom, though. And her brother," Una points out. "Then there's Vivian herself. Eventually they're going to figure out Brian's not the one they want. Maybe this is what your father was trying to warn you about in your dream."

In the pause that follows, reality sinks heavily onto my shoulders. The hard, shiny bitterness in his eyes softens, and he takes a deep breath.

"You're right. I can't do anything for my mom, but maybe we can keep them away from Brian without them finding out about us. Maybe we'll even find out the truth about our fathers."

I'm not so sure I want to know any more truths. I mean *really* I don't. Possibly-alive fathers are one thing, but murdered mothers are something else. I'm afraid to even ask about any details of Elina's death. The ice cream rolls uneasily in my stomach, and even though the night is hot, a bead of cold sweat worms its way down my neck into my shirt.

She swats at another mosquito. "I vote we continue this inside. I think the ice cream is making us taste even sweeter." She gathers the bowls, and Lucas holds the door open for us. As I pass through behind her, these new dangers spinning around me like a dust devil, he touches my shoulder.

"Sorry," he murmurs. "Like I said, I hope my life doesn't scare you away." His anxious eyes latch onto mine, and I hold his gaze, my heart pounding with conspiracies and murder—and because he is so, so near. Even with all of these new and terrifying developments, the magnetic pull between us is practically visible, shimmering like a heat mirage.

"Looks like it's my life too." I smile a lot braver than I feel. Relief relaxes his face as he smiles back, but I'm glad he sees how scared I am. For a moment I feel better, but as we retreat to the living room, I feel dizzy and suffocated again, as if my lungs are full of water.

What have I gotten myself into?

I wobble my way to the couch and sink in beneath the Wolfsong tapestry, grateful for the cool air and the soft cushions. He sits next to me, his crossed knee barely touching mine. One corner of Elina's weaving undulates in the breeze from the A/C. Up close, I can see gossamer strands of silk embroidered around the indigo edge, a whisper trail of feathers, deepening from silver to velvety black... like mine. I don't believe in signs, but this feels almost like one.

Una curls up like a roly-poly on the loveseat. She looks at me, waiting for me to continue. There's only one way through this: keep going.

"Okay. My dad said there's a way to hide Brian from them, to keep him safe. He said I have to go into Brian's dreams and take him back into mine, but since he isn't a dreamwalker, he won't be able to help. Like, not at all."

She considers this for a moment. "Maybe it would be easier if Brian knows you're looking for him. It's also good if he has something that belongs to you."

"Like what?" Lucas leans back, draping his arm across the back of the couch, not quite touching me, but still creating that protective, tantalizing force field around me, like when we were driving or when we were sitting in the kitchen today. His warmth settles the spinning feeling. The dust devil falls away, and I can breathe again. "You mean like in voodoo? You can get into someone's dreams if you have a lock of their hair or something?"

She shakes her head. "I've heard it's the opposite. If he possesses something of yours, *you* can walk into *his* dreams. It's like a doorway."

"It sounds like vampires. You have to invite them in," I muse. I'm not a vampire fan, but even I know about that. Werewolves and zombies never impressed me much, either. Walking around in other people's dreams is *way* scarier.

"Which is why it might be useful for Connor to have your painting," Una speculates thoughtfully. "For a while, anyway."

Her words startle me. Maybe Jackson Connor didn't win today, after all. The idea of peeking into that creepy poser's dreams—when all he might see is a flash of purple light or an unidentifiable hawk—is both fascinating and disgusting at the same time, like driving by a bad car accident. You don't really want to look at it, but you can't look away.

I turn to Lucas, still imagining the surveillance a hawk could make in Jackson Connor's corner of Dreamland. Lucas's eyes have a speculative gleam in them, and I know he's thinking what I'm thinking. But it will have to wait. The most important thing is to find a way to protect Brian.

"I don't exactly know what to do next," I say somberly. I exhale, puffing out my cheeks. "I think I better practice dreamwalking, though. My dad said it would be really hard. Just because it was easy with him doesn't mean I can do it alone."

Lucas's knee nudges mine. "Hey. What's this 'alone' stuff?"

He tilts his head, and the soft light touches his strong brow. His eyes are full of resolve as he looks at Una. "I don't think Dad was warning me away. It was urgent, but it wasn't a warning. I think I'm supposed to help."

Emotions tumble across Una's round face like glitter in a kaleidoscope. Fear and pride, memory and anticipation—each flicker for a nanosecond, then she nods with resignation. "You will do what you have to. But be careful, nephew. *Kúsąą' díńįį' shibéhé.*"

"Well then, you better start practicing too," I point out. He can just barely do it, and whatever happens, I know I'm going to need him. "I guess all I can do for now is keep trying with Mom and hope I can find Dad again."

Una takes my hands warmly in hers as she says good night and heads for the kitchen. Before we go out the front door, I take one last look at Elina's weaving. Five generations of Wolfsong, woven into a tapestry of mystery, magic, and it seems, murder.

[*FILE 201 210614 SANTA FE (13:17)*]

    Raven: Sleeping Beauty underway

    Trigger: Please repeat. Sleeping Beauty? But—

    Raven: REPEAT. Sleeping Beauty. Rolling car pickup Friday 0-900.

    Trigger: Did Black Sky approve this?

    Raven: This is my mission. I don't need his approval.

    Trigger: It'll be your last mission if anything goes wrong. They'll take you down for good, and probably me with you.

    Raven: I am fully aware of the risk, and I'll take full responsibility. Please acknowledge.

    Trigger: (pause) HUA.

CHAPTER SIXTEEN

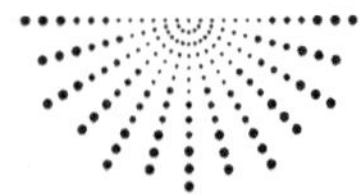

THE KNOT of Dread has been silent ever since Lucas walked into the house this afternoon but stirs restlessly as I slip in my front door. The house is dark, except for the soft light of the kitchen lamp and twin beams from below the bathroom door and Mom's room. The quiet calm of home just makes everything seem worse.

Brian's shower is running, and Mom's door is open, so I peek in. She dozes on the bed, surrounded by laundry. The glow from her TV makes shadows flicker around the room. Even though the volume is way low, the distinctive *Bing, Bing* knell of a *Law and Order* rerun rings out. It's one of the few shows that all three of us like, although Brian's not allowed to watch the S.V.U. version. On *Law and Order*, there are rules. People go missing, people get killed, but in the end, there is a reason. The rules of TV are ironclad: all questions get answered in less than an hour, whether you like the answers or not.

I tap lightly. "I'm back."

"Hi, honey. Come in." She sits up, mutes the TV, and shakes out a pair of Brian's jeans. "I'm extra sleepy tonight for some reason. I nodded off for a few minutes there. Did you have a nice time?"

"Nice" is not how I would describe anything about the last

twenty-four hours—except maybe the feeling of Lucas's lips pressed against mine. That was *extremely* nice.

I step into her room, which is a watercolor version of mine: a cocoon of pale greens and blues, shot through with milky whites and lavender—sea glass colors. Rocks from Arizona and shells from the Jersey Shore trail across her pale wooden dresser to the framed photo of Mom and Dad, taken less than a minute after they were married, surrounded by friends and family in full regalia.

"Yeah, we had ice cream with Una. How did the dominoes go?" I dip into the laundry basket and fold a pair of Brian's socks.

Mom gives me a rueful smile. "You know exactly how it went. Your brother is ruthless."

"Yeah." I grin. "No mercy. Did you meet Hamlet?" Her scrunched face tells me she is aware of the spider, even if they weren't formally introduced.

I fold another pair of socks, and suddenly, exhaustion overwhelms me. Sighing, I tip over backward, landing on the bed with my hand behind my head, staring at the ceiling fan, too tired to say anything but the truth.

"Mom, I'm scared."

She stops folding and takes my other hand. "Your bad dream. Tell me."

"It wasn't a bad dream. It was actually beautiful," I begin. "It all started last week, when I got the jacket. It *is* Dad's jacket, I'm positive."

Her bed is much softer than mine. It's one of those memory-foam ones that make you feel like you are slowly sinking into a marshmallow. Its magic envelopes me one millimeter at a time, and if I'm not careful, I will pass out completely. The ominous news about Lucas's mother makes everything even more urgent, though. I flip onto my right side and focus on her face, which is attentive and gentle, and I don't know how I could ever have been mad at her.

"Okay. I'm not sure how, but the jacket—or maybe that feather— somehow helped Dad connect with me. The first dream was just a few minutes, but this one was longer. Last night, I decided to find him. I remembered what it looked like when he showed up before, and I... I made it like that again. And he came! It's so beautiful there, Mom, more stars than you can imagine. He took me to his part of Dreamland—which I didn't know had parts, but I guess everyone has their own little piece of it. It was really different from mine, and it was hard to walk there, but he sat me down and told me. He told me about Stargate, how they know about Grandma Lily and him, and how they can dreamwalk. He said they think Brian can do it too, and they want to find him. To use him. And he said you know about the project."

Mom nods patiently; she has heard most of this already. I'm explaining this calmly—the opposite of this morning's hair-on-fire panic—but she needs more than just my dream to be won over. I dig into my back pocket and pull out the printouts from the library, now smashed flat, and sit upright.

"This stuff is all about Stargate. It's a real thing, and Dad was in it." I unfold the papers emphatically and hand them to her. There it is in black and white, from several sites, in three different fonts. Now she has to admit it, and she *has* to tell me about Dad's part in this.

"Let me see what you have here." She holds the papers so they catch the beachy glow of the driftwood lamp. Her eyes skim rapidly across the first page, then the second. I resist the urge to cross my arms, tap my foot, or shout, "See, I told you!" Instead, I am silent. Patient. Mature. Believable.

She sets the papers down on the bedspread. "Yes. This looks like the project your father was working with."

Finally. Hope rises in my chest, only to deflate when she shakes her head slowly.

"But Vivi, honey, let me explain what this was about. Your dad was only involved for a couple of years. It was after the Gulf War, before we got married. He wanted to be in the project because some of them were researching how to control dreams, but not as weapons.

It was to help soldiers dealing with post-traumatic stress. You know one of the biggest problems with PTSD is nightmares, right?"

I nod uneasily as The Knot stirs. *This isn't right.*

Mom squeezes my hand. "He was training them to control things in their dreams—how to stop the bad ones and change what was happening in them. He wanted to help these soldiers get their lives back. He called it dream therapy, and even wrote a manual."

I shake my head. This isn't what Dad was talking about at all.

"But Mom, this wasn't about PTSD. He was talking about *this.*" I poke my index finger into the papers on the bed, trying to stay calm. Really, I am. Reasonable and drama-free, even though panic is elbowing its way in. "He said Brian's in danger from these people right *now.*"

"Stargate had other components that had nothing to do with him." She dismisses the psychic warrior project with a shrug. "They tried the dream therapy a few more times over the years, but it just wasn't very successful. Your father was so disappointed. Those exercises really did help the few who could actually do it, but most people can't."

She lets go of my hand and retrieves another pair of jeans from the basket. "Before he went to Bosnia, there were rumors the project was starting up again. A Mr. Cooper from Army Intelligence called a few times, hoping to get your father back in, but all he was interested in was the dream therapy, and they weren't reviving that."

"It says that they tried to use it as a weapon," I insist. "Other countries were doing it. They wanted him back because they knew what he could do."

Maybe he did go back to the program, suggests The Knot. *Maybe Mom doesn't even know.*

She shakes her head. "Your dad would never use something like this against anybody, even if he could."

Even The Knot knows this is true.

She frowns again. "Even after he was... gone, Cooper called a few times. They had the manual, of course, but when we moved, they wanted to know if I'd found any other notes he might have left."

Okay, *now* we're getting somewhere. Phone calls, surveillance—just like Lucas said. *They knew when we moved.* I don't want to interrupt her, but The Knot prods me.

"*Did* he leave any?"

She tilts her head, thinking. "No. I think he put everything he could teach in the manual. Besides, when it comes to dreams and spirit, there are things you can't really teach directly." She smiles gently. "He was very proud of *you*, though. He and Grandma Lily were very strong lucid dreamers—really, the strongest I'd ever heard of—but he said you learned faster than anyone he'd ever trained. You could do things when you were six that he didn't master until he was in his teens." Her eyes are luminous in the lamplight, remembering.

Impatience pushes me, but I push back. She's admitting my dreaming skills are excellent. This should work in my favor. *Deep breath, Vivi. Make your point.*

"See? They wouldn't leave you alone, even when he was *dead*. Dad even told me you had to hide us from them."

Mom considers this. "Yes, we did kind of 'hide' from the world. When your father was home, I didn't want anyone or anything intruding. He went to Bosnia right after we got married, and I spent most of that time alone—and then later, with you. So when he was home, we had our own little family cocoon."

"That's not what he meant, Mom. He said you were hiding us from *them*. The guys in Stargate. You said you hoped I'd never have to know about it."

Mom and frowns as if she isn't sure what she heard.

What the hell is going on?

I'll tell you what's going on, growls The Knot. *She's not going to tell you.*

"If it's so crazy, how did I know the name of the project? How did I know about Stargate?" My voice cracks as my façade of calm starts to crumble.

"Honey, you could have heard that any number of times when you were little. Sometimes dreams bring out things we don't even realize we know." Her practical, logical tone tells me this is over. "I know you're worried about your brother, but you're so overprotective of him. I really think that's where all this is coming from. I'm sure you can stop these dreams, just like any other bad dream."

The Knot and I sit upright. "I don't want to *stop* them. I need to *use* them to save Brian before it's too late!"

"My God, Vivian, listen to yourself." Mom bristles. "Stop being so dramatic. Dreams can tell you a lot, but they tell you about *yourself*. Not secret government conspiracies."

The Knot clenches. *Tell her about Lucas's mom.*

Should I? I'm trying to leave him out of it. I don't want her thinking he gave me these ideas, like she hinted at this morning—like I'm just some blobby, brainless amoeba and I can't even think for myself.

It might be the only way she'll listen, The Knot pushes back.

"Mom, please listen to me. I think we might *all* be in danger, not just Brian. Lucas's dad was in the project too, and these people followed their family around for years. They... they murdered his mother."

"Stop it, Vivian!" Green eyes blaze into mine. "Now you're being ridiculous. I don't know what Lucas has been telling you. He's had a lot of problems adjusting since his mother died, and now he's sucking you into them. Maybe you shouldn't be spending so much time with him." She hands back the papers with a meaningful look.

"He... his mom..." I can't finish whatever it was I was going to say. That hard, bitter ball is back in my throat again, and tears threaten, pushing all rational thought out of my head.

She sighs. The exasperation has passed.

"Vivian, his mother was not *murdered*. She was suffering from deep depression after losing Lucas's father." A knowing sliver of pain glides behind her eyes. "She walked down to the beach one night and drowned herself. Elina Wolfsong committed suicide."

Suicide.

Numb, I head back to my room, clutching the useless Stargate papers, trying to shake that terrible word out of my head. The bathroom door is open, and steamy vapors of soap and organic toothpaste curl through the hallway into Brian's room. He sits cross-legged on his bed in Spider-Man pajama bottoms, tapping his iPad.

"Hey, V." He looks up. "Check this out." The remote speaker on his desk comes to life, and what sounds like Shostakovich rolls across the room.

"Symphony number seven. Hamlet likes it." A hairy shadow shifts slightly in the Space Camp condo. Oh, lovely. Hamlet, the *Dancing* Space Spider.

"Do spiders even have ears?" I sit on the edge of the bed. For a millisecond, I feel Lucas right next to me, and my heart flickers on the spot of our first kiss.

"He can feel the vibrations." Brian reaches over and turns the volume down, peering at me. "Are you okay? You've been acting weird all day."

"I'm good," I lie, leaning back on my elbows. "I hear you stomped Jackson Connor at dominoes."

He yawns. "He made a bunch of stupid moves at the beginning, so I took him to school."

"Good. That's what he gets for underestimating you." Curiosity strikes. "What do you think of him?"

"He's okay, I guess. He knew what all my models are, which is kind of cool." The spaceship models bob in breezy agreement from the ceiling. "He didn't like Hamlet, though." He grins. "He wouldn't even look in through the holes."

"Hmmph," is all I have to say about Jackson Connor's nonexistent coolness. "I think he tries too hard."

Brian scratches a mosquito bite on his leg, considering. "Well, that could be useful."

"Useful?" I look at him sharply. Una said the same thing not an hour ago. "Like how?"

"He could keep bringing us tacos from Del Fuego."

"True... Hey, Bri?"

"Hey, Viv?" He mimics me perfectly, which normally would earn him a punch in the arm, but a fierce wave of big sister tenderness rolls over me. I can't help it. He sits there in clean pajamas, the grubbiness of being nine all scrubbed away. So smart, and so vulnerable. Baby Brian. I will *kill* anyone who tries to hurt him. I don't know how, but they will be deader than dead.

"Be careful, okay? You—you know, going back and forth to Space Camp, walking out in the desert like today," I stammer awkwardly.

He collapses back on the pillow, eyes rolling, letting out a deep, dramatic sigh. "Oh-*kaa-ay*. Mom already told me. What's with you guys? Is there some serial killer on the loose?"

"Not that I know of. Just—you know, be aware."

He raises his right hand, staring at the ceiling, and chants, "I solemnly swear, I will be aware."

"All right, then... oh! There's Macaroonies." He knows where and nods.

"Night, B."

"Night, V."

A few minutes later, I step into the shower, hoping the foamy coconut body wash and the steady downpour of water will somehow squash the spiral of confusion coiling up around me. The weight of the day, and the sheer number of things piling up and snaking themselves into knots—I don't even know where to start untangling them, but I work some conditioner into my hair and try to take a stab at the Mystery Trifecta before the hot water runs out.

Mystery #1. Mom. Hot and cold. We'll talk, and then we won't. We do, and yet we don't. She's concerned and at the same time disinterested. Why is she telling me to drop all of this, but telling Brian to be careful?

Mystery #2. Lucas's mother. What happened to her, really? Una is the one who told Mom about it, but she also didn't contradict Lucas when he said it was murder. And how can I even bring it up? What could I say that wouldn't rip him to pieces? *So, Lucas, what's the deal with your mom? Was it murder or suicide?* No way can I ask that.

Mystery #3. Jackson Connor: building renovator, father of two, real estate tycoon, art and brownie points collector. There's too much there, and I don't know what to think about him anymore, so I rinse him out of my hair with the conditioner. Down the drain with you, Douchebag Connor—for now, anyway.

My thoughts can't stay on anything very long; they keep circling back to Lucas. The way he kept me close to him, just barely touching, almost all evening. The way he touched my face and my hair, the way our lips fit together perfectly, just like our hands. The way he looked at me when he dropped me off tonight, how he leaned over and lifted my chin and kissed me as soft as a butterfly's wings until I was dizzy and clutching the front of his shirt as he said, "I have to go, Vivi, but don't forget tonight—"

As if I could forget one single second of anything to do with him.

It's almost 11:00 by the time I finish all of the post-shower rituals of applying lotion, combing out my hair, brushing my teeth, and inspecting my face for any new flaws.

I place the feather on my headboard again, climb into bed, and call Lorena. I don't have that picture of Lucas she wanted—not yet—but I promised to call, and maybe she can start unravelling at least one of these tangles with me. Ringing. More ringing. Then her cheerful voicemail: "Hi! I can't answer right now, but you know what to do." I hang up before the beep. I bet she's with that surfer guy.

I lie in the dark, breathing deeply and clearing my thoughts. I have to practice getting out of my dreams, and I want to try tonight. Una's idea about being able to walk into someone's dreams if they have something of mine gave me an idea, and I think I have the perfect test object: the $2 bill I left in the jar at Noonie's today. No one ever likes those things, so whoever ended up with it must actually want it. And since I've had it for weeks, it should be—I don't know, imprinted?—more than just regular money. I have to follow it and get that person to do something in their dream.

This will be the perfect warm-up for my date with Lucas.

A date in Dreamland.

CHAPTER SEVENTEEN

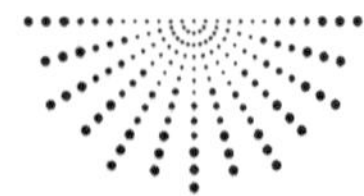

Tonight, the Dreamland stars stretch out and become an infinity of prisms and colors I can't even name. I am instantly in the mountains, and a shower of violet lights skids and scatters out from my feet as I land. This is the fastest I've ever gotten here, and it's exhilarating. Being here on a mission, I'm noticing for the second time, is much different than just hanging out.

The tangy scent of the pine trees gives way to buttercream Macaroonies, and I capture that immediately, breathing deeply. I have to follow that $2 bill, and I'm not sure how to do it, but Macaroonie vapors are a good start. I can't do this the way I found Dad. Changing the dream web to another color—another person's energy—I suspect only works if you know what to change it *to*. All I have is the rich butter-coconut aroma in my nose, a picture of that $2 bill in my head, and the name Noonie's on my lips.

I focus on the tops of the trees, where the coral has deepened to an iridescent violet-pink. I know I have to go over the mountains like last time, but where? I concentrate on the Macaroonie smell. It becomes sweeter, more layered and luscious, settling into my lungs.

I close my eyes to breathe deeper, but then I remember I have to keep them open to fly. I focus on the shifting sky, right where it meets the trees, and picture that flattened out bill, warm from riding in my pocket all day. I push the two visions together, superimposing each upon the other, pressing as hard as I can. It feels like an ice cream headache freezing and squeezing the middle of my forehead. The images give way—there—and merge into each other like a deadbolt sliding into place.

I rise silently, gathering speed over the jagged trees to the crest of the Dreamland Mountains. Suddenly, the two images slip out of place into swirls of butterscotch gold and the deepest pine green. I can barely hold on, but I grit my teeth and push back *hard,* keeping the image of the $2 bill and my tree line pressed together. The spiral waves shiver back into place and go still—but it's no longer the evening horizon in front of me.

The greens and golds have formed themselves into an enormous, ornate building. Creamy caramel marble steps rise into spectacular pillars, leading to imposing, dark green doors with brass fittings that shine like mirrors. The gleaming marble towers endlessly above the doors, disappearing into a misty cloudbank. The silence is still pervasive, but it has shifted, opened somehow, as if I'd been underwater and then surfaced into a silent room. I glide up to the doors, following the steps without my feet touching them. One of the doors stands open, and I slip inside.

I brace for the uneven gravity of another person's dreams, but instead it seems as if I'm looking through a magnifying glass. Whatever I focus on is clear, but the edges seem to curl upwards, as if my vision is trying to fit into a tunnel.

And what a vision.

The marble walls rise upward, just as endless as they appeared outside. There is no ceiling that I can see. The walls are a shiny golden-white eternity of drawers stacked on top of each other, punctuated with glittering brass knobs and intricate locks. Wall sconces cast steep wedges of light above. A marble counter stands directly in front of me, and behind it the entire wall is the deep emerald green of the front doors, with a huge, polished spoke wheel mounted in the middle of it. Golden hinges the size of telephone poles flank the right side, while the other three sides sit flush with the wall, reinforced with thick brass fittings. I finally realize what I am looking at: a vault. A giant vault, inside a bank only possible in someone's dreams.

A shadow moves behind the counter and climbs up onto a tall seat, sliding into the light of one of the sconces. It's Mr. Noonie—but Mr. Noonie from twenty years ago. His graying brown hair is now a deep chestnut, and his weathered skin has gone smooth. He wears a rich herringbone jacket instead of his baker's apron.

Dad said as soon as you enter someone's dream, they start to wake up. I freeze, not sure what Mr. Noonie can see. A cluster of tiny amethyst fireflies? A nighthawk lurking in the shadows? He isn't looking in my direction at all, though. He unfolds something on the counter, just out of my vision, then holds it up to the light, smiling— the $2 bill. He reaches into his pocket, produces a large shiny key, and unlocks a drawer in the counter. He places the bill carefully inside and then locks the drawer, satisfied.

Something pulls on me, a gentle wisp of gravity coming from the direction of the door. I have to go soon, but first, I have to make him *do* something. I've done it with people in my own dreams, but never someone else's—and that's what I'm going to have to do to shield Brian.

Mr. Noonie climbs down from his chair. I look around. The watery tunnel vision wavers a little, and the sensation of being pulled gets stronger.

-Look up. I say it aloud, but it somehow emerges soundlessly from my forehead. *Look up!*

Mr. Noonie hesitates in mid-descent and tilts his head, darting a quick gaze up into the limitless tower of drawers before stepping down behind the counter.

Yes!

I can still see his head as he walks deeper into the shadows.

-Macaroonies! I shout impulsively, as the gentle suction from

behind becomes an insistent tug. Macaroonies? Where did *that* come from?

My vision starts to spin at the edges. As I retreat through the doorway and over the steps, the bank dissolves completely, spinning into gold, white, and green. The green slows down, morphing into familiar pine trees. I drop down lightly, scattering fuchsia sparks flecked with remnants of Mr. Noonie's gold. Home.

A surge of energy flows through my veins as I take a deep breath of sharp, cool mountain air. I did it! The soft scuttling and a barely visible glow in the bushes announce the arrival of the Dreamland menagerie, as if they've all come out to see how it went.

"It was easy," I inform them. My head is still throbbing, but it was definitely a success.

The rosy droplets of my words ripple into the dream web and skip out across the horizon. A few of them gather around a large, pulsing blue glow in the trees. As the glow brightens, the animals make soft skittering noises, and I realize they didn't come out to get a dreamwalk report—they came out to announce the arrival of a visitor. As the glow makes its way toward me, I smell his soap and hear his triumphant voice before I see him take shape in the clearing:

-About time you got here. Look! I made it!

Lucas's glee is contagious, and I laugh too, blurting out: *-Here you are, the man of my dreams.* This would normally cause my face to burst into mortified flames, but we are in my world now—and here, everything I say is the exact right thing.

We stand in front of each other, and the full moon casts silken silver light onto our faces, igniting his eyes and outlining his hair. He takes both of my hands in his, stepping closer, and the warmth radiating from his body envelopes me completely. His touch makes me shiver, as if the velvet tip of a feather is tracing an achy trail of pleasure from my fingertips to my shoulders, around my neck, and down my spine.

-Where do you want to go? he asks quietly, eyes locked with mine.

-You know where. Connor's.

I can barely get the words out. Lucas is so close, it feels like our bodies have begun to merge. Violet and cobalt sparks shiver and pulse between us, and my heart swells like it's going to burst.

-Are you sure? His lips brush mine with a ragged whisper. The effervescence between us begins to vibrate softly like a single note on plucked on a harp. Our bodies draw together like magnets, but I pull away.

-Yes—we'd better—I'm not sure how long we can do this together.

His eyes glint wickedly in the moonlight. I step back, fighting his gravity, freeing my left hand. Our remaining joined hands melt together completely, warm and humming, spun together with sparks of blue and violet.

-Dreamwalk, Lucas. I meant dreamwalk.

-I know what you meant. He grins innocently.

I pretend to glare at him and resist the urge to step back into his arms again, but only because if we touch any more, we will sink into each other and never find out anything about Jackson Connor.

-Okay, he relents. *What do we have to do?*

I point to the summit. *-We have to go over the mountain, and we also have to follow the painting. Keep your eyes open and focus on both things. You have to squeeze them together.*

Lucas frowns. *-Like those 3-D pictures, where you go cross-eyed until a dolphin jumps out at you? I can never see those things.*

-Me neither, but yes. No. It's the total opposite. Instead of relaxing, you have to push really hard.

We face the horizon, still holding hands, and concentrate on the top of the mountain. The gentle hum between us gets louder as I press the Dreamland painting into the sky in front of me, pushing inward until they lock together, becoming one and the same. The wind swirls around us, scattering blue and purple fireflies as we rise and skim across the tops of the trees, until they fall away past the moon, leaving only the two of us and the spinning streaks of a million stars.

CHAPTER EIGHTEEN

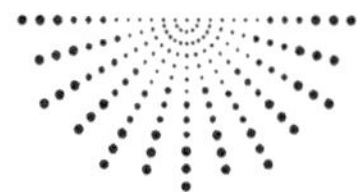

I thought that dreamwalking together would make it easier—and at first, it does.

The prisms of color spin wildly like they did going to Mr. Noonie's, but our combined gravity slows them into bubbling streaks of light that gather and form a wobbly, glowing tunnel. Lucas squints at the flashes that splash across his angular face. Our hands are melded together completely.

-Keep your eyes open, and don't let go, I remind him.

He squeezes my hand in response, sending a sweet ripple of warmth up my arm and into my chest. The lights slow down into brilliant reds, blues, and burnished golds, like those pictures of spectacular autumn leaves against a vibrant sky. As we materialize—or maybe the dreamscape does; I haven't quite figured that out yet—the blues gather and deepen above us. The dark gold and glowing vermilion mingle in layers, and the air grows chilly as the layers finally solidify into... a wall.

The golden-brown granite looms above us, topped with turrets and walkways and dotted with tall poles. We stand deep in the shade, but up on those poles in the sun, long scarlet flags stream out in the wind—wind that's sharp and salty, accompanied by the sound of waves roaring and crashing on huge rocks.

Lucas looks at me, uncertain, and we instinctively press ourselves against the tomb-like cold of the wall. That slithery sensation of being watched tiptoes across the back of my neck. This isn't nice Mr. Noonie's bank. This is Jackson Connor's fortress. Who knows what kind of danger lurks here?

The pulverized gravel and shells under our feet make no crunching noises as we stealth our way to the end of the wall, but I'm not sure if that's because we are barely touching the earth, or if the angry waves are simply drowning out the sounds of our footsteps. Lucas reaches the end and stops abruptly.

-I can't see anything now. The fog is even worse out here.

-What? I don't see any fog. The sky is robin's egg blue without a single cloud. The light is strong and vibrant, like a crisp October afternoon. *Let me see.*

I inch my way around him. Here, way more than in my dad's world, gravity feels... tricky. I don't want to lose contact with the wall or the narrow path around it. I don't want to lose contact with Lucas, either. He stands with his back to the granite, while I turn forward and pass over him, switching hands quickly. I feel his intense gaze on my face, but I keep my own eyes fixed on the end of the wall. We move forward and the ground becomes more solid with every cautious step.

As I peek around the edge, my face is blasted with the stiff, raw wind blowing directly off the ocean in front of me. Dazzling shades of the deepest blues and greens undulate on the surface, seething and rearing back, then exploding on the rocks in massive blooms of glittering white streaked with purple. Huge white seagulls screech to each other above the waves and swoop low over a tiny spit of sand that runs from a narrow opening in the rocks to the walls of the Jackson Connor castle.

-Can you see anything? I can barely see some trees over there.

-I see the ocean, I say, and spin back out of the wind next to Lucas. *I can see pretty much everything.* We are facing steep hills covered densely with dark evergreen trees, sloping into the toothy black rocks that guard the gaping mouth of the cove.

-Let's go to the other end, he suggests. *But you better lead, since you can see better. All I see is fog and the wall.*

-I don't know why that is, but don't you dare let go of me!

-Don't worry. I won't.

I step around him, switching hands again. We creep steadily out of the salty breeze, keeping our free hands flat against the wall for balance.

-Whoa, Lucas murmurs. *Don't look up.*

Of course, I look up immediately and get punched with a wave of dizzying nausea.

-Oh my God. I gasp all the way into the wall, plastering my back from shoulder to hip.

-Told you not to look up.

By the time we get to the other end, we are inching along, arms splayed out like a weird pair of hand-holding starfish. The vertigo recedes along with the sound of the sea, and when I peek around the corner, there is no wind slapping me in the face. All is still in the monolithic slab of shade cast by this fortress. Here, the gravel path widens and parallels a ridge of colorful maples that mirror the golden-brown walls and the scarlet flags. Above us, carved into the castle wall is a domino line of narrow slits, like the kind of tall, skinny windows they made in medieval times. I think if we push up a little, maybe...

-Come on, let's look in. We have to lift up, though... just look up to the windows, not all the way.

-Look in? You mean those slits? You know what they're for, right?

I don't. I look away from the wall to Lucas. His brows are furrowed and his lips are pressed into a grim half-smile.

-They're for the archers.

-Oh... Yikes. I wasn't planning on confronting a squadron of chain-mail clanking bowmen. But this is Dreamland. Any archers here would only see—what? Some blue and purple lights, or maybe a wolf and a hawk. No matter what we look like, nothing can actually hurt us in a dream.

-Let's at least try. We can't stay long, anyway—and when you feel something pulling on you, it means we have about three minutes.

-Yeah? Then what happens?

-I don't know, exactly, but it means he's waking up.

-Okay. We definitely don't want him to wake up enough to know we're here.

I push myself off the ground a few feet, facing the wall. Lucas follows, but he is straining, gripping my hand tightly. I remember he is new to this, and right about now, he's feeling that pushing-the-couch-across-the-floor-with-your-head feeling.

-How about I look, and you stay down and listen for anything coming?

-I don't want to let go of you. His face is sweating now, but his whisper is fierce. The first window slit gets closer.

-Slide down and hold onto my ankle.

This is a terrible, wonderful idea. As Lucas relaxes and slips down the wall, his hand strokes mine, sliding across my outstretched arm to my shoulder. For a moment he is directly behind me, his breath soft on my neck, his hair brushing my face, his whole body humming warmly against my back and legs, just barely brushing me against the granite.

He pauses for an excruciating millisecond—a millisecond that drops my heart into my belly and lights it on fire—then continues descending, trailing that fire with his hand lightly down my side and my leg until he rests on the ground with my ankle firmly in his grasp. By the time he gets there, we are both out of breath and I have lost my train of thought entirely. What am I doing?

Oh. Yes. The windows.

Still shaky, I lift up to the first window, darting my head over the edge like a turtle in and out of its shell. There is no menacing archer lurking in the foot-wide opening, so I drift up for a better look.

It's a library. Thousands of books of all sizes and colors stand silently at attention in the soft lamplight. An enormous atlas rests on a stand, but I can't see what it's open to. The familiar smell of old books startles me, and it curls around another Dreamland pleasure: the sharp tang of freshly ground coffee. How can I have *anything* in common with Jackson Connor?

I work my way over to the next window, tethered by Lucas's strong hand like a human balloon. Again, no armed guard at the window, but there are people inside. It's dark, but it seems to actually be... outside. There are shadowy people, and the faces of men wander in and out of the only source of light: a campfire. I can see the smoke, smell the wet wood. There's another smell underneath—scorched and ugly like burning tires.

Three of the men are sitting; two of the faces are briefly visible in the flickering glow. An occasional hand gestures up and out of the darkness. They are laughing at something, and a third figure is only a dark shape behind the glowing ember of a cigar. As the two men turn toward the fire, I see one of them has a sculpted face, with hooded eyes and a squared-off jaw. I only see him for a brief second, but right next to him, leaning in and pulling a twig out of the fire to light a cigarette, is Jackson Connor.

It's a much younger Jackson Connor, under a black wool cap, but it's definitely him. There are no yacht-club wrinkles around his eyes yet. He looks scrubbed—his Abercrombie cheeks and nose are pink, as if he's been skiing all day. This must be some rich-kid Christmas ski trip. I peer closer, looking for the expensive vest and the lift tickets that dangle like careless badges of preppy bravado. There are no lift tickets, though, and as my eyes adjust to the darkness, I realize this is no ski trip. Jackson Connor and his friends are wearing military camouflage.

The hand on my ankle shifts just as I feel the first pull between my shoulder blades.

-Lucas, are you okay?

-Yeah, but I'm feeling it. What's in there? Can you see anything?

-A big library, and I guess an old Army memory.

Lucas's puzzled *hmph* mirrors my uneasy thoughts. As hard as I try not to ignore Jackson Connor, I would remember if he'd ever said anything about being in the military.

The tug strengthens, tilting the wall away and skidding my field of vision toward the top of the rampart, where the nausea lurks. Oh, no—not doing that again. I look hastily to my left at the next window, curiosity still stronger than the gravity of return.

-Just one more, and we'll go, I promise. As I push up to the third window, I feel a shadow cross at the top of the wall. Too fast for an archer, it swoops by silently—a seagull, most likely. But come to think of it, I haven't heard any raucous cries from the cove for several minutes. Cautious, I peek over the edge.

The final vision is even darker than the previous one. The room is empty, and the gloom is lit by a single tall candle. Its waxy scent is sweet grass and sage, like the ones we sell at Déjà Vu. I squint, trying to see what lies behind that lone, vigilant glow. In the corner, there's a shadow even darker than dark, something solid. The shadow stirs and curves fluidly, and a sigh escapes. A pale, slender hand drops into the candlelight, trailing tiny gems of lavender and palest gold, which disappear into the blackness below. Someone is in there, sleeping. A woman.

-Vivian. Lucas's voice is low and urgent as he squeezes my ankle. *Look.*

-I am. Somebody's asleep in there, but I can't—

-No. His voice is almost a whisper. *Up on the tower.*

I don't want to look up and risk another punch in the stomach. The candle smells sickly sweet, and the thick smoke from the greasy campfire next door is billowing around me. But I can't really see anything more in the room, and the pull between my shoulders is becoming insistent.

I tilt my head and flick my eyes quickly up to the imposing turret at the far end. On a wrought-iron railing that circles the top of the tower, a large raven perches, watching us closely. The sun gleams across its powerful blue-black head and shoulders. It cocks its head, coldly assessing the intruders, more unnerving than a whole squad of archers. The raven looks me over, and as its eyes meet mine, I get walloped by a new ball of nausea and chills from the acrid, burning smells of Jackson Connor's dreams—and because the raven has blue eyes.

-*Shapeshifter*, Lucas murmurs, uneasy. *Vivi...*

It lifts its wings ominously, still looking at me. Challenging me to —what? I concentrate on it, defiant. If I can make Mr. Noonie look up in his own dream, I can surely turn this big ugly bird the other way.

-*Go away!* I focus and strike my thoughts at it as hard as I can. It takes a step and then drops like a pendulum swinging along the side of the tower, heading directly for us.

-*That way!* Lucas shouts, pointing to a break in the trees. *Go. Go!*

I scramble to get my bearings as the tug becomes suction, and before I can take his hand, the red-gold-blue world recedes and spins into turbulent pinwheels of light that roar like a freight train. I call out to him to keep his eyes open, but I'm not sure he hears me above the din. Lucas still holds my ankle, but he is heavy, and instead of soaring through the sky, we brush through large, anonymous tree branches that claw and grab at my legs. At least I hope it's the branches and not that raven, but I don't dare look back and find out.

He breathes hard, his grip on my ankle like iron, and I can feel him scrambling to negotiate the alien landscape of Dreamland. But the campfire smell has evaporated, and I can see my sky clearly ahead. With a final surge of energy, I propel us high over the summit of my mountains into the clean twilight stars. Blood pounds in my ears. I feel an exhausted Lucas let go of my ankle as we tumble into the soft pine needles and leaves.

My heart pounds, trying to claw its way out of my chest. I stare up at the silent, spangled sky and take a few deep breaths, then prop myself up on my elbows.

-Wow. That was—Lucas?

He made it out. I *know* he did. He didn't let go of me until we had crossed the summit and cleared the trees.

But Lucas is gone.

CHAPTER NINETEEN

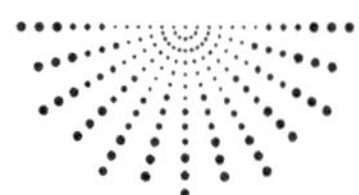

WHEN I PEEK through one eye, the red glow of the clock reads 4:18.

My bed is warm and cozy, and outside the covers, the air is cool. The air conditioner hums serenely, and bands of moonlight push their way through the blinds, slanting pale streaks on the spot where we stood close and—my heart squeezes tight and both eyes fly wide open.

Where is Lucas?

I roll over in the dark, gulping for breath, feeling around on the nightstand for my phone. I *know* he made it out. I brought him back with me, and it's just Dreamland, not a place he could get left behind for real. So why is my hand shaking when I read his last text, *See u in Dreamland,* and hit *reply?*

V: *Are you OK?*

I lie back in bed, resting the phone on my stomach, trying to get my breath back into my body. He's all right (*in,* two, three, four). He'll answer in a few minutes (*out,* two, three, four). My mouth tastes like baked sawdust, and The Knot is wide awake. Amber-colored dreamwalk glitter flickers at me from the side of my vision—residue from Noonie's bank or Connor's wall?

Sixteen more breaths and still no answer from Lucas. The Knot squirms around my stomach again, trying to climb up into my throat.

Way to go. You can barely do this yourself and look what happened —you lost him in Dreamland. What if that thing, that raven-thing, got him? That shapeshifter, he called it.

I don't think that's even possible. He just didn't have the strength to stay longer. Even Dad was barely visible when he brought me back.

"Shut up, you," I order The Knot and swing my legs over the side of the bed. A drink of cold water should settle my stomach and wash the sawdust out of my mouth. I shiver a little. Behind the cool breath of the A/C lurks a deeper chill, one that feels like the shadow of a thick, stone wall. I shove it behind me and stand up.

4:37 glares the clock. I glare right back. "You shut up too."

I pad silently down the hall to the kitchen, grab the Brita out of the fridge, and take a few long, icy, purified gulps straight out of the pitcher. The cold slides all the way down into my stomach, chilling The Knot into submission. One more swallow and I close the door. I slip out the back door, across the dark patio, and into the platinum moonlight of the backyard.

It's warm. The pre-dawn stillness greets me with the burbling of a cricket and the heady scent of unseen jasmine. I stand there, feeling like an inside-out hurricane; the eye of turbulence in the middle, surrounded by peace and stillness. Soon the moon's patient glow calms the thoughts and worries spinning and twisting inside me, smoothing them out in the soft night air.

One thing is all too clear: I don't know what the hell I'm doing. Here I am, jumping around in other people's dreams, trying to—do what, exactly? Save Brian? Find Dad? Teach Lucas? Maybe I'm just finding a way to make Jackson Connor go away and leave us alone. I can't get Mom to talk to me, I don't know where Lucas is, and even Lorena doesn't answer my calls.

But as agitated as I feel, I do remember what she said—was it only yesterday morning?—to be *still*. If you don't know what to do, then don't do anything right away. Yeah, well, that's easy for her to say. She has almost as much patience as Mom, and I have *zero* patience for just about anything. When something needs to be done, I say do something!

Even if it's wrong? The Knot pipes up.

"*Especially* if it's wrong," I retort, "and I thought I told you to shut up."

The moon hangs a little lower. The faintest tinge of dawn shrinks the darkness and makes the sky somehow smaller and less infinite. My panic seems smaller too. The internal turbulence subsides, for now. Okay, I will be *still* and see what shakes out—but only for a little while.

I step back into the kitchen and silently close the door. The coffee machine has come to life, gurgling a loud greeting and filling the room with its irresistible richness.

"Good morning." Mom's soft voice comes from the deep shadow behind the table. Somehow, I'm not surprised to find Ninja Mom waiting for me. "You're up early, honey."

"Yeah, I woke up and couldn't go back to sleep."

She doesn't say anything, so I add vaguely, "There's a lot going on."

I can see her smile in the lifting gloom. "There is, for sure. Vivi, I don't like how our talk ended last night. I didn't mean to just dismiss your concerns."

Now it's my turn to say nothing. If she wasn't trying to dismiss my concerns, well, she could have fooled me.

"There were so many secret things about Stargate, things your father couldn't tell me, and even more things he didn't know about. In these research programs, you only know about the part you're doing, with just a general picture of the whole thing. They say that's the only way to keep things from being compromised. I don't know about that. It seems to me all the secrecy just causes rumors and exaggerations. Sometimes it felt like we were just standing in the middle of a river. It's all around you, but all you can see is the surface. You can let it pick you up and take you, or you can stand there and let it flow through you, but you cannot push the river, Vivian. Believe me, I've tried. Sometimes, all you can do is stand your ground and wait to see where everything is flowing."

In other words, be still. First Lori, now Mom. Sigh. This has all the makings of a trifecta. I grab two mugs out of the cabinet and splash cream into both of them before filling them with coffee. Mom doesn't object to the cream when I hand it to her. She must really be sorry.

"Don't worry, Mom. I'm a good swimmer." I smile and lift my mug in an imaginary cheer, with imaginary confidence, and start back to my room.

"And Vivi, about Lucas."

I stiffen and stop in the doorway. Now what? *Here it comes again,* sniffs The Knot, *stay away from the big, bad Wolfsong.*

"I didn't mean what I said, about spending less time with him. You two seem to be good for each other. It's just that it's happened so quickly, and, well, I guess I'm a little overprotective myself," she admits.

"It's okay." I'm glad we're back to normal, but one thing here is definitely not a mystery: any info I get about dreamwalking or Stargate won't be coming from Mom.

Ruffled feathers smoothed over, Mom starts breakfast, and I go get dressed for painting class. When I close my door, a tiny blue light flashes on the nightstand. Lucas! I flop onto the bed with relief and flip open the phone.

LUCAS

Wild ride, but still in one piece. You?

That was crazy! I thought I lost you there for a minute. I start to type that I was afraid the shapeshifter had gotten him but decide not to share all of the early morning head-drama, at least not in a text.

Nah. A van turned around in my driveway
and woke me up right when we cleared the
trees. Still seeing crazy stars. Is that
normal?

Yeah, *they* go* away* **

haha you going to class?

Are we driving after?

Definitely!

A FEW HOURS LATER, the moon has retreated and the sun wields its scorching path across the windless sky. I ride as fast as I can, but even the pecan forest can barely hold off the relentless heat. Doppler Dan the Weatherman says no rain in sight for a few more days.

I duck into the Fine Arts wing with the smaller sketchbook in my backpack and a picture in my head for the mural. I don't need much to sketch out what I want. After all, I know the painting and the place by heart.

But I have another picture in mind, another image that's been following me around since I woke up. Three shadowy faces lit only by a small fire. Maybe if I can figure out what that scene, or memory, or whatever it was in Jackson Connor's dream was, I can figure out what he wants. I was pretty sure before, but after that dreamwalk I'm absolutely *positive* that Jackson Poser Douchebag Connor is not what he seems to be.

The Knot agrees.

The drawing takes only a few minutes, and I'm still not sure it's exactly right when I pedal over to Welding and Automotive. People aren't my best subject, but I think Lucas will recognize Connor. The second face is all planes and angles, and as for the third, I felt his jovial presence last night more than I could see what he looked like. All I can capture is the charcoal-y shadow of Guy #3.

Lucas comes out of the double doors carrying a printer-paper box full of twisty metal scraps. "Hey!"

I never knew someone's eyes could actually light up, but his are glowing sparks under the unruly hair. They lock with mine, which sends a fresh jolt of happiness down my spine. He grins and sets the box down to jump off the loading dock.

"I was going to bring the truck around to get you. You ready?" His smooth voice is calm and cheerful, as if we were never chased by a blue-eyed raven over the Dreamland Mountains.

Meanwhile, my voice has betrayed me again, and all I can manage is a squeaky, "Hi. Yes!"

He sets the box in the bed of his truck, and then my bike, giving me a brief, sweet glimpse of muscled arms and shoulders outlined by his dark red T-shirt. Instead of the levee, we decide to head for one of the farm roads that runs between the pecan orchards and the chile fields at the edge of town. Unlike the levee, there are a few shady spots there, where it might be a blessed 100 degrees instead of 105.

We ride in silence for a few minutes. I itch for another chance to drive, wanting to redeem myself after crashing his truck twice in the same day. But mostly I want to show him the drawing and hear what he thinks about last night.

Route 28 is deserted. There is nothing to crash into for several miles. This makes me feel relieved and mortified at the same time, because yay, I can't crash anything—but wow, is he worried I will? I wait for him to stop and switch places, but he doesn't.

"Where are we going?"

"Just a little farther, where I can turn around." He keeps glancing in the rearview mirror, while the quarter-sized dreamcatcher dances in time to the bumps in the old road.

I twist around. "Is someone back there?"

"No. Just in case." His voice is casual, but his eyes are wary, as if he's used to being followed and knows how to get around it. The reality of those years of surveillance on their family and what Mom said about Elina committing suicide hits me hard. The Knot, usually sleeping when Lucas is around, suddenly sits up, horrified.

"Lucas, do you think someone knows about last night?"

He swings into a long driveway and backs up so we are facing away from the late morning sun. Heat waves shimmer all the way back to the turnoff on Valley Road. He puts the truck in park and leans back, unbuckling his seat belt.

"Well," he says thoughtfully, "I don't see how anyone could know —except for maybe Jackson Connor."

"Okay, that's not making me feel better," I reply glumly, undoing my seatbelt. "I was thinking we just looked like lights, but do you think he actually saw *us?*"

"I don't know." Lucas shifts sideways, facing me, and takes my hand. His thumb strokes mine gently, melting my whole arm into warm butterscotch. "I couldn't see much when we got there, maybe because I'm new at this? The longer we were there, though, the clearer it got. But even in *your* dream, I only see lights until we get close, so I don't think he saw us, if he even remembers the dream. I guess I'm just being paranoid."

The Knot listens anxiously for any telltale note of artificial reassurance, but there is none. And it's true; even I can only see him as lights when he first arrives—and he's actually been invited. Satisfied, The Knot drops back down and waits.

But only for a moment before anxiety coils deep in my gut again.

"What about that raven? What was *that?* You said it was a shapeshifter. It scared the crap out of me." I shiver, remembering the cold blue eye, the nauseating fear.

I know what a shapeshifter is; doesn't everyone? A person that can briefly take the form of animals, other people, and sometimes even trees. They're part of Native tradition, but shapeshifter stories are all over the world, from European werewolves to the Japanese kitsuni, and they are almost always seriously evil.

"How did you know?" I ask.

"I don't know that for sure, either. Whenever something is out of place, it gets my attention. Sometimes it's a good thing, like finding an unusual stone. But when it's creepy, when something about it is wrong... my mom used to say to stop and listen to my instincts. Hear what the universe is trying to tell me."

There it is. The "be still" trifecta is complete: Lorena, Mom, and now Elina Wolfsong.

What happened to you, Elina? The question bubbles up again, begging to be asked no matter how much I don't want to know. How do I find the words?

I sigh. "Yeah, I've been getting a lot of that lately."

"Well, that thing was definitely *wrong*. I just wanted us to get out of there as fast as we could." Lucas pauses, then squeezes my hand gently, leaning a little closer. "I was hoping to get back to our spot in Dreamland."

My face flames scarlet, remembering that dreamy embrace, as well as that excruciating, delicious moment on Jackson Connor's wall. When our lips touch, the warmth spreads from my face to my chest, swirling down through my knees and radiating across my whole body. This must be what they mean by "chemistry."

Our kiss is deep and sweet, and our bodies pressed together leaves me breathless. At this moment, I would gladly be breathless for a few centuries, but we break apart long before even one century has passed. He hugs me hard and smiles.

"Vivi! This is supposed to be a driving lesson. And we *are* sitting in the middle of the road." He cocks one eyebrow and glances toward the long stretch of Route 28.

"For sure," I answer promptly, scooting over to open the door. Chemistry is one thing, but I want to *drive.*

I turn us around in that same driveway, pointing away from Valley Road. "You can keep watch for stalkers," I inform him.

"Okay." He laughs. "Oh, wait." He digs his phone out of his back pocket and drapes his arm across the top of my seat, holding the phone up in front of us. "In honor of our first dreamwalk."

Ridiculously happy, I rest my head against him, smiling as he takes a couple of pictures.

"One more," he announces and quickly pulls me close to him again, kissing the top of my head while the phone clicks a final time. "Mmmmmwaah! Hey, your medieval phone can get pictures, can't it?"

I shove him away, laughing. "Yes! Shut up and let me drive."

His arm plops down behind me again, but I fight the urge to lean back into it and focus on the road instead. Five miles later, I have accelerated up to freeway speed several times, practiced stopping fast ("Watch out for that white van!" "Haha, very funny!") and changing lanes smoothly. I have not crashed anything or anyone. Best of all, I'm holding the steering wheel like a normal person instead of clutching it like someone dangling from a bridge. We are deep in the chile fields, not a car or tractor in sight.

Perfect.

"Lucas, there's something I want to show you. I drew what was in Connor's window, the one with the soldiers. It's in my backpack."

"Yeah?" Interested immediately, Lucas digs out my sketchbook and flips it open.

The road is empty, so I risk a few glances over to his side of the truck. He thumbs through the heavy pages, nodding his approval at a sketch of the neighbor's cottonwood tree and another of Rufus the cat. Both eyebrows fly up and he tries not to smile at a lame attempt to draw my bike. I groan. Ugh! I meant to throw that disproportioned mess away. It looks like a kindergartner drew it.

"Next," I urge.

He finally gets to the last one in the book and turns it sideways.

"I didn't put too much detail. I just wanted to get the gist of it," I caution, worried it's just as awful as the bike sketch. He stares at it, not saying anything. At least he isn't laughing.

"It's, you know, just a rough drawing," I offer. Does it suck *that* much? I pull over and put the truck in park. He still hasn't said anything, and I cringe inside, torn between babbling some random excuse for my crappy drawing or falling as silent as he is.

My own pulse throbs in the silence, so I opt for something in between. "What do you think? Why is Jackson Connor keeping this in Dreamland?"

Lucas sets the book aside thoughtfully. "I don't know. This one is Connor, right?" At least he tapped the right face. "It reminds me of something, but I don't know what."

He glances out his window, and his eyes narrow as he leans away from me, zeroing in on something. "Well, look who's here. Speak of the devil, and he will arrive." He turns and grins at me, flipping his thumb toward the distant intersection. "Wanna go take another shot at him?"

Dust clouds are billowing up from the shoulder, but I can see what's idling down Valley Road even from here: a white van.

I punch him lightly on the arm and head in that direction because really, it can't be the same one. By the time we switch places and get to the intersection, it's nowhere in sight.

When we pull up in front of my house, I can't wait any longer. The bubbles of fear that simmered all day break the surface. I take a deep, even breath, hoping to fill my lungs with courage as well as air. I don't want to hurt him, but I have to know.

"Lucas, can I ask you something?"

"Sure, anything." He rests his hand on mine, stroking my thumb with his.

"What exactly happened to your mom?"

The gentle caress halts, and his soft gaze sinks into that hollow, thousand-miles-away look. His wounded eyes paralyze me, and my heart drops. He doesn't say anything for a few agonizing seconds.

Oh God, what have I done?

"We were in California. She had trouble sleeping for weeks, going days at a time on only a few hours. Then she started crashing for fifteen, maybe twenty hours at a time, saying weird things and not eating." His hand shifts, holding mine tighter. "Then in the middle of the night, she walked out of the house, half a mile to the beach, and into the ocean."

"Oh, Lucas," I exhale miserably.

"They checked for drugs, of course. They thought maybe she took those sleeping pills that have weird side effects like sleepwalking. She did have a prescription from when my dad went MIA, but she never even filled it. My mom never took any kind of drugs. She wouldn't even take Tylenol. So they decided it was suicide, and they wouldn't listen to me or Una. It was almost like someone told them to do it."

"But why?" I wonder. "Couldn't it have just been an accident? Maybe she woke up and couldn't go back to sleep, so she decided to go swimming?" It's not the smartest thing to do, swimming alone at night, but people do weird things when they are grieving. Mom has stayed up all night lots of times, cleaning furiously and reading tarot cards for hours. She had read the cards before, but that's when she began booking clients regularly. I think it was her way of trying to get a grip on our future—a future without Dad.

"No." His mouth is a flat, bitter line. He runs his hand through his hair, the hair he'd cut in mourning two years ago. "First of all, my mom would never have killed herself. But especially not like that." His voice breaks and his face contorts briefly, but he swallows hard and continues. "Even though we spent a lot of time at the beach, she would never go in. *Ever*. My mom was terrified of the ocean."

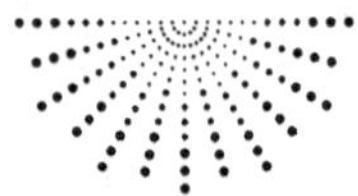

Lorena

OMG he's so freakin HOT!!! Is that the
only pic?

2 more otw

I send Lori the ones where we are looking at the camera, but not the one where he is kissing the top of my head. I can't stop looking at any of them. Two have flaws—little things no one would notice but me. But one of them is perfect. We are leaning into each other, and not just smiling, but almost... glowing.

Happy.

LORENA

Wow. Just WOW. And he knows about your
dreams and everything?

His dreams are like mine. I hesitate, then
add, His dad was MIA in Iraq the same
week as my dad.

I can't even remember the last time I didn't tell Lorena every-thing, but even if they're all tangled up together, Lucas's secrets are not mine to tell. So I'm keeping the mystery of Jackass Connor and his creepy dream castle on the down-low for now.

> It's FATE. There is a reason for all of this. He
> is too hot for it not to be

>> He. Is. The. Best. Kisser. Ever. <3 <3

>> Well, he is. And as my former relationship
>> coach, Lorena has the right to know. In fact,
>> I owe it to her. It has nothing to do with
>> provoking any little tweaks of jealousy, like I
>> get when she goes on about her new
>> boyfriend/haircut/license/iPhone. I swear.

> That must be the reason! Ha! But maybe
> you two are supposed to find out about
> your dad. Things better with your mom?

>> Pretty much, but Mom being weird, saying
>> all those things. She's actually sick, she
>> stayed in bed and slept all day.

> She's never sick! Hope she's better soon.
> How's my BBF?

>> Fine, launching a tarantula into space
>> tomorrow :-o or a space chamber?
>> Something Brian-y.

> Smarter than all of us put together. Hug
> them both for me ok? Gotta bounce,
> sending u pics of me n Todd at the beach.

>> Cool, ttyl

The pictures she sends are exactly what I expect. Lorena's hair is streaked with blonde spirals, springing to riotous life in the California humidity. She is wide-eyed across oversized sunglasses, making a big smoochy-lipped selfie face, cheek to cheek with the Fabulous Todd. He is the perfect, good-looking surfer cliché: longish hair, some kind of shell on a cord around his neck, very white teeth, and instantly forgettable.

I snap my phone closed and survey the landscape of Déjà Vu. Mom thinks she has the flu. She skipped dinner and went to bed early last night, and today I'm on my own. Everything looks good except for the customer refreshments. There's an acute shortage here and at home, so I lock the front door and cross the dew-soaked morning grass to Noonie's, ignoring the tiny star-flashes on the edge of my vision. I have more in mind than just a Macaroonie mission.

The heavy wooden door to the bakery is propped open, and the blackboard easel out front already boasts today's lunch specials. Mr. Noonie scurries like a squirrel, sliding fresh trays of bakery heaven into the display case and serving up large cups of gourmet caffeine. This early, most of his customers are the artists and entrepreneurs of Zia Square. The lady who owns a gallery full of glass—everything from huge colorful vases to tiny spun-glass animals—pays for her triple espresso and cranberry-almond scone, then nods at me as she whirls out the door in a cloud of jasmine oil.

All alone, just me and Mr. Noonie. Suddenly, I feel both anxious and ridiculous. Will he take one look at me and remember a strange dream with a hawk, or maybe a shimmer of purple lights hollering, "Macaroonies!" in his regal-looking Dreamland bank?

"Hello, Miss Vivian!" He beams at me, and as usual, his big mustache, round brown eyes, and curly hair remind me of Super Mario Brothers. Or their dad.

"Seeing anything new at Déjà Vu?" he jokes for the thousandth time and winks at me. "How is your lovely mother these days?"

I think Mr. Noonie has kind of a crush on Mom, but who doesn't?

"She's fine, Mr. Noonie." I smile and follow the script. "Nope, nothing at Déjà Vu that hasn't been seen already."

Unless you count the emerald fireflies following me from your dream.

"The usual?" He peels off a few white bakery bags from the stack and opens one with an efficient snap.

"Yes, sir. A dozen of each kind and a medium house blend. With cream."

Mr. Noonie deftly fills each bag. "Oh! You have to try my latest creation. Strawberry-lemon ricotta." He lifts out a Macaroonie in tissue paper and hands it to me.

Golden-white with flecks of dark pink, and still warm. I can smell it, rich and sweet and tart all at once, and I know this scent is going straight to the Dreamland Top 40. I refrain from popping the whole thing in my mouth and instead take a delicate bite like Mom would, and wait for the flavor bomb. *Boom!* There it is, like warm, crumbly cheesecake with chunks of sweet, moist berry and startling flecks of lemon. My eyes widen as they meet Mr. Noonie's.

"Wow! Amazing. Maybe the best yet."

"You and your brother are my toughest critics." He beams. "Here, take a few for him to try too."

"As if," I protest. "I'm not sharing. He can get his own."

Mr. Noonie smiles and places a few in a separate bag... then a few more... and yet *another* handful. He snaps the lid on my coffee. "Here's my new card too. You can put it on your tray, okay?" It's a rich dark green, embossed in gold, looking like it was chiseled directly off his huge Dreamland vault.

When I leave Noonie's, the sun has already sucked the dew from the grass, and the star-flashes have been replaced with the whining clamor of power tools emanating from Jackson Connor's renovation project. The oily metallic odor tries to follow me across the square back to Déjà Vu, but I open the bag and inhale some still-warm strawberry-lemon paradise, trying to balance the anxiety and triumph teetering precariously on a tightrope in my head.

Mr. Noonie often tests out his newest flavors on the people of Zia Square. But never—*never*—has he just given away a dozen Macaroonies. Did I make this happen? Did I make some kind of post-dream suggestion, and he did it?

The Knot flips open and lights up like my phone. *You tell* me. *Isn't this exactly what Dad was talking about? Stargate, hellooooo!*

Yeah, right. The Amazing Vivian, Dreamwalker Extraordinaire. Not likely. After all, this is why the Stargate Project ended. *It doesn't work.* Lucid dreamers can control some parts of their own dreams. Maybe some of us—the dreamwalkers—can visit other people's dreams, and *maybe* even make small things happen. I'm pretty sure I made Mr. Noonie look up in his dream, but I sure couldn't make that Jackson Connor shapeshifter raven-thing go away. In fact, just the opposite.

There's no way someone can go into another person's dream and cause them to do something after they are awake. The Knot sits up in protest, but I firmly push it back down. *No.* That kind of mind control is simply not possible.

Unless it is, whispers The Knot. I unlock the door, flip the sign to OPEN, and pretend I didn't hear that.

Business is steady most of the morning. I keep extra busy for Mom's sake, and to keep The Knot quiet. I water the potted herbs in the back room and clean the front window. In between customers I make a list of supplies for the mural. Procrastination has reached its limit; I'll start painting tomorrow, when Déjà Vu will be closed along with most of the other Zia Square shops.

In honor of Mom, I have a healthy salad for lunch. Well, not so much in honor of, but because of. She made it last night, and when I brought her tea this morning and sat on her bed to get the groggy-sounding marching orders for the day, she told me to take it for my lunch. I added some ham and an avocado, then picked out as much of the kale as I could because leaves should not have hair.

By midafternoon, things slow down. Lucas is almost finished transforming that twisted hunk of Chevy into an eagle—wings pulled back, talons outstretched, ready to snatch its unsuspecting prey—but when I told him that Mom's sick and I'd be alone at the shop today, he said he would come by. All day long, he's been on the edge of my thoughts.

Okay, I admit it, he's right smack in the middle. It's a good thing too, because when I think of him, I can't hear The Knot, which has been making noises about the Macaroonies and the drawing of Connor and his dream buddies, which went to the trash as soon as I got home yesterday, before it could humiliate me any further. Ten minutes later, I fished it back out and put it under my bed. As bad as it is, something about it nags me. There's definitely something *there*.

A small box of Zuni animal fetishes in the office needs to go in the display case. There are sixteen, including turtles, a butterfly, a mottled marble badger, a raven with a coral berry in its mouth, and a bear carrying a turquoise bead on its back. They are beautifully detailed, with contrasting eyes of white jasper or onyx, but they are made to sell. Empty. They have no history, no spirit. Yeah, I know, I don't believe in signs, or spirits, or unseen forces. But lately, it seems like weird stuff happens whether I believe or not.

I stand behind the counter, bending over the box for the last of the fetishes, when the front door jingles.

"Welcome to Déjà Vu," I say automatically, and when I stand up, I'm staring straight into the arctic blue eyes of Jackson Connor.

"Oh! Hi, Mr. Connor. *Jack*," I amend, prompted by the friendly pout he puts on to remind me we're *friends* now. He rewards me with a megawatt smile, which immediately puts my radar on full alert and sends The Knot into a defensive coil.

"Hello, Vivian! It's hot as blazes out there." He wipes some imaginary sweat from his brow and hoists a plastic bag onto the counter. The outline of a cardboard drink holder with two large slushees resting inside peeks through. "I brought you guys something cold to drink." He looks behind me, sweeping his chilly gaze from the back hall to the ice cream door, tilting his head like a well-groomed dog. "Is your mother busy?"

"Mom took the morning off. She has some things to do today," I inform him pleasantly as his smile dims by a few kilowatts. This is not actually a lie. Just because I don't tell him she took the afternoon off too, and the "things" she's doing are sleeping, drinking a lot of fluids, and sleeping some more. Not even "friends" tell each other *everything*.

As if he hears what I am thinking, he asks, "Is Summer feeling okay? There's something going around." He looks genuinely concerned, and before I can stop myself—

"Oh, she's okay. A little tired."

His smile softens. "Nothing serious, I hope?"

Shut up, The Knot groans, *don't tell him anything!*

I recover quickly. I arrange my face into a patient, opaque smile. A wall of courtesy.

"No, she's fine, just busy. Off tomorrow, back on Saturday. Did you have a reading?" I know for a fact he doesn't, but I reach for the day timer that has all of Mom's appointments.

"No, not 'til next week." He shakes his head. "This is the craziest town. Who closes on *Fridays?*"

"Everybody here," I observe, but that uneasy feeling is prickling around my neck again. I wish he'd hurry up and leave, or that Lucas would get here and rescue me.

"Only in the Land of Entrapment," Jackson Connor mutters and flashes a quick smile as if this is a hilarious piece of wit I've never heard before.

"Mmm-hmm," I murmur, not amused.

Lucas, where are you? Hurry! As if to answer me, a blue spark pulses at the edge of my sight.

Connor lets go of the bag, then peers into the case below. "Well, what do we have here? Carved animals?"

I don't answer Captain Obvious, but I can't stop a slight flinch as he plucks the raven off the countertop.

"Now, *this* one is lovely." He lifts it up on his palm, but he isn't looking at it. He's looking at *me*. "Especially the eyes. Can you see them?"

"Yes, they're all like that," I say—but then I *see*, and my mouth goes dry. The tiny raven's eyes were white, *I swear*, but now they're different. They are a brilliant turquoise.

Like the flash on a camera, Déjà Vu blinks away. I'm paralyzed, pinned to that granite dream-wall, while Lucas clutches my ankle and a huge black bird dives toward us, its blue eyes burning nause-ating holes into mine. *Don't look at it!* His dreamwalk command echoes in my head.

I blink hard, and the wall is gone. The nausea isn't, though. A cold sweat shivers across my body, and my healthy lunch is threat-ening to make a comeback. Desperate, I yank my focus away from the bird. *Don't look, don't look.*

"Really amazing, isn't it? Some people have such a talent for these things. Have you ever tried anything like this?" Jackson Connor watches me intently, and I have no idea what he's searching for, but there's no way I'm going to let him find it.

"Nope, I stick to painting." I shrug like an indifferent teenager, hoping he can't hear my heart pounding. "This kind of work is way beyond me."

I finally meet his spearpoint blue gaze with what I hope are two impenetrable green shields and blink once. Two heartbeats go by—I know, because I can still feel my heart knocking against my lungs—and as the front door jingles open, Jackson Connor glances away.

I don't care who it is—even one of the Peppers would be a welcome sight at this point—but it's Lucas. Finally. Relief floods through me, but I hold steady, sending *Go away!* vibes to Jackson Connor.

Lucas looks at both of us, and his eager face swiftly shifts into deflector-mode.

"Hi Vivian! Hey there, Mr. Connor," he offers cheerfully.

"Hello, Lucas." As Connor carefully sets the onyx raven back on the counter, a wave of something—Annoyance? Speculation?—crosses his face the way a quick gust of wind passes over a field. He turns to Lucas with his usual toothpaste-ad smile. "You're supposed to call me Jack."

"I know. Sorry, Jack. I was raised to call my *friends* by their first name, but not my elders," Lucas points out.

"But we are friends, aren't we?" Connor's voice is light, but his smile falls away from his eyes.

Lucas pauses and shoots him a level gaze. "Don't worry. I won't forget next time, *Jack*."

Connor runs his hand through his hair and looks at his watch. "Well, I'd better be getting back. You two enjoy these." He waves in the direction of the drinks and adds, "Vivi, please tell your mother I came by, and that I'll call her tomorrow."

"I sure will. And thanks for the slushees, Jack." My smile-mask hurts my face, but I hold it until he goes out the door.

It's not until Jackson Connor is off the front porch that all the air whooshes out of me, and I lean my elbows on the glass counter with my head swimming in my hands. Icy bands wrap around my chest, and I can't catch my breath. Lucas is behind the counter in an instant, his arm around me, scooting the stool close so I can sit down.

"Vivian, are you okay? What the hell was that? What *happened?*"

"Connor..." I shake my head. Little black dots prickle in and out of my vision, and Lucas sounds as if he's at the end of a long, long hallway.

"Put your head down between your knees. *Breathe*, Vivi."

My knees dissolve. The hardwood floor ripples like a muddy pond, and I am desperately trying not to pitch into it head first. *In, two, three, four.*

"That raven. Blue eyes."

Out, two, three, four.

"Shapeshifter." The mud stops quivering and settles back into solid boards again. My blue-jeaned knees emerge as the tide of black dots rolls away. The stool is solid underneath me, and Lucas's arm holds me gently against his chest, safely away from the abyss. I sit up and lean back into him, getting my bearings.

"The raven? In the dreamwalk?"

"Yes. No, the one on the counter. I was talking to Connor, and the eyes turned blue."

He reaches over me and picks up the fetish. "This one? What did he do?"

How do I explain what just happened?

"Connor didn't do anything. He just pointed out how interesting the eyes were, and… and then they were blue, and I was suddenly back *in* the dream, like a flashback. Then it was over, and he was just holding that raven and staring at me."

Lucas picks up the raven, then scoots around sideways to show it to me. His arm never leaves my shoulder, but his face is troubled. "Look, Vivi, the eyes are white. Chips of white jasper."

"I know. I knew it even when I was looking at it. Maybe it was just a flashback to that dream, like a side effect or something? But for a second, it was like *he* turned the eyes blue."

"What, a Jedi mind trick? Making you see something that isn't there?"

"Worse. Like the little star-flashes. As if the raven followed me back from the dreamwalk."

A hideous thought makes my heart skid to a halt. Stunned, I turn and face him.

"Oh my God. It's just like the Macaroonies."

"What?" Lucas has been following so far, but now he's mystified. He stands in front of me, patiently holding both of my hands, and I scramble to make him understand.

"When I went to Mr. Noonie's dream for practice, I suggested… well, actually, I *yelled* 'Macaroonies' at him. And this morning, he gave me extra ones. Not just a few, but a *lot*." I close my eyes. "What if this is the same thing? What if Connor did this? What if he's a—"

I can't even say it out loud.

Lucas is quiet for a moment. Then, "You made Mr. Noonie give you extra cookies?"

I nod miserably. "I'm pretty sure." My eyes are still closed, but tears fill them up with the unthinkable, and I can't bear to look at Lucas's face. He must think I'm a lunatic.

"Vivian." He pulls me gently to him and wraps himself around me, folding me gently to his chest and resting his chin on my head as my arms reach around his waist. "This is it; it's what our dads were working on. And we can do it, too—well, at least *you* can, kind of. This is huge.!"

Nesting in Lucas's arms and feeling our bodies humming together from head to toe for one sweet moment, I let him hold me up with his optimism.

"But what about Jackson Connor?" I step back. "What if *he's* a dreamwalker?" There, I said it. The word ripples through me like a shock wave.

"I guess it's possible," Lucas speculates, "but I don't think so. There aren't very many of us. He's an annoying dickweed, but I think that's all." His eyes are soft. "I think you just had a flashback to the dream. Like you said, that bird scared the crap out of you. Both of us. And we were probably there for way too long."

I remember. And I also remember how strained he sounded when I wanted to stay in the dream and peek in the last window. How he found the way out and wouldn't let go until he knew we were safe. He's right; I shouldn't have kept us there. I should've followed my own instructions and left as soon as we felt that first tug.

Doubt still nibbles at me. "Then why was he staring at me like that?"

"Probably because you were as white as a sheet! When I came through the door, I thought you were going to either puke all over him or pass out."

"I almost did both."

Lucas gestures toward the melting slushees, which are leaving sweat rings on the counter. "Speaking of puke, do you want any of that?"

As if I would drink anything Jackass Connor set in front of me? I make a face and put them back in the bag. They're going straight to the trash.

"Okay, you're probably right," I admit. "He's probably not a dreamwalker or a Jedi master. But I'm staying away from him, awake or asleep. I'm just glad you showed up when you did."

"Me too. You know what's weird is when I was getting out of the truck, I thought I heard you call me."

Our eyes lock together as I recall my silent plea... but no, that's impossible. Sometimes you know exactly what someone is thinking, but people can't hear each other's actual *thoughts*.

"I don't trust that asshole any more than you do. That drawing you did of his memory, his dream, whatever that was? It reminds me of something, but I don't know what. It's really bugging me. There's something *there*."

Maybe Lucas *did* hear me call him. When he echoes my thoughts like this, our connection feels so strong. It gives me courage. I need that more than ever, because no matter what Jackson Connor is, I can't take any more chances. I know what I have to do.

Tonight, before it's too late.

CHAPTER TWENTY-ONE

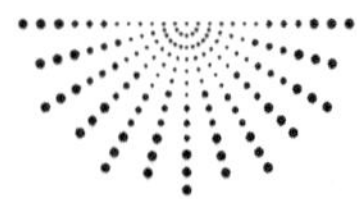

4:18 AM.

I should have known better.

I can't stop crying, I can't breathe, I can't think. The bitter trifecta of failure.

My twisted sheets tangle around my body, and I'm as limp and flat as my pillow, paralyzed by my spectacular incompetence. Even The Knot is silent, a cold, stunned lump of misery. The sun's not up yet, but at least it will eventually rise out of the dark, low dawn.

As for me, I'm not so sure.

I keep replaying everything in my head. I should have known this would be harder than I ever thought possible. Dad said it would be, but I didn't think it would be such an epic disaster that even *he* couldn't salvage it completely. And now, he may be gone for good.

Everything started out the way it always does. The veil of stars rolled and effervesced as I passed through them into Dreamland, and when I skirted the tops of my trees heading for Brian's dream, I *knew* I could do this. I had experience now, I knew how to keep my balance, and I especially knew not to stay too long. I felt invincible!

All I had to do was step into his world, take his hand in mine, and show him where to go to be safe. This was a simple mission: touch down, get him, push hard, and fly out. What could go wrong?

I found him easily too. From high in the violet sky, his world was a buzzing island of pale yellows and bright greens out on the horizon. I didn't have to crunch anything together or hold it in my mind. I saw the lights and pushed forward, eyes open. It was like swimming through a layer of summer heat, a dense wavering curtain of energy, but then it gave way, and I popped through. When I landed, the air was cool, as fresh and dark as the desert at midnight.

I was on a thin, high bridge, overlooking a city of prisms. At least, I thought that's what it was, even though it was like no city I'd ever seen. It was like in the movies when they show a metropolis at night, with all the traffic moving in fast motion but through layers of translucent, multi-angled prisms. Like a hive full of millions of bees, the prisms hummed with pale gold energy and Kelly-green electricity. More than just three dimensional, it was four or five or twenty dimensions deep, layered and pulsing. Almost... thinking.

The bridge I rested on swayed gently, its golden suspension wires as thin as hairs, interlocked in a perfect looping pattern, like those animations that show how gravity bends time and space at the edges of black holes. A perfect geometric grid, curved down to a dense point of infinity. Where the golden wires intersected, tiny, bright green spangles shivered like droplets of water, first bright and then dimming, pointing the way.

I smelled spaghetti sauce and knew he wasn't far away.

-Brian. The violet drops of my voice rolled along the wires, like beads sliding down a gilded string.

I took a cautious step forward, testing the gravity here. The thin strand held me, but I kept myself light, with my fingertips grazing along one wire for guidance, because in someone else's dream, you never know. I gained speed, gliding along quickly like an ice skater, following its spiral path lower and lower.

-Brian.

With every featherweight step, the bridge vibrated and hummed like a violin string. I could now see the bridge spanning above and across the entire city of prisms, almost to the horizon. The wires telegraphed the vibration of my movements like a web, and when I looked back up to where I'd started, I realized that's what it *was*—an enormous, golden spider web.

I was in the right place for sure. Hamlet the Space Spider is only the latest arachnid in Brian's long history of spider obsession. When he was just a toddler, he was fascinated with Grandma Lily's stories about patient, precise Spider. He has admired their engineering skills his whole life. They are *tenacious*, he says.

Then I realized if dreamwalkers appear as animals sometimes, he might be a humongous spider, which I was definitely *not* ready to see. But then, he's not a dreamwalker, so hopefully he'd just be Brian. A hint of those strawberry-lemon Macaroonies drifted by as I stepped off the web and onto soft beach sand, and there he was, his normal non-spider self. Here in this spot, the night had disappeared, and the tart ocean breeze swirled with hazy morning sunshine.

He wore his favorite board shorts. He was on his hands and knees, making a sand-dribble castle like the one in the picture in my room—but on steroids, with dozens of towers and levels, topped with intricate, dribbly spires and decorated with hundreds of pearlescent seashells. His hair stuck out in salt-water spikes, and patches of sand were stuck to him in places as if he'd backed into a sandy paint roller. A look of intense concentration furrowed his round face as he scooped wet sand from the edge of a tidal pool, packing it densely into a bucket before upending it for the next wing.

His eyes were closed.

-*Brian,* I said. The purple sparks rippled toward him and simply evaporated. He didn't stop what he was doing or even raise his head.

-*Brian!*

Dad said Brian wouldn't be able to help me. It never occurred to me he wouldn't be able to see me or even *hear* me. The dreamwalk clock was ticking, so I dropped to my knees directly in front of him and put my hands on his shoulders. Unlike Dad and Lucas, who felt warm and solid, I could barely sense my hands on him. It was like trying to hold Jell-O.

-Brian, it's me. It's Vivi. I need you to listen.

His slippery arms twisted easily through my numb fingers as he turned back to the bucket and began packing it full of sand again, humming. My heart fluttered like a frightened bird. Now what?

-Brian, look at me. Look! I lifted his chin up, stuck my face an inch away, and yelled as loud as I could. *You have to come with me. Right now! It's an emergency, come on!*

He stayed still, and for a hopeful millisecond, I thought I saw his eyes flutter under the eyelids. But no, it was gone, and he wasn't seeing me at all. He kept humming and turned away for more sand.

That familiar nudge deep in my chest meant three more minutes, tops. The fluttering bird in my stomach turned into a whole surging flock, and Dad's instructions echoed back to me:

You will have to push, Vivian, as hard as you possibly can. You will have to fly.

Brian stopped moving and was standing in front of his architectural creation with that quizzical, intense look he has when trying to remember something. The tug had tied itself to my spine, and while the pressure was still gentle, I knew I had to get him up and out of there with me. I had to show him how to get to my mountains like Dad said, and I had to do it *now*. I grabbed onto Brian's hand and squeezed as hard as I could, trying to find something solid to grip.

Dad's voice whispered across a dozen years, *Look at your hand, Vivi. Try.*

I'm trying Dad, I'm trying! I stared at our hands, straining to fuse them together—like Noonie's $2 bill, the Dreamland painting, and the flowers turning inside out into diamonds.

I was hunting and pushing for the latch that slides into place— *push, Vivian, push*—and suddenly our hands merged with a grateful *click*, and we lifted up slowly. *Yes!*

The tug became more urgent; the prisms collapsed and began to spin.

-Hang on Brian, don't let go!

But I couldn't lift him far or fast enough. The sky slipped out and grew dark again, the prisms shimmered back into place, and there we were at the top of the web. Far below, the transparent canyons undulated, and I looked away quickly. A wind from nowhere circled around us, swaying our precarious perch.

-Don't look down, I yelled, but he was oblivious. Our hands were still locked together, and his closed eyes were frowning down at them, as if wondering what had gotten hold of him. He wasn't humming anymore.

The wind began to howl, and the suction was dizzyingly strong, pressing the air out of my lungs, smothering me. If I couldn't drag him out of there in about thirty seconds, I was sure it would rip us to pieces. I looked at my brother, stunned, as the horrifying reality of our situation hit me.

I couldn't do it.

There I was, stuck at the top of a massive Brian-web, and I couldn't let them find him—whoever "they" were—but I couldn't get him out, or show him where to go, or even tell him anything. Hot fear blackened my vision as I realized I would have to leave him here and try to come back again with Lucas. His strong grip that had held me steady along Jackson Connor's wall might be enough to help get Brian out.

But what if I couldn't come back? This might be my only chance. No, it had to be now, *right now*. But how?

There was only one desperate thing left, the one thing that worked before, and maybe—hopefully, please—might work now. The wind roared as I swept my gaze across the web to the little green lights. I braced myself against the golden strands, took my deepest breath and said the name, summoning... *diamonds.*

Diamonds.

Push, Vivi, push as hard as you can— oh, God, push! Don't let go. This is it. This is all there is. DIAMONDSDIAMONDS- DIAMONDS

The green droplets bubbled thickly and began to turn, blossoming into brilliant, clear crystals.

-Dad, Brian said, opening his eyes wide as the web turned inside out to silver, and something strong gripped my free hand, pulling us up and out of the rising tornado. The three of us spun away into the Dreamland stars.

THE FIRST THING I heard when I opened my eyes to my own Dreamland sky was the warbling of a cricket. My hand was clenched tight, holding nothing except cool mountain air. I bolted upright, and my forehead punched me back down, throbbing like a drum. I leaned up on one elbow, getting my bearings.

Where—?

Brian was sitting a few feet away, eyes closed once more, thoughtfully rubbing the hand I had held. Under a huge pine tree beyond him, a shadow moved, and a silver wisp of cigar smoke curled around a familiar silhouette.

-Dad?

-Hello, sweetheart. That was a bumpy ride out. You all right? He sat down between us, bits of crystal phosphorescence settling around him, and took my hand, resting his other one on Brian's shoulder. Soft, smoky warmth wrapped around us. Safe.

-I tried, Dad, I really did! I'm sorry I couldn't get him all the way out by myself. Is he okay? Is he going to be okay now?

-I don't know, Dad said quietly. *I hope so, Vivian. Don't be sorry— you did a great job. You just had a little stall out on the runway.* His affectionate smile was quick, but gone just as fast as it came. *Did he hear you? Did he say anything? Did he see you?*

-Yes. No. I don't know! He opened his eyes for a second. He said 'Dad,' I added hopefully.

-But did he respond to you or say your name? Dad pressed on. *When he opened his eyes, did he see you?*

I remembered Brian's eyelids fluttering, trying to open down on the beach.

-I don't think so. He was kind of trying before you came, so maybe. He's here now, though, isn't that what matters? He's safe now, right?

-He's safe for *now. What really matters is if he knows how to get back here, knows how to find you when he's not safe.*

-But he's here, so we can just tell him.

-You can try.

-Me? But you're the one he felt, Dad. He opened his eyes when you came.

-I can't stay, Vivi. They are very near, and I can't let them find you.

-Won't they get sucked out when I wake up?

-Some of them can stay longer. They can keep you asleep.

-Who? Who are they? Wait, there's this guy, Jackson Connor. There's something wrong about him. Mom and Brian don't see it, but Lucas—

-Lucas? You mean Joseph Wolfsong's son? His dark eyes caught mine and held them intently.

-Yes, he's the one I was telling you about before. He's a dreamwalker too. And his dad.

-Joseph can help you. Talk to him.

-But he's gone, Dad. Missing in Iraq, the same week as you. Lucas thinks he's still alive. You knew him?

-Joseph's missing? Dad took a sharp breath. *Yes, I knew him on the rez. We were in Bosnia and Iraq together. And Stargate. Vivi, I have to go.* He stood up in one swift, fluid motion. The soft cocoon of our togetherness slipped to the ground.

-But this guy, Jackson Connor. As hard as I tried, I couldn't keep panic from creeping into the edges of my voice. Dad placed his hands on my shoulders, dense and warm, and his hug surrounded me like the buttery smoke of his leather jacket.

-He could be anybody—or nobody. You have good, strong instincts, Vivian. Trust them.

-When can you come back?

-I don't know if I can. It was dangerous to come tonight, and I don't know if we can do this again. There are limits. He spoke so softly, I barely heard him. His solid presence was dissolving, flattening out so he looked like a picture of himself.

-Not ever? But you have to! I don't know what's going on. What do I do? What do you mean, limits?

-Brian. Get back into his dreams. Get him to see you or hear your voice. Lucas can help too. I don't think they know about him. But do it soon, Vivi. There's not much time.

His voice was fading, rising up into an unseen tunnel that would take him from me again, this time maybe forever. Hot tears stung my eyes as I tried to grab his hand before he dissolved completely.

-No, Dad, no!

My desperate shout came out as single droplet of amethyst, and I watched, helpless, as it chased the tiny diamond-remnants of Dad over the trees.

-Walk with me.

-Nil' hish ash. *I walk with you always, Vivi,* the wind said as the last diamond twinkled out. *Always.*

CHAPTER TWENTY-TWO

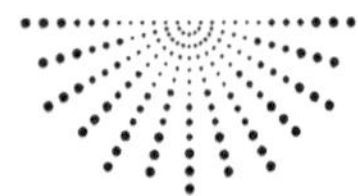

Two desolate hours later, the soggy mess of my life still refuses to melt into the mattress and take me with it. I have finally run out of tears, lying here motionless on the edge of my black hole of failure, when Brian flushes the toilet and I twitch a little. I'm a total dreamwalking disaster, but it seems I'm not completely paralyzed.

Get up. Do something! urges The Knot, which is also apparently not paralyzed.

Even if it's wrong? My tired reply rings hollow in my own head.

Especially if it's wrong! scoffs The Knot. Having my own sarcasm tossed back at me is double mockery.

I used up all of my wrongness last night. I sigh.

My phone buzzes, breaking the evil spell. Lucas. This might be the sign that I will live after all. Warm hope drips into my frozen veins, and I roll up onto one elbow, breaking the surface of this pool of misery with a deep breath. White crystal and gold dream-sparks scatter behind me, trailing my father's voice. (*Lucas can help. I don't think they know about him.*)

LUCAS

Can't sleep. Weird dream, not sure what it
was, but my dad was there.

> OMG, your dad? I saw mine too. What
> happened?

It was real fast. He couldn't stay. He wants
me to find something, a picture. I don't
know exactly what but I know where to
look.

> I found Brian, but I don't think it worked. My
> dad was there for a few minutes. Groping
> for words, this is as much as I can say
> about my catastrophic failure.

I yank my legs out from the tangled pile of sheets and swing them around to the floor. A pair of gold dream-sparks skips across my bed and disappears over the edge.

> Lucas, our dads were in Stargate together
> for sure. He told me.

See, we were right! My dad didn't talk, just
showed me in my head… ugh hard to
explain, have to do some digging in his
stuff. How's your mom? Una's worried.

There are noises in the kitchen, but they're loud and Brian-y spoon and bowl sounds. No voices. No coffee smell. Wide awake now, I hop around the room, yanking on clean bikinis with one hand, texting with the other. This is the one and only advantage to having a dinosaur phone—actual keys instead of a screen.

> Not much better. This isn't like her at all.
> She's never sick, never tired. She's kind of
> confused too.

Confused like how???

> She wasn't sure what day it was yesterday. It's like she's not completely awake, even when she's awake.

> Like sleepwalking. Like my mom.

I freeze, staring at my phone. Like Elina? No. No, she's not *sleepwalking*, just tired.

> IDK. She says it's a virus or something. Maybe it's mono?

> Hope that's it. OK gonna start digging. Hope I find what I'm looking for, whatever it is. See u in a while.

> Me too. See u there.

I grab some clean jeans out of the drawer. My "KARMA IS A BITCH" shirt doesn't tempt me; after last night, I need a less depressing message. How about OBEY? Maybe if I wear that one, the universe will listen. Then again, I don't need the whole universe to listen—just my little brother. I can't wait until he's asleep again, either. I have to make him understand *now*.

I set a record for the fastest casual stroll into the kitchen, bunching my hair into a quick ponytail. Brian stands at the counter, dressed and ready to go, pouring milk on a huge bowl of Cinnamon Crunch.

"Hey, B. Where's Mom?"

"Hey, V. Getting dressed, I think." He stops pouring the milk just as it reaches the brim, then leans over and slurps up the excess before moving to the table, where a motionless Hamlet waits in his box. Meditating before his antigravity adventure, I guess.

I grab a bowl and shake out a pile of toasty cinnamon sugarbombs, plucking one out for Ophelia. Even hamsters deserve Cinnamon Crunch now and then. But Mom would rather buy rat poison than something with this much sugary wonderfulness.

"Where did this stuff come from?"

Brian shrugs and answers with his mouth full. "I froo 'em in the cart an she 'idn't hay any-hing." He swallows, considering. "She must really be sick." His brown eyes have faint dark smudges under them.

"You look tired. Did you sleep okay?" I plop down in the chair across from him, ignoring the hairy spider legs visible through the translucent Hamlet Hotel. "Did you have weird dreams or something?" I crunch my cereal, eyeing him. *Please say yes. Please say, 'I saw you and Dad, and we went from my dream to yours. I could do it again if I tried.'*

"You know I never dream," he reminds me. "I woke up a couple of times, though. I thought I heard someone talking."

"That's funny, so did I. What were they saying?" Maybe he heard us. Maybe he heard *enough*.

But he shrugs. "I don't know. Someone wanted to go somewhere or something. What did *you* hear?" His face is solemn, like he really wants to know, and as he looks at me, a spark of gold seems to dart through his brown eyes. This may be my best chance.

This may be your only *chance*, The Knot reminds me.

"I thought I heard someone calling me. It almost sounded like... Dad. And you were in it too." I hold my anxious breath for a second. I can't tell if this means anything to him. Better keep going. "Just one of those dream things. But it reminds me of something Dad told me. If you hear someone calling you in a dream, you can go to them. He said to just push up and fly with the sound. Be a hawk."

He considers this, kicking the chair leg with his sneaker and chewing. "Can *you* do that?"

"Sometimes. I was trying to last night."

"What were you trying last night?" Ninja Mom's voice arrives just before she appears in the hall entry, yawning and cutting off any further attempt to reach Brian.

Her wild hair is subdued into a thick braid, and she's wearing an old, flowered blouse over capri jeans.

"I thought we'd get some gardening done today, so come home

right after your class. Are we out of coffee?" She sounds better than she has all week. A bubble of relief lifts off my chest, reminding me of just how worried I've been.

"I was going to prep the wall for the mural today."

"Maybe not. Doppler Dan says it's supposed to rain." She walks unsteadily to the counter and picks up the Cinnamon Crunch. "Where did this come from?" She turns toward me, but her eyes are out of focus. "Did you buy this?"

"No." I see why Mom is walking so oddly. She has one ancient, checkered Van on one foot, and a wedge-heeled leather sandal on the other. "Mom, your shoes."

"You know I don't want you two eating this stuff. It's just garbage." She picks up the box of evil bliss and waves it around.

"You got it yesterday at Albertsons, remember?" Brian pipes up. He notices her shoes and then looks at me, uncertain, but I'm *absolutely* certain. Something is seriously wrong with her. That happy bubble pops in my chest and sinks back down, adding another layer to The Knot.

"Mom, you have on the wrong shoes. Are you feeling okay?"

"I'm *fine*, Vivian," Mom announces. "I am finished being sick, and I have work to do. Now, I know there's coffee around here somewhere."

She hobbles across the kitchen—up-down, up-down—a walking hiccup. She opens the oven door and sets the cereal box down firmly on the rack, then hesitates, frowning. Turning toward Brian, Mom stares at something behind his left shoulder, something no one but Mom can see. Brian's round eyes dart from her to me then back to her.

"We went to Albertson's yesterday? Didn't we get coffee?"

"No, just cereal and milk and some fruit." He drops his gaze to a tiny splat of milk on the table and concentrates on rubbing it in with his finger.

She opens the silverware drawer and rummages around. "Well, that's ridiculous. I would never forget coffee."

She's right. She never would. *Or put a box of cereal in the oven, or wear two different shoes, or stare off into space like some kind of zombie,* hisses The Knot.

"You're still tired from being sick." Panic rises in my throat, but I swallow it back down. "I'll get some on my way home, okay?" I stand up, collect our bowls, and glance at Brian. "How about I walk Brian to the bus while you change your shoes?" I point to her mismatched feet.

Mom finally looks down, bewilderment rippling across her face. "Well, *that*'s not going to work. For heaven's sake. Vivian, why don't you walk Brian to the bus, and I'll go change these gloves." We are silent as she wobbles down the hall and closes her door.

"I guess Mom's still sick." His troubled gaze follows me to the sink.

"I'm pretty sure." I rinse the bowls and put them in the dishwasher, trying to hide my shaking hands. "But she's a little better, right? She just needs some more rest. You ready?" He nods. "Hamlet ready?"

He picks up the box and peeks through one of the holes. "You ready in there?" The spider waves a leg. "All systems go," he reports. "Wait, I need my thumb drive," he adds, and darts through the back hall to his room.

I grab my backpack and peek in Mom's room. The mismatched shoes are still on, and she is almost asleep again. I carefully slip the shoes off and kiss her on the cheek. "We're going now. See you later. Get some sleep, okay?"

She nods, already sinking down into the twilight zone. "Love you," she whispers.

Tears prickle my eyes, but hers are closed, and she can't see them. "Love you too, Mom."

Brian is petting Rufus in the driveway when I wheel my bike out of the garage. Two cat tails stick out of his backpack like an old TV antenna, and Hamlet's box is hooked to the back with a small bungee cord. Rufus bumps his big orange head against my leg, and the three of us walk past the neighbor's house in silence while my heart and brain are chasing each other in circles, like the clickety-buzz coming from my bike wheels.

I can't shake the vacant look in Mom's eyes, or the feeling that this isn't the flu, or mono, or any other normal virus. Is this what Lucas's mom had? When he first told me about her, I couldn't imagine anything that would make a person so disoriented they would walk into an ocean and drown, but now I'm not so sure.

"What's wrong with Mom?" Brian blurts out as we reach the corner of Valley Road. Rufus has turned back toward his house, stalking a butterfly as it flutters down the side of the road. "She should go to the doctor."

"She'll be all right. It's only been a couple of days," I lie, pretending Mom hasn't been careening away from normal for over a week. No cars are coming, so we trot across and head for the next turn that leads to the bus stop.

"No, she was weird last week too. She wasn't sleeping all the time, but still. She didn't hardly eat anything, and she kept telling me stuff like 'be careful.' Like you," he remembers and shrugs to shift his backpack a little. "I think it's African trypanosomiasis."

"African *what?*"

"Sleeping sickness. I was reading about it last night. You get it from tsetse flies. Maybe she got bit."

"Tsetse flies? Aren't they just in Africa or Brazil or something?"

"Yeah, but they could get here by accident on a plane or a ship. Like that spider in *Arachnophobia*." Brian was probably the only kid in America who watched that movie and rooted for the poisonous spiders.

"Maybe." Inspiration strikes. "Hey, you know what? There was a big web in that dream last night. Huge! I thought it was a bridge, but it was a big gold web, and we were up on it." Okay, not very subtle, but there's no time for subtle.

"Cool! Were you scared? You hate spiders."

"Scared? No, not really." Scared doesn't even begin to describe the suffocating terror of being stuck up there, knowing I couldn't bring my little brother to safety. "It was just a web. No spiders."

"What did I do in it?"

"You were holding onto my hand real tight. We were going to fly. I was telling you to hang on and stay with me no matter what. Like Dad said, be a hawk."

He smiles up at me as we reach the last turn. "You're the expert. If we ever have to fly out of a dream web, I promise to hang on."

"You swear?" I stop walking. I bore into his eyeballs with my most intense laser stare. "If you have to leave a bad dream, you call me, and I'll fly you out. I'm not kidding, Brian, *promise me you will.*"

He goes still, his eyes serious as he raises his right hand. "I solemnly swear we will soar through the air."

My relief that maybe he got it, *maybe it will be okay*, wavers as he drops his hand, laughing, and continues down the sidewalk. I scan the deserted street, half a block down to the stop. Brian's bus isn't there yet.

"Whoa, there, wait! Security breach. Hamlet's trying to escape." Hamlet's yellow prison is slipping out of the bungee cord, and the flimsy plastic latch is partially open. I snap it shut with a loud click and reposition the box. "Guess he's rethinking this zero-gravity thing."

"Don't worry. You're going to love it," Brian assures the would-be fugitive from over his shoulder.

"Hamlet smells weird."

"He ate a lot of crickets yesterday. He has gas," he informs me solemnly, then giggles. "You smelled a spider fart."

Spider farts. Great.

My phone buzzes.

OMW. I found a picture of Jackson Connor.

A picture of Jackson Connor? Where? The growling rumble of the bus drifts from around the corner.

"The bus is coming, so you can just go from here. Remember what I said."

"Okay, V, see you later." He marches toward the bench, then stops and turns. "Look up sleeping sickness! I'm pretty sure that's it."

I wave, then hop on my bike and pedal furiously to Community College. As soon as I get to the parking lot, I flip open my phone to call Lucas.

No answer. His truck isn't at the welding dock. I decide to wait under the cottonwood tree and intercept him when he gets here. For a second, I think I hear someone say my name—the way sound sometimes echoes in a crowd—but it's just the wind and the traffic playing tricks on me. I feel better already. Obviously, Lucas found something —a clue, a connection, maybe even an answer

And he'll be here any minute.

CHAPTER TWENTY-THREE

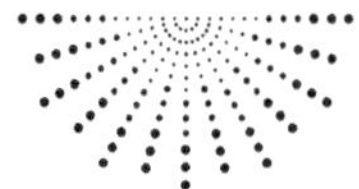

I'm not worried. Everything's fine.

He probably just stopped at the Piggly Wiggly for coffee. Or gas. Probably there's a line. Or maybe he forgot something at home and had to go back.

I'm not worried, even though it's been fifteen minutes and there's still no sign of him. He hasn't called or texted, and The Knot is curling over itself into a fist, but he said he's on the way.

Then where is he? The fist tightens, complete.

I ignore it. My eyes are glued to the parking lot entrance as I clutch my phone, willing it to ring. Willing it to OBEY, like it says on my shirt. I'm not actually worried. I'm just anxious to know what he found out. A few more cars pull into the parking lot, but no red truck. I wait a few minutes and call him again. *Come on, Lucas, where are you?*

The Knot wiggles restlessly. What if he had an accident? He's a cautious driver when I'm there, but what if he was speeding down the road to get here, and someone pulled out in front of him? What if I'm sitting here all impatient while he's lying mangled and bleeding in the street at this very moment?

Suddenly I see it. A transparent vision descends, layering over the parking lot: the edge of a street sprinkled with broken glass trailing ominously to a dark bloodstain. Not just a few drops, either. It looks like someone splashed a cup of blood against the curb. The hair on the back of my neck stands on end. Like yesterday's shape-shifting raven side effect, the gory hallucination tries to take hold of me and drag me under like an ocean wave.

I shake my head furiously, trying to vibrate the vision of blood and glass out of my head. It spins away but still lingers, deep in the shady pockets between the trees. I strain my ears for the sirens I'm sure must be heading this way, but hear only the grinding gears of a big truck out on Valley Road and a rousing chorus of protest from the cicadas. The heat must be making me hallucinate because I hear my name again. But it's only the traffic and big, buzzing bugs hissing, *Viviiiii…*

That's it. I'm out of here. There's a totally logical reason why he didn't meet me, like some truck problem or a dead phone, but I'm not waiting another second. I slip onto my bike and take the back way to Una's, avoiding the truck traffic on Valley Road.

The road behind the Pecan Forest is a trail of uneasy magic. No bloody visions follow me, but heat curtains shimmer under the canopy, and blue-gold dream sparkles dance just out of sight. Up above, little kernels of clouds blaze into popcorn in the brilliant blue sky. Maybe it will rain later, but right now there isn't even a hint of a breeze. Burnt, oily truck fumes linger in the stillness, and I pedal faster to keep their stifling smell from clinging to me.

By the time I get to Una's, long tentacles of sweaty hair have escaped my ponytail and wrapped themselves around my neck. The coneflowers by the mailbox nod sleepily in the heat, while the gate wolves look to the sky in a silent, permanent howl.

Lucas's truck isn't there.

I hop off and roll my bike under the carport next to Una's Jeep, and she opens the front door as soon as I ring the bell. Her anxious face only feeds my fear.

"Where's Lucas? Did he find you? Did you see the picture?" She motions me inside.

"No, he texted that he was on his way, but he didn't show up at the college. He's not answering his phone either, so I waited a few minutes and decided to come here."

"He left more than twenty minutes ago." Una frowns. "Your face is really red. Go sit under the A/C while I get you some water."

The living room is a cool and quiet refuge from the blistering furnace outside. Una returns with a huge glass of ice water, and I gulp it down, feeling the icy relief slide down my throat and into my stomach.

Heat stroke defeated, I notice the shoebox on the coffee table. Hundreds of photographs stand vertically in the box, while a dozen or so lay scattered across the table.

"So what happened? Lucas texted me and said he found a picture."

"He did. He spent an hour going through these, hundreds of them, but he found the one he was looking for. The one Joseph wanted him to see." Her face clouds over. "A picture of him with your father—and someone who looks like Jackson Connor."

The room spins, and I clutch my knees, leaning forward in the loveseat.

"*Together?* Where? When?" I gasp. My thoughts spin out faster than I can reel them in. The Knot tightens, listening.

"I don't know. It was a group of soldiers in the late '90s. The picture is really dark, and I only saw it for a few seconds." Una sits on the couch. "I'm not even 100 percent sure it was him, but Lucas was positive. He said he had to find you and tore out of here like a bat out of Hell."

She picks up the loose photos from the table and hands them to me. "My brother took a lot of pictures, but that was the only one with Jackson Connor in it. Or your father."

I flip through them. Soldiers. Like the men in the second window.

The memory I tried to draw but couldn't. Like dozens of other pictures at home. Like the ones on Dad's memorial web page.

"These dark ones are from Bosnia, I think. Why would Jackson Connor show up here and not tell us he knew my dad? Even if he didn't know it was us, which I guess is possible since Mom goes by Hawk, what about *your* last name? It's not like there are a lot of people named Wolfsong."

Her eyes meet mine. "Maybe he doesn't want us to know who he is."

My brain tries to squeeze this information into some kind of shape I can recognize. Dad said to trust my instincts. And my instincts have been saying—no, *screaming*—that Jackson Connor is not what he seems. Ever since he walked into Déjà Vu, he moved too close too soon, bringing nothing but turmoil and doubt into my life.

"But my dad was there last night. I even asked him about Jackson Connor, and he had no idea who that was. He said Connor could be anybody, or nobody."

He also said there are limits, The Knot points out. *And he didn't know Joseph was missing.*

"There's that," Una agrees, sitting on the couch. "But what about yesterday? Lucas told me about the raven's eyes, and how you thought Jackson Connor might be a dreamwalker." She taps the loose pictures together on the table and slips them back in the box.

"Una, that was *terrifying*. I almost passed out." I rub my hands across my face and rest my chin on my hands. "But we decided it was a hallucination, a side effect from staying in the dream too long."

"That's what you guys thought yesterday. I thought so too, but now..." She takes both of my hands. Her voice is low and urgent. "Vivi, I think it was a test. You went into that man's dreams, and somehow he suspected you were there. Maybe he only saw you as a hawk, but you and Lucas got past his defenses, so he had to find out who you were. And that little raven? I think he wanted to see if you recognized those blue eyes from the night before, when he chased you out."

A dizzy, sick residue from yesterday passes through me like a ghost.

"He was pushing, Una. I felt him. It was like he was pushing me back into that dreamwalk, and for a second, he almost *did*. But I-I sidestepped him."

"You're stronger than he is. I bet he still doesn't know for sure." She leans forward and squeezes my hands. "Okay, there are a lot of 'ifs' here, Vivian. But *if* Jackson Connor is a dreamwalker, and *if* that's really him in the picture, there's only one reason he could be here." Her face goes still.

The missing piece falls into place.

"Oh my God. *Stargate*." The word strangles me, and I can barely breathe out the next one. "Brian."

Wait, wait, *wait*. Jackson Connor, a CIA thug from the Stargate Project? He's definitely a phony and a snob, from his expensive haircut down to his designer shoes, but he doesn't exactly fit the part of the dangerous mastermind of a CIA dream-warrior project—even if I don't know what that would actually look like. No, it can't be. If he was in both Bosnia *and* Stargate—

"But if they're in that picture together, *and* they were all in the same project, Dad would definitely have known him or known *about* him, wouldn't he?"

"Maybe. Like I said, there's a lot of 'ifs.' I can't get into the dream world like you guys, so I'm just looking at the things in *this* world that aren't adding up."

"Mom said in these classified projects, people only know their own part," I remember. "Maybe Jackson Connor was in it but with a different group? That might be why there's only one picture. Maybe they didn't really *know* each other."

"Could be—and that's another thing. We can't wait. We have to talk your mother about this." Una stands up. "Is she any better today?"

"I thought she was. She got dressed and was acting normal, looking for coffee, but then she—I don't know—she slipped *out* of normal. She was taking a nap when we left." I follow Una to the front door. "I'm worried about her. Even Brian is. He thinks she has African sleeping sickness. Can you come over now? She never wants to go to the doctor, but maybe she'll listen to both of us."

"I think I better follow you over there. I'm worried about her too," she says. "We could be totally wrong about this, but I think we should stay together until we know something for sure. And I wish that nephew of mine would call. It's been over half an hour."

I pedal out of the carport into the desert heat. A trifecta of worry —*Mom, Brian, Lucas, Mom, Brian, Lucas*—is wheeling around in my head all the way to Valley Road. Tumbling right behind it is The Knot, whispering *Knew it, knew it, knew it,* and everything I've wondered about for the last two weeks is rolling into a big, fat, Jackson Connor-shaped lump.

I *knew* that raven wasn't a side-effect.

I *knew* Jackson Connor was a poser from the minute I laid eyes on him, since the day he rolled into town in his luxury Douchemobile. Ironically, it was the same day Dad's jacket came to me, when I touched the hawk feather for the first time and got slammed with icy-hot lightning. The day someone was watching me, deep in the shadows by the big tree.

Was it him? Why would Jackson Connor be watching *me?*

Maybe he wasn't watching you, The Knot chimes in. *Maybe he was watching* us. *Like they watched Lucas's family.*

The man who was watching me was big and muscle-bound, I remind The Knot, much bigger than Jackson Connor. There's no way that was him. *This is crazy.* The heat is broiling my thoughts into total nonsense. Just like this morning's bloody hallucination, which was just some kind of visual slippage, and not related to Jackson Connor at all.

Una's picking up some coffee at the Piggly Wiggly, and as soon as we get home, we'll wake Mom up and figure this out like rational human beings.

THE HOUSE IS cool and dark, blinds closed against the sun. Ophelia is scampering around in her cage, squealing for her overdue lunch. "It's okay, food is on the way," I call to her, thinking a scoop of hamster chow and maybe a spinach leaf would make her happy.

Then I see the kitchen.

All the cabinets are hanging open. Dishes and glasses are all over the counters, and the water runs in the sink. The freezer door is open too, with small, drippy pools of water on the floor below.

"Mom?" I walk through, closing the cabinets, turning off the water, and throwing a dish towel down on the puddle. "Hold on, Ophelia," I murmur, heading toward Mom's room.

Her door is open and the TV is blaring, but she's asleep. A dozen of her handmade coffee mugs line her dresser and nightstand. Some are brimming with water, others only half full.

"Mom!" I switch the TV off and turn on her light. "Mom, are you okay? What's going on?"

She opens her eyes and turns toward me. "Vivi! I'm so glad you're here. I hardly see you anymore..." She trails off and sighs, eyelids fluttering closed again.

I tug on her shoulder, gently. She feels a little warm, like maybe she has a low fever. Brian's diagnosis of African trippy-something-osis flits across my mind.

"Mom, what's with all these cups of water?"

Her eyes open and she struggles up onto one elbow. "Oh. I wanted to have a drink near me while I take a nap. You know those are my favorites." She sweeps her slender arm in the direction of the army of mugs.

"You've been sick for a week. You should go to the doctor. Una's coming over, and we'll all go. I'm worried about you, and so is Brian." I rarely play the Brian card. Mom always expects me to be anxious about something, but if he's the worried one, she pays more attention.

"You want me to go to Doc-In-A-Box?" She groans. That's what Mom calls the small clinic on the other side of Zia. "I don't know. Maybe tomorrow. Actually, I feel fine, I'm just really tired. Did you see my phone anywhere? I thought I heard it ringing."

I dig through the purse on her dresser and retrieve the phone. "One missed call, at ten. There's a voicemail." I hold the phone out to her.

"Would you check it for me, sweetie?" Mom gropes around and sips from a mug on her nightstand. I tap the screen.

The call is from the Alamogordo Space Camp. An ugly chill slithers up my back and grabs the back of my hair. I speed-dial her voicemail, listening over the roaring in my ears, and the message sucks all the air out of the universe:

"Good Morning, Mrs. Hawk. This is Janet Lopez, from Alamogordo Space Camp. I'm calling because Brian didn't come today. I know he was looking forward to today's experiment, and I just wanted to see if he's sick, and when we can expect him back. Please call back and let us know. The number is 505-555-2267. That's 555-CAMP. Thank you."

CHAPTER TWENTY-FOUR

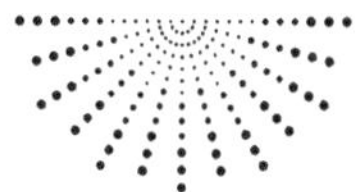

Brian...

A dizzy wave of dread sends me staggering into the dresser, and I drop the phone. How can that be? I took him to the bus stop myself.

No you didn't! You were in a hurry, and you left when you heard the bus, remember? The Knot shouts and kicks me in the ribs, hard. Then the horrifying vision of glass and blood in the street slams into me for a second punch. There *was* an accident this morning, but instead of Lucas, it must have been Brian. And the blood...

Shaking uncontrollably, I look at Mom. Her eyes are closed again. I take a breath, trying to remain coherent.

"Mom, that was Space Camp. They said Brian didn't get there this morning. Did anyone else call? The police or the ambulance? The hospital?"

I remember waiting for the sirens this morning, the ones that never came. If he was in an accident, someone definitely would have called. I pick up the cordless landline buried among the mugs and check the caller ID. The only call to the house in the last three days is from a telemarketer.

"Oh, Vivi, that's right. If I'm going to the doctor, you'll need to take him to the bus stop. Wait, is tomorrow Saturday?" She is drifting down into sleep again. Panicked, I grab her shoulders and shake her. "Mom! Brian's *missing*. He didn't get to camp today. Did anyone call?"

She shakes her head quizzically. "Brian? Missing?"

"Mom, you have to wake *up*. I think there was an accident. We have to call 911. We have to find Brian!"

"Tsk. Brian's just at camp. Star camp... no, that's not it. Stargate?"

Stargate?

The word hits like an iron weight, crushing the air out of my lungs.

They took him.

They didn't invade his dreams or his thoughts, they actually *took* him.

They've got him, and it's all my fault. I was so focused on Lucas and the pictures all morning, trying to convince myself nothing was really wrong, and *they took Brian*. Struggling against the darkness closing around me, I gasp for breath, suddenly compelled by every force in the universe to go. *Go now.*

"I'm going to the bus stop. I'll be right back. Then we're calling the police!" I choke out the words, flying through her bedroom door, and running smack into Una. Relieved, I catch my breath.

"They took Brian. Can you get Mom up? I'll be right back." The tug under my ribs is practically dragging me out of the house.

Una looks as if she's been slapped. "They took him? Physically *took* him? Okay, I'll try to get some coffee into her. Hurry!"

"Sure, honey, just call before you go? That's always the polite thing to do." Mom's voice calls after me and drifts into oblivion.

I slam through the side gate and leap onto my bike, pedaling furiously to the bus stop. I don't know what I'm looking for, but something pulls me as hard as the whirlwind that sucks me out of a dreamwalk. I dart across Valley Road, bouncing off the sidewalk at each street until I swing around the corner near the bus stop, the last place I saw Brian—and there, right by the bench under the sign, is Lucas's truck.

I skid to a wild halt and lean my bike against the rear bumper. Some miracle holds up my legs as I run around to the side of the truck and follow it to—*oh God, no*—little pieces of the turn signal lens shattered in the street, and on the curb, a thick splash of dried blood the size of a dinner plate. The cold lump of nausea in my stomach turns hot, and before I can take another step, a bitter flood of bile and the remnants of Cinnamon Crunch doubles me over and splatters out all over Lucas's passenger door.

Bent over and gasping for breath, I avoid looking at the blood— Brian's? Lucas's? Whose blood is it? Did Lucas hit Brian with his truck? *Where the hell are they?*

The window is rolled down, the keys still in the ignition. An unopened bottle of water lies on the passenger seat. I reach in, careful not to lean on my own puke. I don't care if the water's been heating up all morning—anything to get the taste out of my mouth.

Under the bottle there's a faded photograph, so old the edges are curling up. I pick that up too, then swish some hot water around in my mouth and spit it out. I try a tentative swallow. Blue and gold sparks rise up and spiral around my vision, then fall away. *Breathe, Vivi. Breathe.* As long as I don't look at the blood, I'll be okay. I lean against a non-pukey part of the truck and look at the picture.

It's one of the Bosnia pictures. Not the exact one on Dad's memorial web page, but like the ones from Una's, they look like they're from the same night. Cold twilight illuminates the background, and a half-dozen soldiers stand around the fire, posing for the camera.

My focus goes straight to Dad on the far right, just like in the photo I've seen hundreds of times. He's wearing his jacket—my jacket—with his caduceus pin glinting and a cigar clenched between his teeth. The man next to Dad is tall, with sharp brows slashing across his angular face, the one I only saw for a second and couldn't capture in the drawing. But here, the light from the camera's flash shows him plainly. It's Lucas.

No, it's an *older* Lucas, somehow standing in a twenty-year-old photograph. Then it hits me: this isn't the freak time-travel accident it looks like. This has to be Joseph Wolfsong. And standing next to *him,* grinning in all his rosy-cheeked, preppy-toothed glory is Jackson Connor.

My head is swimming. I take a few incredulous breaths. How did I miss this? True, I could barely see him in that gloomy castle window, but I didn't even recognize the man with the cigar—my own father.

I flip the photo over for any information. "S-Bosnia 1995," it says, with a line of names I don't know except for the one at the end, Ian Night Hawk. Next to that name is "me"—Lucas's dad—and the next one, the name assigned to the man I know as Jackson Connor, is "Jim Cooper."

S-Bosnia 1995. These are the men from the Stargate Project. And that name, *Cooper.* The one who called all the time, trying to lure Dad back into the project. The *Mr. Cooper* Mom never met, the one who checked on us after Dad was gone and somehow knew when we moved. The *Mr. Cooper* who somehow found us in Zia and came here for Brian—who has him right now.

The vibration in my pocket makes me jump out of my skin. I flip open my phone, and relief floods though me. Finally, it's Lucas! There's no message though, only a picture. A screen of white with numbers at the bottom. I tilt the phone away from the sun's glare, realizing it's the picture he took of the van I hit—yes, the little smudge of red paint is there under the government license plate. The van that was in this very spot, right by the bench, when we came to pick up Brian and... my stomach drops to my knees.

They were here that day to take him. They must have come back today, and this picture can mean only one thing: the man who calls himself Jackson Connor has both of them in the van, and the blood on the street—

Trembling, I start to text back, then stop. Lucas sent only the picture. No message. If I answer him and the phone makes a noise, what might happen next is something I can't even think about.

I pour the rest of the warm water over the door. Sheer panic jump-starts my run to the back of Lucas's truck. I lift my bike over the tailgate and drop it on its side. As I climb into the driver's seat and turn the key, the blue and gold sparks return, darting just out of sight.

The three minutes to my house feels like half an hour, and the panic only gets worse. I run inside, all the way to Mom's room. "Mom! They're *both* gone!" I yell incoherently. "Lucas and Brian are gone, and Jackson Connor took them!"

She's propped up with pillows, and Una's at her side, but Mom's eyes are closed. Una stands up and sets a fresh cup of coffee down on the nightstand.

"Connor took Brian *and* Lucas?" Fresh alarm washes across her face.

"That's not even his name. He's really Jim Cooper. He followed us here, and he *took* them. He took them for Stargate."

Mom stirs fitfully in her sleep and murmurs, "Cooper again? I don't like him, Ian. Tell him to quit calling."

"Mom. Wake up!" I shake her shoulder, hard.

She turns away and sighs deeply, pulling the sheet up over her head. Stunned, I'm almost as paralyzed as she is. How can Mom find out Brian has been kidnapped and simply roll over and go back to sleep? This is not some kind of sickness that has a hold of my mother —it's something else, something deep and terrible. I grip her shoulder, fighting the urge to shake this out of her as hard as I can.

Be still, Vivian. Is this the instinct Dad wants you to listen to? The Knot hisses. *Breathe!*

Five breaths later, I turn to Una. "What do you think? Should we take her to the doctor?"

She shakes her head, her eyes somber in the lamplight. "This is not the flu, or mono, or even Brian's African sleeping sickness. Vivi, this is just like Lucas's mother." She bends over Mom, straightening the covers. "It's not a normal sleep. It's more like a trance. Someone is controlling this." Her voice is grave, and the relief I felt when she got here pours out of me like sand from an hourglass.

"*Someone?* A dreamwalker, you mean. Like Jackson Connor!" I sag against the door frame, picturing the ocean rising up and swallowing Lucas's mother forever. "How much time do we have?"

"It's hard to say. We had no way to help Lucas's mother. We didn't know what was going on. But she stopped talking the night before she died. Your mom's still talking, so I think she'll be okay for a while. Summer is fighting hard, and she's ferocious." The conviction in her voice pushes hot tears out of my eyes and down my cheeks.

"Lucas sent me this." I show Una the picture of the van. "There was blood on the sidewalk, and I'm positive they're in this van. We have to call the police." I reach for the landline to call 911.

"No police." Mom struggles to sit up, her eyes straining to open. "It's not safe."

"Mom, we have to. We have to find Brian!"

She twists in the sheets, shaking her head vehemently. "No, *no—* they'll find us. It will start again. No police. *Promise me.*" She groans and sinks back into the pillows.

Una and I look at each other, frozen by her words. *They'll find us.*

"But they've *already...*" I begin when The Knot rears up. *The police, Vivi? Just what are you going to tell them?*

The mocking tone sends chills up my spine: "*Hello, yes, this is an emergency. My nine-year-old brother was kidnapped this morning, and I know who took him. This guy who's posing as a real estate broker? He's really a CIA agent, and he stole my brother to make him into a dream warrior. Yes, that's right, a dream warrior.*"

I throw the phone on the floor, my mind spinning. There's no way I can call anyone with that.

"Vivi," Una says, "your mother knows something. Even though she's barely conscious, she *knows*. What are we going to tell the police, besides the fact they're missing? And that government plate, there's no way to trace it to any one place or person. It might not even belong to that van."

She's right. They'll come over, ask questions we can't answer, then put out an Amber Alert. That will take at least an hour—while Brian and Lucas are taken even farther away. And Mom is so sure about this. I scrub the tears from my face, and the blue-gold sparks shoot across the inside of my eyes like firecrackers.

"Well then, I'm going. I think I know where Jackson Connor took them. Pacheco Canyon." The words tumble out before I even realize I've decided.

Her face goes still. "Are you sure? We could take Summer to the clinic, and I could go with you."

"You know they can't do anything, and we can't leave her alone." Fresh tears choke my voice down to a whisper. "You have to protect her, Una. You have to stay here and keep her awake and keep *him* away. *Please.*"

"I will, Vivian. Ń *dáh.* Go."

I grab my backpack and step out to the garage for some bottled water. I also throw in some beef jerky, a couple of Cokes, and the last of the Macaroonies from our stash. It's not like I'm hungry, but Brian always is. He'll want to eat when I find him, and I will find him. *I will.*

Next stop, my room. I take a deep breath, trying to exhale the terror faster than it can flood my body. It's 100 degrees out, but I don't care. I need my Dad. His voice echoes in my head as I slip the jacket on. *You're very strong. You're going to have to be even stronger now.*

"Dad, I'm so scared," I whisper aloud.

You are the only one who can do this, Vivi.

When I return to the living room, Una gives the jacket a quizzical look.

"My dad's," I explain. "It was in a box you brought. Mom said Dad had lent it to a friend before he went to Iraq."

"He must have lent it to my brother. That jacket was in a box of his things, and I knew it was way too short to be his, so I threw it in with the rest of those clothes. That same day when I met you, I knew it was supposed to come to you. Maybe I should have told you, but I didn't think it meant anything at the time."

I shake my head. "I don't get how you just *know* stuff."

"You know a lot of things too, Vivian," she points out. "You've known Jackson Connor was not what he seemed from the beginning. Sometimes the universe tells you, but the hard part is learning to listen. Oh—" she adds, "make sure you take the first-aid kit from the Jeep. You don't know what's been going on up there. You might need it."

Oh, great. Kill my heroic moment with a looming unknown injury. The reality of the situation must be showing on my face, because Una opens her arms and draws me in for a hug.

"Don't be afraid, Vivian. *Doo nénłdzig da.* You can do this."

"Oh, I'm not afraid. I'm terrified. But I'm going."

Una steps back, her eyes resolute. "Brian first. That nephew of mine is okay, I know it. But first, you have to get Brian out of this nightmare, wherever he is." A shadow of doubt crosses her face. "What are you going to do once you get to Pacheco Canyon? There's no cell tower back in those mountains, and if you get into trouble... how are you going to find them?"

"The lights. I'm following the lights. They usually come back with the dreamwalks, but I've been seeing them all day. Blue and gold—I think it's Brian and Lucas."

Mom's room is cool, and the overhead light is now blazing. Una has cleared most of the mugs away. "I brought sage to smudge the house. I'll get some coffee into her and keep her talking, so she doesn't fall asleep all the way." She doesn't explain what she means by "all the way," but I have a pretty bad idea what it means.

I shove that thought away. She has to wake up. She has to! I hold her soft face, struggling not to start crying again. "Mom, open your eyes. Una's here, and I'm going to get Brian."

Her eyelids flutter open. The fog inside them lifts, and they become lucid pools of green. The sleepwalker falls away for one brief moment, and it's *Mom* who gives me the faintest smile. "You're going to roast in that jacket, honey."

"It's Dad's. I need it."

"I know." As she drifts down again, Mom clutches my arm like a vise and whispers fiercely, "Vivian. Find Brian. *Find him and don't let go.*"

"I will, Mom. I promise." It's hard to sound strong when my voice is shaking like this.

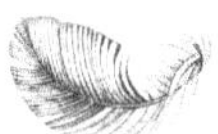

I HEAD for the freeway in the only vehicle I know how to drive. The Land of Enchantment stretches out gold and green in all directions, ringed with purple-gray mountains stabbing into the sky. The popcorn clouds from this morning are expanding and simmering behind the unsuspecting mountains, threatening to boil over into dark, menacing mushroom shapes by late afternoon and unleash torrential thunderstorms.

In a warehouse parking lot near the entrance to I-25, I take off the jacket and open the map from Lucas's glove compartment. Mom was right, Dad's jacket is too warm to wear, but it's right next to me on the seat with his iPod. I'm by myself, but I can feel them all with me. Brian and Lucas, Mom and Una. Even Elina's dreamcatcher swaying on the rearview mirror seems to be urging me forward.

I lean back and close my eyes. "So, you guys, which way are we going?"

A dozen amber and blue fireflies dart from my right eye to my left. North to Albuquerque, Santa Fe, and beyond—to whatever waits in Pacheco Canyon.

CHAPTER TWENTY-FIVE

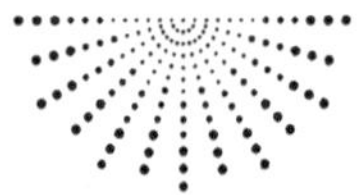

The rain starts just outside of Albuquerque. By the time I pass the Santa Fe exit, it's coming down in sheets and the colored flashes have merged with the rainy swoosh of windshield wipers. Ever since I turned onto Route 591, the sparks have been fewer and farther between. I have no idea what this means, but every bone in my body hums like a plucked guitar string. Brian and Lucas are *here*.

When I pass the big brown sign that says I'm entering the Santa Fe National Forest, I pull over to call Una. There's only one bar on my phone, here at the edge of civilization, and her voice echoes like she's in an empty gym. She reports no change in Mom, which I guess is a good thing.

"Are *you* okay?" Una's concern penetrates the drumming of rain on the truck.

"So far. I'm turning onto Route 102 now. Where does it go? On this map it just... ends." Fortified by some beef jerky, I roll down the window a few inches and let the cool, rain-washed air roll over me and sink into my pores while I look over the map.

"It follows that ridge for a while, then runs into 475, which loops back down to Santa Fe," she explains.

"Any place where Jackson Connor might be buying a cabin?"

"There's a few cabins way up near the ski lodge, but nothing along that ridge you're on. Everything behind you is Tesuque land, and the land to the north belongs to the Nambe Pueblo." Her words become garbled, and the call drops.

Time to get moving. The storm is getting worse, and I have a long way to go.

Two miles after I turn onto Forest Route 102, the pavement gives way to a rollercoaster of gravel and mud, cutting my speed in half. I drive another half mile, then bring the truck to a crunching halt. The rushing waters of an arroyo have breached its embankment, cutting off the road with an instant river twenty feet wide. How deep the swirling brown foam is, there's no way to tell—true desert landscaping. If I try to cross it, I could be washed over the side of the ridge into the canyon below.

I shift into reverse. If I go back to that last fork, maybe I can go up higher and cross this arroyo at a better spot.

A bouncy, grinding quarter mile higher, the road is even narrower and more twisted. Under the trees it's as gloomy as twilight, but the rain is deflected a little. I get out to look at the arroyo, and it's not any better than it was below. The truck can go no further.

Dark, heavy cloud banks are clotting around the mountains, and the wind picks up, hammering the rain through the trees. There's a saying here in the desert: If you don't like the weather, just wait ten minutes and it will change. I decide to take the universe up on that offer and wait it out in the truck, where it's safe.

But there's another reason I can't go on. The little blue and gold fireflies that brought me here are gone. That primal tug urging me forward has fallen to a low-level hum. I know they're here, but *where?*

Fear bubbles up and The Knot whispers, *This is just great. You're halfway up a mountain with no idea where to go or what to do next. For all you know, they're both drugged. You'll never be able to find them without the lights.*

Drugged.

"That's it," I say aloud. If Brian's drugged, that's like he's *asleep*. That means I can try to get into his dreams again and take him to safety. But how? There's no way I can just close my eyes and insta-sleep right now.

There's only one way. I'll have to dreamwalk *awake*.

But how? How do you get into someone's dreams when they're not even asleep? This must be what Dad meant all along, but I have no idea how to do it. And what happened when I *knew* what to do? Total, epic disaster. Hopefully it will be different this time; maybe I'll be stronger if I'm awake.

None of that even matters at this point, because there is no other choice.

I slip the jacket on and settle back into the seat, closing my eyes. *Breathe.*

In about two minutes, I'm warm and heavy, and I can barely feel the seat. As the sound of the storm fades away and darkness closes in, The Knot rises up again, but I squash it down. I already know what it's going to say, and I'm not listening. Today's possible trifecta of failure is clear:

1. It might not work.
2. This time, Dad won't be able to help.

And—ding-ding-ding—for the bonus:

3. If I get stuck there, Jackson Connor will have all three of us.

THIS TIME, I pass through the web of stars faster than ever before. They are only a blink of light as thin as a soap bubble.

The sweeping ridge of majestic pines rises above me into the endless starry sky, but the light is different now. It's not the usual sunset, or the long rays of late summer afternoon, either—it's an odd layering of light and color with mountains from both places. I can't see the truck or the ridge, but I can feel the seat beneath me and the sound of the storm is there, but far below me.

I am effervescent, as if my molecules have all shivered loose and could simply scatter like dandelion fluff in the wind. I rise up effortlessly, weightless, surrounded by my own purple glow. I turn toward the mountains, ready. There are no pictures to merge, no visions to lock together, no spinning of time and space. There is only one direction: Brian.

-Brian. Where are you?

The words rise up, bubbles of royal purple, and the stars drop out of the deep sapphire sky. They spiral around me, twinkling gold and green, and then stretch out into a trail over the ridge. I follow them, skimming my fingers along the glimmering web of droplets, up and over the mountains. For a brief moment, I can see my ocean under the enormous moon.

As I enter a thick bank of clouds, his voice emerges from all around me: *-Help me, Vivi, help!*

I feel him from every direction at once, and I know I'll be standing on his dream web any second now. *-I'm coming, B, hang on!*

I feel myself materializing on the web, and my feet are touching something, but the cloud bank is still there. I can hardly see, but I definitely don't see a city of prisms. I take a step forward. Feel the crunch of gravel. A cold, salty wind whistles through unseen trees, and somewhere in the fog, seagulls shout their raucous laugh. When I take another step, I run smack into a wall. A cold, granite wall... My heart sinks when I realize Brian isn't trapped in his *own* dream.

He's trapped in Jackson Connor's.

I've been here before. I know what lies around each corner—and what's probably watching with beady blue eyes from above. I press my back against the fortress, but I can barely feel it. The purple incandescence shaped like my body has almost no weight. The fog thins a little, and I can make out the three narrow windows to my right. The archers' windows, Lucas said. There are no other entrances to this fortress, so I face the wall, tap the ground with my toes and bounce up, remembering the sweet warmth of his grasp on my ankle.

As I glide over to the edge of the first opening, a single yellow firefly zigzags past me, rising and dancing farther down the wall. I only glance in as I pass the deserted library, but I slow down at the second window. I want to see this scene again. I want to see my Dad. After last night, I may never find him again. Even if this is someone else's memory, even if he can't see me, this is still Dad's face moving in the shadows, and still his smile.

The firelight flickers the same way it has for twenty years. The men are laughing and talking, but it sounds like they are under water. Joseph Wolfsong leans against a big rock with his long legs stretched out, crossing them exactly the way Lucas does. Perched on the rock behind him is a Dad-shaped shadow. The glow of his cigar catches the curve of his cheek and brow, his white teeth. I know he can't hear me; this is a memory from long before I was born, but I can't help it, and my heart silently whispers, *I love you, Dad.*

In the movies, this is where he would pause and look around—maybe in my direction—as if he'd heard his name in a crowd, or near a swarm of buzzing cicadas. But this isn't the movies, and he just sits there smoking, wearing my jacket while I wear his.

My eyes fall on young Jackson Connor. Jim Cooper. He has already lit that cigarette and is standing up. He is not laughing anymore. His eyes are narrowed, blazing with reflected firelight.

He is looking right at me.

Oh, *shit.*

I snap back out of view, blood thundering in my ears. Shit, shit, *shit!* Did Connor really see me, deep in a twenty-year-old memory, or was he just looking in my direction? I have no time to wonder or be scared. I have a mission, and I have to *do* something.

Even if it's wrong?

Suspended in midair by the window, I realize—no, I *decide—it won't be wrong.* Connor may be a dreamwalker after all, but Dad said no one he ever worked with learned as fast as I did. *No one.* That would include Connor, wouldn't it? He couldn't keep Lucas and me out, and he couldn't force that blue-eyed raven hallucination to stick. He couldn't keep me out today, even if he did see me—because Jackson Connor is trapped by his own dreams, his own memories. He's a prisoner in his own fortress.

I inhale deeply, feeling the power surge through me like electrical sparks, and my incandescence glows brighter because I *know.*

I am stronger than Jackson Connor. I can go wherever I want, do whatever I want, and he can do nothing about it.

I am a Dreamwalker.

I look over the edge of the window. Connor is still squinting in my direction, his head cocked as if he's listening for something. Fine, because I have something to say. I rise and breathe in, expanding to fill the narrow slot. He doesn't seem to see me, but he senses *something.* He takes a step backwards, and the tiniest ripple of fear rolls across his eyes. The words resonate from my whole body in a swirl of purple thunder.

-I'm taking Brian back, and you can't stop me. You can't have him and you can't have Mom. You can't have Dad, either. You stole my family, but I'm taking them all back!

Jackson Connor stands frozen in the firelight, as if a church bell has rung and he's the only one who heard it.

Brave words can't stop the clock. Time is slipping away, and I can't stick around to see if he heard me. The firefly darts frantically around the third window. Something pulls me, deep under my ribs. I let it reel me to the last opening.

-I'm here, I'm here!

Is that Brian's voice or mine?

I peer into the gloom of the third window. The sweet grass candle is burned down to its last inch. In the darker-than-darkness, the sleeping woman lies very still, barely breathing. Long, familiar wavy hair is tumbling over the side of the bed into the last glimmer of candlelight. *No, please no, not...* I'm so fixed on the hair, I almost miss the small shadow shivering on the end of the narrow bed, hugging his knees and rocking back and forth.

Brian.

It doesn't seem like anything wider than my head will fit through the opening, but when I lean in, my body compresses itself and pops through, like a slippery, amethyst grape. I fly to the bed, and what I've known all along closes my throat: the sleeping woman is Mom.

The tug wraps around my spine, and a whisper of salt air glides through the tiny room. The candle sputters a little, reminding me that time is slipping away, and Jackson Connor knows I'm here.

I reach out and pluck Brian's cold hand away from his knee, holding it as tightly as I can with both of my hands. He stops rocking and lifts his head. His eyes are closed, but his mouth opens and a whisper escapes.

-Vivi? I can't see you.

-I'm here, Brian. I'm going to get you out, but you have to open your eyes. Can you feel my hands?

-Yes, I feel them. They're warm.

Our hands start to tingle and merge like they did at the top of his dream web. The glow that is me ignites his hand and spreads down to his elbow like a living watercolor. By the time it reaches his shoulder, he is lit from within, swirls of yellow spun with bright green. His eyelids struggle to open.

-Hold on tight, Brian. Look at our hands and focus. Push harder than you ever have in your whole life.

He clenches his teeth and his grip on my hand tightens. His dream-lit body goes very still and warmth courses through him. His eyes open slowly, blinking at our clasped hands. He leaps to his feet and clings to me.

-Vivi! I called you just like you said.! It's bad, it's really bad. Look at Mom! Jackson Connor made her sleep.

Tears shimmer down his cheeks. The candle wobbles in the

growing breeze, and my shoulder blades tighten against the force pulling us out.

-*Come on, we have to wake her up.* I take her left hand in my right. *Hurry! Grab her other hand and squeeze hard. Whatever happens, don't let go.*

Brian bolts to the other side and grabs Mom's right hand, completing the circle. Her hands are icy, but they begin to glow faintly.

-*Mom, wake up! It's us. Open your eyes.* Brian shouts, and I shout along with him.

-*Mom, I'm here! I've got Brian. We have to get out!*

The lightest squeeze warms my fingers, and her eyelids flutter. The cold breeze in the tiny room spins upward like a dust devil—and riding on that wind, the sinister smell of burning oil. Jackson Connor has found us.

-*Mom, open your eyes. Hurry!* I scream as the candle sputters one last time and goes out, plunging the room into darkness.

The total blackness disorients me for a moment. I can't even see the window, but I know where it is by the invisible rope around my rib cage trying to pull me out. Then the faintest outline of our hands appears—barely there, but all three of us joined together. The oil fire smell rolls around the room like a living thing languidly closing in on its prey.

-*Hey B, you all right?*

-*Yeah.* I can barely hear him, and his voice is shaking. *I want to go home.*

-*Me too. Just told on tight. We're almost out of here, buddy.*

-*You'd better hurry, Vivian.* Mom's voice is low, but clear and solid in the rising wind.

-*Mom!* We chime together. *Are you okay?*

The wind is howling now, the oily serpent spiraling in closer.

-*Get Brian out of here. I'll be fine. Go!* I can see the faint outline of her face now.

Her eyes are open, and I know that determined set of her mouth.

There's no arguing with it. My knees go weak with relief. She lets go of our hands and sits up, taking deep, even breaths, filling with swirls of watery light.

-But Jackson Connor—Mom, are you sure?

She stands and puts warm, strong hands on our shoulders. Droplets of pale yellow and lavender trail her movements.

-Don't worry, I'll see you in a little while. Just get him out. Now. Go!

We slip out through the window and into the dead of night, dropping lightly onto the path. Brian has a tight grip on my hand. Gravity is dragging me, but to where? The last time I left this world, Lucas was with me, I could see where we were going, and even then we just barely made it. I can't see a thing now—not the trees, not the rolling hills, not even the ground we're resting on. Only Brian's faint glow.

Oh, Lucas, the desperate, silent plea surges through my veins, *which way is out?*

Before I can decide where to go, something large swoops down from above, rustling so close it almost touches my face. Feathers.

The raven.

-Don't look up, I whisper. Unlike me, Brian always follows directions and immediately lowers his chin to his chest, peeking at me sideways.

Shhhooop! Shhhooop-shhhoop! Three sharp clicks on the gravel tell me it's not only the raven chasing us. I groan silently. *Archers.* I press him back against the wall and slide to the left. The world starts to shift and drag, and my lungs feel like they're full of water. The faintest curl of oily smoke worms its way past us. Panic closes my hand around Brian's in an iron grip. This can't be the end.

I manage to find my brother and wake up Mom, only to be pinned down by Jackson Connor's oil-fire dream-archers? Frantic, I look everywhere for a hole in the coal-black heart of Jackson Connor's dream world.

-Vivi?

-What?

-*What's that?* He points to where I think the trees are.

A dozen neon blue sparks are darting back and forth. More and more come out of the inky darkness, doing figure eights until they are a swarm. They stop and form a glittering column, then tumble down and begin circling around again, strong and sure of where to go. A single blue light zips close to me, bringing the smell of soap and fresh limes.

The tension that has stretched me to the edge all day snaps like a rubber band, and I almost collapse with relief. Even this weightless dream-body feels lighter. *He's okay. He's all right—and he's here.*

-*Come on, let's go. That's Lucas, and he knows the way out!*

-*But what about* them? *Won't they get us?* Brian keeps his head down, but his anxious eyes roll up to where the archers are reloading, or whatever it is archers do.

-*No, I don't think so. This is just a dream; they can't hurt you. But remember what I said: push as hard as you can and don't let go of me, no matter what. And keep your eyes open!*

We crouch low, then spring off the castle wall like a pair of swimmers, focusing on the cloud of tiny blue spangles. I desperately hope what I told him is true. It's just a dream, and we can't *really* get hurt.

Two seconds after we push off, the chilling rustle of wings followed by a slew of arrows speeds past us on the right. Another round misses us again, but something stings me in the leg, and a dull, wet throbbing drums my calf.

Only a dream, I insist silently, *not the raven, not the archers, not real not real not real.*

The darkness tilts and cracks apart, sliding into a cold, relentless whirlpool, sucking us out of Jackson Connor's Dreamland. There is no up or down; it's all directions at once, and the only thing keeping us from going under and spinning into oblivion is the zipline of blue lights guiding us over the trees to safety.

My Dreamland forest is quiet and warm, with late afternoon sunlight slanting through the trees. I lie on fragrant pine needles, feeling my body lose its fizziness and become solid again. Brian is asleep, wrapped in my arms and the soft leather that cradles us both. I slip my arms out and tuck the jacket around him.

-Brian, can you hear me?

He nods, eyes closed.

-You're safe now. Don't be afraid. Stay here until you wake up, okay?

-K. He nods again.

I look around for Lucas, but the only sign of him is a trio of blue lights fading quickly under the gardenias.

-Lucas?

I barely hear him as the lights fizzle out completely:

-Hurry.

CHAPTER TWENTY-SIX

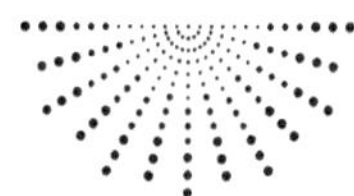

A crack of thunder tears open the sky, yanking me out of Dreamland. The world stops spinning, spiraling down until it's just me and the truck. The wind has dropped to a hiss through the evergreens, and the rain has subsided to a light, spattering drip. It's almost dark.

I take a few long gulps from a Coke, exhaling the last remnants of Connor's smoky prison, and reach for my phone. I know there's no chance, but a miracle appears on the screen: one bar.

Una answers before the end of the first ring. "Did you find them?"

"Yes and no? I sort of... meditated my way into Jackson Connor's dream and pulled Brian out. Mom was there, and I tried to get her to come, but she stayed behind. I'm going ahead on foot."

"You went into Connor's dreams when you were awake? Vivi, *he* must have been awake too. There's no way he's sleeping right now."

Static clogs the last of her words. I jump in before she's gone. "How's Mom? What's she doing?"

"She's awake. She's exhausted, but Vivi she's—"

The words echo and bend as the call collapses into the space between us, but it sounds like Una said, "herself."

Mom's herself.

For a moment there is no sound but the water dripping on the truck and my breathing. Una's right—Jackson Connor had to be awake when I went into his fortress. And if he wasn't asleep, then it wasn't a dream. So where was I? In his subconscious? Maybe that's why it was so dark and foggy. I was in Jackson Connor's murky, evil mind.

This must be what the Stargate Project was working on all along. Not just controlling people's dreams, but actual mind control.

Told you, crows The Knot. *Told you, told you, told you.*

I turn this over in my brain. I told Mr. Noonie to give me Macaroonies in a dreamwalk, and the next day, he actually did. Does that mean that when I find them, Connor will take one look at me and let Brian and Lucas go?

"Not likely," I say aloud, and hop out of the truck.

On the other side, I open the door, slip on the jacket, and stuff Una's first-aid kit into my backpack. I have no idea where I'm going, but somehow, I have to find them before it's completely dark.

There's a path going straight up that looks like it winds around to the ridge overlooking the canyon. The trail is rugged and steep for a hundred yards, but it levels out above the arroyo, and I stop to catch my breath. My legs are feeling it already.

I massage my cramping right calf through my jeans, and my hand comes away smeared with blood. A three-inch gash in my pants reveals a matching one in my leg.

From the archers?

That's impossible. Dreamwalks aren't physical. They're real, but even if I went into Connor's actual thoughts, they're still just *thoughts*. Uneasy, I dig out the first aid kit. Dad said for dreamwalkers, dreaming is the same as being awake, but I didn't think he meant that literally. I tape four Band-Aids over the gash, thinking my definition of *impossible* may need some serious rethinking when this is all over.

The water swirls far below, but thunder rolling in the distance means the storm is circling back. Out over the vast desert floor behind me, the sinking sun has burned a volcanic hole in the clouds, igniting a crimson fire in the towering thunderheads. An ominous rumble confirms it—I am gazing at the gates of Hell. I turn away and continue up the darkening path, trudging deeper into the forest.

The climb gets steeper. My legs are on fire, and my lungs grab for air as I push onward. Sweat drips down my face and stings my eyes. Pine branches grab and slap at my arms in the rising wind, slowing me down and laughing as the storm closes in, sniffing me out, making my hair stand on end. Where is the top of the trail?

Desperate for a breath, I stop, looking wildly around. Thunder bursts the air above me, and lightning splits the darkness. The cold, sharp smell of desert rain spirals around me, raising goose bumps on my skin. I try to bolt, but just like in my nightmares, my legs feel like they're stuck in concrete.

It hits me with the next crack of thunder—*this is the dream*, the one I can never change, the nightmare that stabs me with panic, sucking the breath out of me until I only have enough strength left to jump out. Well, not this time. If I can't control it when I'm asleep, I can damn sure control it when I'm awake. I put one aching foot in front of the other, hoping the universe doesn't call my bluff.

A broad swoosh of feathers brushes above my head from the right. Startled, I watch the—owl? Hawk? Raven? *Please not the raven* —circle back and dip down again, like it's waiting for me. It's a nighthawk. I take a tentative step toward it.

Circling once more, he glides away. Following the dark bird through the trees, I veer to the left. The forest opens to a small clearing above the ridge, at the edge of the storm, overlooking the edge of night itself. The nighthawk swoops out over the abyss, and its raspy screech echoes back to me before it disappears. I silently thank my namesake. I know it's just a coincidence—he was out for his twilight hunt and got caught in the storm—but it feels like more.

It feels like Dad.

I spot a pair of headlights on the road ahead of me. They aren't moving. The dark silhouette against the slate-colored sky is tall and boxy, and I stop dead in my tracks.

The white van sits diagonally across the road, one headlight shining out over the ridge, the other spotlighting the front bumper crumpled against a couple of boulders and a small aspen tree on the edge of the cliff. A muscled giant moves in and out of the cock-eyed beams, snarling and cussing like a pirate.

He's been out here a while—his T-shirt is soaked, and his dark hair is dripping. I creep up through the trees until I'm directly behind the van, hoping this WWE reject doesn't hear the hummingbird fluttering in my chest. I peek around to see the passenger door and a few leafy branches in the twin beams.

Far out in the canyon, there's a pale curtain of rain sliding through, slowly closing over the deep shadow of the other side. And just a few wet feet beyond the tree, where the reject is inching around carefully, is a 500-foot drop.

"Hey, Viiiiiktor...!"

Brian's cheerful, singsong voice cracks my heart wide open. He's all right! I crouch by the rear bumper, inching my head out to see the giant growling in the headlights. His nose is swollen, bruised, and bent to one side.

"What?" snaps the thug.

"Fetch!"

Brian flings his arm out the window, gleefully releasing a large, flat rectangle. It sails like a Frisbee over the ridge and crashes into pieces with several heavy, rocky *thwacks* somewhere on the slope below. Looks like Viktor just lost his laptop. He roars and strides toward the van. While he scrambles awkwardly over one of the boulders, I bolt back across the road, out of sight. I can't see Brian anymore, but I can see Viktor. He rips open the driver's door, turns the motor off, and slams the door. I hear another stream of profanity and the chirp of automatic locks.

"You'll be sorry you did that, you little shit!" Viktor stomps over to the edge of the road.

There is no guard rail here, and he zigzags slowly down the side of the slope, muttering at the evergreens and mesquite. I kneel in the mud, waiting to move in on the driver's side where he can't see me, but he has to get pretty far down before I can try to spring Brian from the van. If that giant starts chasing me, I want a good head start.

I creep along the side of the van, willing my feet not to make any noise. The headlights are still burning and the windows are now only half open. He is closing his backpack when I whisper, "Brian. It's me. Be real quiet, and let's get out of here!"

"Vivi!" He turns to me, relief washing over his small face. "I thought I heard someone back there. Is Mom here?"

"No, but she's better." *I hope.* "Where's Lucas?"

"At the cabin. Jackson Connor took us."

"Ssh, I know. Escape now, talk later." I can't hear Viktor mothercussing at the bushes anymore. "Look out your window. Can you see where he is? Is he still going down?"

Brian kneels and looks over the top of his window, scanning the darkness. "I see his flashlight way down there. He's never going to find that laptop. Jackson Connor is going to be sooo mad." He nods, pleased at his handiwork.

"This window's open a little more than yours. Can you squeeze through it?"

"I think so. Here." He shoves his backpack through, and I drop it on the ground. "Careful, Hamlet's in there, and he's a hero. He made Viktor crash the truck!"

"What?"

"Hamlet got out, and he crawled on Viktor." He snickers and shakes his head in the light of the dashboard. "So Viktor started screaming and jumping around—Ah! Ah!—" Brian bounces on the seat and the van creaks, slipping back an inch—"and he crashed into that tree. He's pretty dumb, that Viktor, and he's not a very good driver, either."

The rain is still light, but steady now, and the gravelly mud is getting softer by the minute.

"We better get out of here before he comes back, or this van slides over the cliff."

Oh... hell, yeah. An awesome idea is igniting in my brain. "Hey, B. What gear is this thing in?"

Brian peers at the dashboard. "It's in 'N'. Neutral. Why?"

"You said Viktor is going to be in trouble for the laptop going over the cliff... wanna add the van to the list?"

He stifles a snort and nods. "He'll have to make up some new cusswords."

"We'll have to get it away from the tree, then push it over. You sure it's in neutral?"

He peers at the dash. "Yeah."

"You're gonna pop the parking brake." I don't see a handle sticking up between the seats. "Look over here by the door at the bottom of the dashboard, but don't pop it yet."

Brian feels around below the steering wheel. "Okay."

"Now, this is the tricky part. You have to pop the brake, then get through the window as fast as you can in case it starts rolling. I'll help pull you out. All right, then, on three."

"Wait." He turns the wheel all the way to the right until it locks. He gets off his knees and crouches on his feet, hand on the brake. "Okay, ready."

We count together. "One... two... *three.*"

The brake pops with a satisfying clunk, and Brian pokes his arms and head through the window. I grab him under the armpits, but it's a little too high and I don't have much leverage. I brace myself with one wet sneaker on the door and pull. He wriggles through a few more inches.

"Ow! It's scraping my stomach." Brian groans.

"Shh—I hear something."

There's a rustling in the bushes below, and then—way too close—a barrage of F-bombs.

"It's him. Hurry! Suck in your stomach. Put your feet on the steering wheel and *push*."

I take a deep breath, plant my foot as high on the van as I can, and heave back with every bit of my strength. The van creaks and rocks, and a few more inches of Brian emerge with each pull. Then the horn blares as he pushes off the wheel and finally wriggles through—sending both of us butt-first into the mud. The van comes loose from the tree and rolls slowly back as we scramble out of the way to the edge of the woods.

I can't see Viktor, but I hear his mystified "What the—?" when the van loops drunkenly around, momentum swinging its back end up to the ridge side of the road. It wobbles and shudders, and then the rear wheels drop, the crooked lights tip skyward, and the van slips off the edge of the world.

The victorious sounds of crashing metal, snapping branches, and tumbling rocks freeze us both in our tracks. I hold my breath, waiting to see what Viktor decides to do. A new string of profanity and hurried footsteps crunching back down the cliff snaps us free, and we run deeper into the woods. When we get to the trail, we stop by a fallen tree, gasping for breath. Brian looks at me.

"'What the...?'" he mocks, and laughter bubbles up between us, taking our last bit of air as we collapse into the wet pine needles.

"We have to get going, we can't hang around here," I urge. "Follow that path."

"That was the coolest thing anyone has ever done." He pants as we trot through the trees. His eyes are shining in the gloom. "That was superhero-style."

"Hell yeah," I say, but I don't feel much like a superhero. My calf is throbbing, and Viktor could come back up the cliff any minute. "Keep moving. In a few minutes, it's all downhill. What *happened?*"

"Jackson Connor. He came to the bus stop and that guy Viktor grabbed me. Then Lucas came. He crashed into the van and jumped out, and he broke Viktor's nose, and there was blood all *over*." Brian sighs in admiration. "But Viktor hit him in the face really hard and knocked him down. Then they tied us both up and put us in the van and came up here to the cabin."

Horror and gratitude tumble around in my heart. I saw the damage Lucas inflicted on Viktor trying to save Brian—only to be captured himself.

"Where is this cabin? What's going on there? Wait, hold on." I pull off my shoe and tap out some gravel, holding Brian's shoulder for balance.

"It's over that way." He points higher up the mountain. "First, he asked about my dreams. He didn't believe I don't have any, so he gave me a shot. Probably sodium pentothal—that's truth serum—then he started asking about *you*. I didn't tell him anything—I'm no squealer! I just remembered the directions from when I made the Moon Rover and started telling him how to do it. But then he got mad and told Viktor to get rid of me."

"Get *rid* of you? Meaning *what*?" I stop tapping my sneaker. Get rid of Brian, as in *kill* him? Jackson Connor would kill a nine-year-old? Rage ignites my heart. *You are so dead. They will find chunks of you scattered all over this mountain. They'll put "rest in pieces" on your tombstone, Connor.*

"I don't know. I didn't hear everything they said." Brian shrugs. "But then you came. How did you get here?"

"I drove Lucas's truck, but the road is washed out, so I came up this trail."

"You drove by yourself?" He digests this. "But how did you know where we were? Did you remember about his cabin?"

When you're talking about something crazy, like the trail of lights and the gravitational force that brought me all the way to the top of a mountain, it's better to keep it simple.

"Yeah, I kind of remembered that. I had this dream while I was waiting for the rain to quit, and when I woke up, I knew you were here."

"I had a dream too. From the truth serum, I think. I don't remember it much, but at least I had one."

He did open his eyes, deep in the fortress. Just long enough to help us get out, but he did.

"Maybe you'll remember it later. Are you okay now?"

"Yeah, it wore off pretty fast. You know how truth serum is." His offhand tone cracks me up as we stumble down the steepest part of the trail.

"Oh, sure I do. How could I *possibly* have forgotten the aftereffects of sodium whatever-the-hol?"

It's so dark and wet under the trees, we almost walk right into the truck. We climb in and pop open two waters.

"You're going to have to stay here while I go back for Lucas." My voice sounds confident, but it's totally an act. What I'm going to do when I find him, I have no idea. But now that I can breathe normally again, I feel him nearby, the same way you feel the presence of someone in another room in your house.

"First, let's move this truck so no one can see you." I park the truck a few yards away from the path, behind some bushes. "How far is the cabin?"

"Maybe a mile up from the van? There's a dirt driveway on the left." He spots my leg. "Vivi, you're bleeding." His eyes search mine, anxious.

"Nah, it's just a scratch. I already taped it up."

He tilts his head as if he's searching his memory, deciding whether or not to believe me.

To avoid any further questions, I dig the beef jerky out of my backpack, along with the Macaroonies, which are now pulverized Macaroonie crumbs. "Look, I brought you some food. You have your phone, right? I'll call you when I'm heading back."

He rolls his eyes. "You know there's no bars up here."

"Well, there might be a bar when the storm passes. Just turn it on and wait for me."

I don't tell him that his phone won't work any better than mine did. I don't tell him the reason I want his phone on is in case people in helicopters have to locate him out here in the middle of nowhere.

In case I don't come back.

He looks at me for two heartbeats, and then nods. "Okay, V." His solemn expression shifts. "If you're going back up there, you should take Hamlet."

"Why?" Even if he did help Brian get away, he's still a huge hairy spider in a box that won't stay closed.

He holds out the box. "You don't have any weapons or anything. Maybe you can put him on Jackson Connor and he'll freak out like Viktor." He grins at his own suggestion.

After everything he's been through today, I don't have the heart to say no.

"All right." I sigh. "C'mon Hamlet, let's go." I wedge my new secret weapon under the first-aid kit, hoping it doesn't pop open, and slip my arms through the straps.

"See you soon, B. Don't be scared, okay?" I hug him hard and whirl toward the path.

"You, either. Remember, superhero-style."

Trudging up the path again, I feel more like a super-wimp, but from the moment the van went over the cliff, The Knot has been quietly unraveling thread by thread. With each step, I exhale some dread and inhale a little hope.

"Hey, Vivi," Brian shout-whispers from behind me, "be careful. There's rattlesnakes up there. I heard them."

"Cool. If they start any shit, I'll let Hamlet take care of them."

The profanity makes him giggle, and he closes the truck door.

This night is far from over. But tarantulas, rattlesnakes, whatever, it doesn't matter. Brian is safe. I take one last look at him, a look that is my final breath of air before I plunge underwater, back into this nightmare.

CHAPTER TWENTY-SEVEN

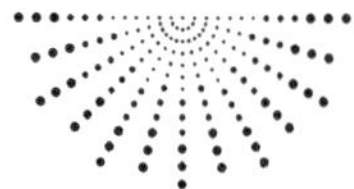

Twenty minutes later, I'm totally lost.

Well, maybe not *totally*, because if I turn around and go downhill, I will eventually come to the path—or to the ridge road, with a pissed-off Viktor climbing out of the canyon. I thought this was the driveway, but it's just another trail. I don't see lights from any cabin, and the thunderstorm that left the Gates of Hell a while ago is churning all around me.

"Lucas, where are you?" I croak through my parched throat.

I stop, trying to listen to the universe like everyone keeps telling me to do. No blue lights, no nighthawk. I spin around as the dark, familiar fear slithers across the back of my neck. The storm bellows in the treetops, daring me to show myself. Then a single blue spark blinks to my left, instantly swallowed by the roaring wind, and I take a few steps back into the trees.

The next flash of lightning reveals a dilapidated wooden shack with three steps leading up to a rickety porch. The sagging porch roof is barely held up by a couple of spindly poles. It looks like the whole place could collapse with a couple of good kicks, but a faint glow comes from the open door.

The rain stings my face like needles as I run to the side of the cabin. The idea of looking into another one of Jackson Connor's windows—and maybe seeing him looking right at me, *awake*—makes my blood run cold. But the glass is layered with years of dirt, and I'm pretty sure he won't see me, so I hold my breath, stand on tiptoes, and peer in through the grime.

The stingy light of a battery-powered lantern reveals a battered wooden table with a briefcase on it and two ancient folding chairs. One of them is tipped over on the floor. Murmuring shadows and a scuffling noise spill out of the front door, and I dart to the right and peek up over the crumbling porch.

"...just as stubborn as your father was." Hands tied behind him, Lucas staggers out the front door, followed by Jackson Connor with another lantern.

Lucas's gold T-shirt is covered with a heart-stopping bloodstain, and his hair is covering his face. Connor shoves him between the shoulder blades, and Lucas stumbles, falling toward me. I jump back behind the cabin wall as he hits the splintering wood, landing hard on his side with a groan. His back is to me, and I creep behind him, into his shadow. I'm out of the rain, but the sound sizzles all around, even echoing up from under the porch.

"You still don't get it, do you? You can shape the future, Lucas. What you have can change the world, change *humanity*. Imagine it— no more wars, no more terrorism. No hate. No enemies. You and the others just spend a little time in their dreams, and it all goes away. Hearts and minds, Lucas. That's what I wanted, for all of us. And the money's not so bad either."

Connor's seventy-two perfect teeth gleam in the dim glow of the lantern. He reaches into his shirt pocket and pulls out a cigarette and a lighter. As he turns away from the wind and cups his hands to light it, I take Lucas's hand and squeeze it gently. He inhales sharply, then squeezes back.

"Hey, it's the love of my life," he mumbles.

I can barely hear him over the sound of the rain, but his voice is groggy and slurred. Drugged. I scold my heart for jumping at his words—he's obviously delirious—but if he doesn't shut up, it could be a very *short* life for both of us.

My lips are almost touching his ear. "Are you bleeding?"

He shakes his head almost imperceptibly. His wrists are bound with a pair of zip-ties. Maybe Una's first-aid kit has something sharp enough to cut them. I slip out of the backpack and crouch in the shadows, while Jackson Connor paces a few feet away.

"Too bad about Brian." He sighs. "I really wanted to bring in both of you. He's really remarkable, even if he didn't inherit Ian's abilities. The Night Hawks have been hard to track, but when he started at Duke, it was easy to log his activity on that tablet. When I saw a search for Stargate and the parapsychology studies, I was so *sure*. But now..." He takes a regretful drag on his cigarette.

And now you've sent Viktor to get rid of him. As I feel around inside the first aid kit, I will the murdering, smoking douchebag to choke to death from instant cancer.

"Viktor will be back, and we'll be leaving as soon as this rain quits. You have a few more minutes to make your decision, Lucas. Your father was my friend, and I'd like for us to be friends too."

"Hmmph." Not likely.

Connor takes another drag from his cigarette and exhales a long, thin stream of smoke. "Maybe you can get Vivian to join us. She's a loose cannon, but I know she's got something, and being Ian's daughter, she would probably be trainable."

Trainable! Indignant heat floods my cheeks. *I'll show you trainable.*

"Or, you can go as a prisoner. No one knows where you are. You'll just... disappear. People might even think *you* took Brian," he muses. "Either way, I bring them Joseph Wolfsong's son. Then I'll be back in, and Stargate can pick up where we left off."

Lucas lies on the porch as I crouch just below, but we both stiffen as if we just swallowed the same marble.

He'll be back in? As in, he was kicked out?

My hands close around what feels like a steel pencil with a cap. An exacto blade? No... yes! A scalpel. I draw it out and slip it carefully behind the first zip-tie. The thick plastic resists and seems to grow even denser as I press the scalpel through it—then it snaps apart. Now for the second one.

"What do you need us for, if you already have 'others'?" Lucas asks.

Connor doesn't answer.

"Look, if I'm going to work on this, it's stuff I need to know," Lucas points out, sounding more like himself.

I recognize the tone he always uses with Connor—casual, polite, and totally guarding what he's actually thinking. Whatever drug Connor gave him must be wearing off.

"Well..." Connor considers, then continues cautiously, "The people who are born with it are much stronger than the ones we train. Ian and Joseph taught us to control our own dreams in the PTSD project, but some of us were able to walk into someone *else's* dreams and change those. So, we practiced that on each other in our group."

His caution gives way to admiration. "But those two were always able to go deeper than the rest of us. They could dig into the subconscious and actually plant suggestions that subjects carried out when they were awake."

Connor flicks his cigarette out into the rain as I slice through the second zip-tie. Lucas keeps his hands together, flexing his fingers and rubbing his wrists.

"Small things really, but I saw the possibilities, and so did the agency. This is true mind-control."

"My dad would never—"

"Oh, yes he would. Your father liked pushing the envelope more than anyone. But he and Ian wouldn't pursue it outside of the group. They said it was too unstable—and unethical."

Sounds like your dream job, Connor.

Then I remember those possibly unethical extra Macaroonies Mr. Noonie gave me.

Small things, really, but...

"After they were gone, the agency put me in charge, and I had all of Ian's notes. I worked for *years* trying to perfect the technique. I even kept track of you, waiting for you, hoping for any sign that you had inherited your father's talents. Years and years of nothing!"

"Sorry to disappoint you," Lucas mutters, pushing himself up from behind and leaning against the dried-up broomstick of a post.

I stand directly behind him, wondering what to do next. The scalpel fits comfortably in my hand and *do something* is ringing in my brain. *Rest in pieces* still feels like a good plan, but I can't just jump out waving a knife. That would give new meaning to *even if it's wrong*, not to mention *epic fail*.

Connor shrugs off years of disappointing surveillance and walks to the other end of the porch. The rain has almost stopped. "It doesn't matter. You're ready now, right? We'll show them." He turns his back to us, looking toward the road, and wonders, "Where the hell is Viktor?"

"Down at the bottom of a cliff," I whisper, and place the scalpel in Lucas's palm. His shoulder blades tense with the unasked question, so I add, "He's alive. Brian's safe."

Lucas clears his throat. "I don't know how ready I am, but if you need me to get you back in, I think I should know why they kicked you out."

Connor wheels around sharply. "They didn't kick me out. I'm still with the CIA. They just suspended the program."

"So, what happened?" Lucas draws his knees to his chest, sitting up straight, boots flat on the floor.

His back expands with each deep, slow breath. The rain has slowed to a drip, and I hear something shifting under the porch. Is this whole cabin going to come down on us?

Connor hesitates for a second. Then, "Back when we started researching dream control, I figured out how to make someone stay asleep. Usually, we can only stay in someone's dreams for a little while, as I'm sure you know—but I could stay longer than most. That became my specialty. I would work with the subject, keeping him asleep long enough for him to take control of his own dream."

I freeze in my shadowy hiding place. His specialty?

"You were keeping someone asleep, planting suggestions? So, basically trapping them in a nightmare?" Lucas's tone is dangerously calm.

"I was *helping!*" Connor snaps. "It worked fine with the soldiers in our group. They started being able to face their fears, not just in their dreams but when they were awake. It's just that I tried it on someone outside of the group, and—"

"And what? It didn't work?" Lucas inches himself up into a crouch, but Connor doesn't notice.

"Just the opposite. It worked *too* well. The subject had a very common fear, so I thought I could do it alone, but they were untrained, and I couldn't... she couldn't come back." His face is defensive in the lantern's light. "I did everything I could to save her. But with you as my partner—"

"So you killed some random woman and got kicked out for it, and now you want *me* to try it? You are one sick son of a bitch!"

"I don't have to justify myself to you. This was after *years* of practice. And she wasn't some 'random woman.' I chose her very carefully. She wasn't in the program, but she knew all about us."

No.

A woman with a common fear... it can't be.

I drop below the edge of the porch, blood pounding in my ears. Lucas pushes against the pole, sliding quickly to his feet, fists clenched behind him.

"The only people who knew about Stargate were the men in it—and their wives. Vivian's mom—*and mine.*" His voice shakes with disbelief and fury. *"You killed my mother?"*

Connor's voice rises in panic as he says, "I told you, it was an accident! I would *never*—"

Lucas erupts with a shout of rage, springs from the pole, then lunges forward. I hear Connor's surprised "Uunh!" as they go down in a heap on the porch, and I leap to my feet. All I can see is a furious tangle of arms and legs, accompanied by thuds and scrapes, shouts and growls as they pound each other across the creaking boards, making the waterlogged roof sway in protest.

Suddenly, Jackson Connor flips them both over. In one quick motion, he pushes Lucas face down, one knee pinning his right arm, the other in the small of his back. He bends Lucas's left arm up behind him and twists it hard. Lucas groans, as Connor plucks up the scalpel.

"Nice try, Lucas," he pants, "but you're no match for CIA training."

The scalpel gleams in the light of the lantern. So does the angry streak of red dripping from Jackson Connor's left cheek. He wipes his shirt sleeve across it, wincing, while the creaking porch protests loudly under their combined weight.

"Lucas, I really didn't want you to find out. I'm truly sorry, but you have to understand. I couldn't use Summer. She was too far away and way too strong. I had nothing to work with. Elina was my only choice—and I've paid for it, believe me. That mistake ruined my life."

"Ruined *your* life?" Lucas bellows, struggling. "You're going to find out what ruined really means!"

"I truly hoped we could work together, but you've obviously made your choice. Prisoner it is. Don't worry, you won't be the first." Connor weighs the scalpel in his palm, considering. "Of course, I have a few choices myself. I could rearrange your face a little. I could hobble you so you never walk again. Or," he leans forward and sneers, "I could just end your misery right now."

"*No!*" I shriek, running up the steps. I grab the lantern and swing it with all my might. Jackson Connor looks up, startled, as the lantern connects above his eye. The scalpel clatters to the boards. Connor twists away fast—too fast—clutching his head. He loses his balance, falling hard into the other post.

The post snaps in two, and Lucas rolls away as the corner of the roof crashes down, trapping Connor in an avalanche of rotten boards and rusty nails, and spearing a hole in the crumbling floor boards. I stumble back down the steps and around to the destroyed corner, shouting for Lucas, but he is already crawling clear of the wreckage.

"Get back!" he shouts.

As Connor struggles to pull himself out, the whole end collapses, sliding him headfirst toward the hole. He throws out an arm to stop himself.

Just before he howls in pain, I hear the rattle under the porch.

CHAPTER TWENTY-EIGHT

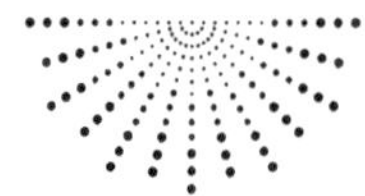

"Looks like we have a few choices here," Lucas announces. "Personally, I'm for just leaving him here with the snakes. I'm sure they'll be back soon." A large bruise is blooming on the side of his face, and he's cradling his left wrist.

Connor groans. He has elbowed himself out of the hole, but his foot is twisted and caught in the pile of broken planks. Two telltale spots of blood are spreading through his shirt sleeve.

"Lucas... Vivian, please. I've been bitten. You can't just—"

"We can't just leave? Sure we can." Hostility jolts through my body like lightning. "You had no problem sending his mom—or my brother—off to die!" I hold the lantern, glaring at him and keeping my feet safely out of his reach. There's already a big, satisfying lump forming where the lantern cracked into his forehead.

"Your brother?" Connor tries to sound mystified and fails. "What are you talking about? I told Viktor to take him down to the rest stop and leave him there. I would never hurt Brian."

"You would *never* hurt Brian. You would *never* hurt my mother," Lucas spits. "Who else are you *not hurting* while you destroy their lives?"

"Mom was sleeping all this time because of *him*. He was trying to get her out of the way so he could get to Brian." Saying it out loud pisses me off even more, and I wonder if just leaving him here would be enough. Would anything be enough payback for the lives he's destroyed?

His gaze latches onto mine, searching for something he knows is there, digging into my thoughts like he did in Déjà Vu.

"She's just sleeping," he says. "She'll be fine. I took every precaution. Believe me; I would never put Summer in danger."

Lucas makes a wild noise that is half laugh, half growl. "There's that *never* again!"

Connor's breathing is faster, shallower. He's bleeding, broken and bitten—an awesome trifecta of pain—and I couldn't be happier. But he hasn't stopped watching me, hasn't stopped digging. His eyes narrow as he finds what he was looking for and asks, "*Was* sleeping? Did you—is Summer awake?"

I meet his uncertain gaze for two expressionless heartbeats. He doesn't look away, but something wavers in his eyes.

I hope it's a whole lot of pain.

I turn away, feeling his eyes on me as I walk back to my hiding place in the shadows. As if I'm telling him anything. He can just wonder about it, but though I have a feeling he knows.

Even if it was a twenty-year old memory, Jackson Connor saw me in his fortress window.

"There must be something in the first aid kit to tie up your wrist." I kick my backpack away from the porch before picking it up.

The rattlesnake may have slithered away from the cabin, but everyone in New Mexico knows rattlesnakes often have friends. Lucas retrieves the other lantern from inside the cabin and perches on the far end of the porch, flexing his swollen hand and wincing.

"I don't think anything's broken," he decides and removes an ace bandage from the box with his good hand.

Connor struggles to sit up. "You can't just leave me here. I know you think I deserve it, but Elina was a terrible accident, and I'm *sorry*. Leaving me to die would be murder."

"Shut up!" Lucas roars, leaping to his feet. "Don't you say her name again, not ever!"

"Okay, okay. I'm sorry. I won't, I swear." Connor moans, falling back to the ground, his breath coming in shallow gasps.

"You better quit moving around so much," Lucas informs him. His eyes are cold, narrow slits. "It just makes the poison travel faster through your body." He sits back down, breathing hard as I help him bandage his wrist.

"Lucas," I whisper, holding his hand gently in mine. "I can't believe I'm saying this, but we can't just leave him here."

He shoots a venomous glance at the man on the ground. "The only way I'm helping that murderer is to throw him off that cliff over there, so he can die faster. A life for a life."

"But he's right. We have to do something, or we'll be just like him. Worse, even."

The wounded look on his face hardens. "You actually want me to help the man who killed my mother? He'd have no problem killing *your* mom, or Brian, me, you—anyone who gets in his way. And you're okay with that?"

My head spins as I choke out the words, "Of course I'm not *okay* with that. But Lucas, I keep thinking about my dad. Your dad too. How they found us, wherever they are. They brought us together to save Brian. Maybe to save *all* of us."

I take his other hand, leaning in close so Connor won't hear. "I keep wondering what they would want us to do. It's like I feel my dad watching. After all we've been through, they'd want us to be strong together and do what's right. They wouldn't want us to let him die." I raise my voice and turn in Connor's direction to say, "No matter how much he deserves it!"

Lucas drops both of my hands. "My dad was a Marine, a *warrior*, and this guy is the enemy. I know *exactly* what he'd do."

"Connor's the enemy, but he's also a government agent. If he dies because of us, we're as good as dead ourselves. We have to do something."

"You go right ahead, then. I won't stop you. But I won't help you either."

"What? I can't." I stare at him, incredulous. "You're the one who knows how."

He lifts his wrapped hand. "I'm left-handed. I couldn't do it even if I wanted to. Which I don't."

"You can tell me while *I* do it then."

His gaze burns into mine, two fiery coals of misery. The dark bruise shadows his face like the secret that has shadowed his whole life—the secret of Jackson Connor and Stargate.

"I'm sorry, Vivi. I just can't."

A hot wave of anger breaks over me. "Fine, then, I'll do it myself! You can just sit here and wait. I'll probably screw it up, and he'll die anyway, but at least I won't be a murderer."

I grab the first aid kit and the lantern, spinning toward Jackson Connor, half expecting Lucas to follow. He doesn't. I shove the rotten boards away from Connor's foot, grab him under the arms, and yank him a few groaning inches before letting go and plopping backwards onto the ground.

Lucas perches on the other end of the porch, his back to me. Panting for breath, I peel off my jacket and drag Connor a few more feet, until he's clear from the precarious wreckage. I glare at Lucas's back while I catch my breath.

"Thank you, Vivian—" Connor rasps.

"Shut *up*," I instruct him grimly. "Don't talk to me. Don't even *look* at me. I hate your guts, and I would rather be doing anything else besides helping you."

I take out the coiled snakebite tubing and dig out the microscopic directions by the light of the lantern. Tears blur my vision, and I don't see the tiny blade inside before it nicks my thumb.

"Ow!" I scream in frustration as much as pain, loud enough to echo across the ridge.

Lucas doesn't even look up. My chest tightens with fury. How can he abandon me like this? I squeeze my thumb hard to stop the bleeding, but that doesn't help the stinging in my heart.

From out in the canyon, through the still, rain-washed air, my own voice comes back to me.

"Ow... ow-ow-*oo-oo*..."

It's not my voice. It's not an echo.

Connor turns his head. "What's th—"

"Shh!" I stand up. A chill sparks up my spine, raising the hair on my neck.

A second, closer voice chimes in: "*Ah roo-oo-oo!*" The wolf song drifts up and coils around us, lifting into the trees, where unseen night wings rustle.

"Lucas," I whisper, "is that the wolf preserve?" It has to be, but that's at least ten miles away. This feels as if it rose from the canyon itself.

He is hunched over, shaking. Anger forgotten, I join him by the porch. His breath comes in harsh, rasping gulps, shuddering through his body as the past battles the present, until he raises his head and lets out an anguished cry, tears streaming down his face. A moment later a pair of wolf calls answer him, then fade away into the night.

He pulls me in hard and holds me tight, sobbing silently until the waves of grief subside. He takes a deep breath, throwing a bitter glance at Jackson Connor.

"Okay, let's get this over with. Let's save this murdering piece of shit's life."

CHAPTER TWENTY-NINE

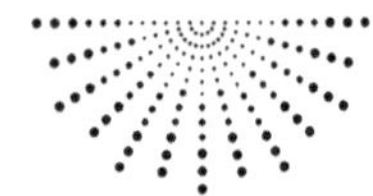

"I'm not very good with blood," I whisper, uneasy. "When I saw that blood on the sidewalk at the bus stop, I threw up."

"That's because you thought it was Brian's." Lucas steps carefully into the crumbling cabin and brings out one of the folding wooden chairs.

"Well, asshole, today's your lucky day." He snaps the chair open and looms over Jackson Connor's pale, sweaty face. "Don't think this changes anything. I'm helping *her*, not you."

Maybe this won't be as gross as I think. After all, Connor's got a nasty scalpel slice across his cheek, and that doesn't bother me a bit. Well, not too much. If I don't look at it.

Lucas brings out the other chair and Connor's briefcase. He sits holding one lantern, while the other rests on the ground. "Use the briefcase to keep his arm flat. Okay, Vivi, first you gotta cut that sleeve off."

I kneel in the wet gravel and use Una's scissors to cut the Armani sleeve away from Connor's arm. His forearm is swollen, with angry dark streaks surrounding the two pinpricks of blood.

Lucas picks up the sleeve and twists it around into a rope. "Tie this right here." He points to his own upper arm. "Tie it really tight."

I slip the twisted sleeve under Connor's arm, feeling him watch me as I tie it snug.

"Vivian—"

"Stop *talking*."

He winces as I pull the knot tight but closes his eyes and doesn't say anything.

Lucas unrolls the clear, flexible tube and sets down a suction cup the size of a dime.

"Okay, you're going to have to make a few cuts. A small 'X' right on each bite mark, then a horizontal slit about half an inch below each one." He traces an underlined "X" on his own forearm. "You have to cut all the way through the skin. Where's that scalpel?" He jumps up and heads toward the remains of the porch, calling, "You better hope it's there, Connor. This isn't nearly as easy with that little razor blade."

Connor shivers, eyes still closed, teeth starting to chatter. "I'm cold."

I refuse to answer him. I couldn't care less if he's comfortable. But if he keeps shivering, he won't be able keep still, and I'll probably slip and cut an artery or something. The only thing around to keep him warm is the jacket. Someday, maybe I will appreciate the irony, but right now all I can do is grit my teeth, place my father's jacket on top of my family's worst enemy and try to keep him alive.

"Thank you." I can barely hear him. He closes his eyes and says faintly, "It smells like cigar."

"Found it," Lucas calls out. "Well, look who's here."

He comes over and squats beside me, and in the lantern light, I see Hamlet's yellow Space Camp box. Connor watches as Lucas cleans the scalpel with an alcohol wipe and hands it to me.

"Are you ready, Vivi? Connor, you better lie still. I'll hold your arm steady, but Brian's friend here is going to keep watch on the rest of you." Lucas places the box on top of the jacket, a few inches from Connor's face. Hamlet pokes a friendly foot through one of the holes.

Connor stiffens. "Get that thing off me," he whispers hoarsely.

I make an ick-face at Lucas and clean Connor's arm with a wipe. I don't care about him, but amateur surgery is hard enough without a hairy arachnid waving at me from a foot away.

Lucas leans over Connor. "Are you sure? I'm just trying to help you face your *fears*." But he sets the box aside, holds Connor's arm flat on the briefcase, and nods at me.

I close my eyes for a moment and take a few deep breaths, thinking of Dad and how many times he had to do something bloody and gross and scary to save a life. And I don't know if I can do this, save the man I wish would just die, but it's the only thing *to* do. So I open my eyes and say a quick, silent prayer.

Dad, please don't let me screw this up.

The cuts are quick, like brushstrokes, and they bleed a lot less than I thought they would. Connor says nothing, but inhales sharply and grimaces as I use the tiny suction cup on each bite mark. That's when there's blood—not a lot, but enough to make me a little queasy. I need to concentrate, but at the same time I need to distract myself from the sight of what I'm doing.

"That picture, Lucas. The one in your truck. How did you find it?"

Keeping Connor's arm immobile, Lucas tells me about opening the boxes of Joseph Wolfsong's belongings, not sure what he was even looking for. "I just figured I would know it when I saw it. I thought it wouldn't be in the clothes, but I looked there anyway because of your jacket. There were books and papers—a lot of Marine Corps stuff I need to actually go through when I have time—but then I found it. The shoebox packed solid with pictures. I haven't looked at them in years." He'd pored over a hundred of them until he found the picture of the memory I couldn't draw. The memory that set our families on a collision course, trapping us all in a hideous web of government secrets and Jackson Connor's obsession.

"Bosnia," Connor murmurs.

"She told you not to talk," Lucas's voice is sharper than the scalpel.

Finally, I blob out some antibiotic ointment on each cut and bandage his forearm with gauze and about ten Band-Aids, feeling Connor's eyes on me again.

"Okay, I'm done. *We're* done." I untie the Armani tourniquet and stand up. The rain chill has gone. The mountain air is warm and piney, and the full moon is pushing its way out of the clouds.

Lucas looms tall over Connor. He looks at him for a long time, his eyes as black and hard as obsidian, then says quietly, "Consider yourself very, very lucky."

He walks over to retrieve my backpack, and Connor grabs my ankle.

"Vivian. Thank you," he croaks.

"Believe me, it was nothing," I say stiffly, and reach down to retrieve my jacket. "Let go of me."

"You... your father... listen to me..."

"What about my father?" I give him a hard stare.

"You have his power. You and Lucas. I never had it, not like him, no matter how hard I tried," he whispers. "I may not make it, but you can continue his work. Dream therapy, like when we first started. We *helped* people."

I shake my head. *Never.*

He holds tight to my ankle. "Not with the agency... they'll be looking for you two, now that they know it's not Brian."

Lucas comes up behind me. "And whose fault is *that?*"

Connor closes his eyes. "I can't change the past, but I can give you the future. The Stargate files, Ian's notes, everything. Your father, your grandmother, Joseph, and Elina... it's all there. Yours now. On my laptop..." He lets go of my ankle and slips into unconsciousness.

I freeze, rooted to the spot. I *know* this isn't what it feels like.

There's no way.

This is *not* because of the dreamwalk. He's just giving me all this information because he thinks he's going to die, and now he's trying to get some brownie points for the afterlife or something. It can't be because I stood in the window of his fortress and yelled at him to do it. That kind of Stargate mind control simply doesn't exist.

Except if it does, whispers the last remaining thread in The Knot as it dissolves, finally and completely.

No matter how or why it happened, Jackson Connor just gave me back my family.

On the laptop.

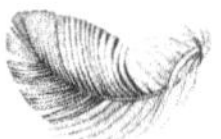

Lucas holds my backpack as I push my arms through. My body is numb, and my head is spinning as he crouches over the still figure on the ground.

"Well, he's still breathing," Lucas reports. "He's warm, and his pulse is strong. You were right; we couldn't just leave him, but now we have to. We've done everything we can, so let's go find Brian. *And* find that laptop. We need to get out of here before Viktor comes back."

He stands up facing me and takes my hands. His eyes shine in the moonlight, and his battered face is proud. He draws me close and kisses my forehead. "I don't know how you found me, but I *heard* you, I heard your voice. I think I answered you, but I was pretty out of it from whatever those drugs were. I even dreamed I saw you with Brian. You guys were following me, and we were running through the woods."

"That wasn't a dream. I mean, it *was*, but—"

Our hands meld together as we walk down the muddy driveway to the road. The moonlight pours silver on us as I tell Lucas about my final dreamwalk into Connor's fortress, finding Brian and Mom, the archers—and Lucas's swarm of blue lights that found us and led us to safety.

About the trail of fireflies that led me to Pacheco Canyon and how the van ended up at the bottom.

And about the laptop.

CHAPTER THIRTY

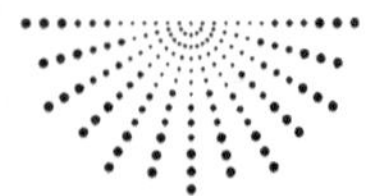

"Where exactly did he throw it?"

"Over that way, to the right."

Lucas takes a dozen cautious steps down the rocky cliff that was scoured by the storm and is now drying in the moonlight. He sets the lantern down and reaches back for me. I grab onto his good hand, sliding to his side in a cascade of rocks and mud. The sound of rushing water surrounds us as a dozen arroyos empty out at the bottom in unseen, hissing whirlpools of gritty foam. Somewhere down there, scattered in the abyss, lie the muddy remains of Jackson Connor's laptop, and all the answers we're searching for.

"Look, there's the van." Lucas points to a sliver of white gleaming deep in the mesquite.

It's much farther down than I thought it would be, and his face tells me what I already realize; even in the bright moonlight with a lantern, we aren't going to be able to see a thing until we step on it—and some of those things might be snakes washed out of their hiding places. I've had enough snakes for tonight, thank you.

"This isn't any good... We can't see more than three feet in front of us." His voice sounds as hollow as I feel.

"I guess we could come back when it's light out and try to find it," I offer, but he shakes his head.

"Even if we do find all the pieces of the laptop, I doubt anything would work after being rained on and bouncing down the side of a mountain. And we still don't know where Viktor is." As we start back up the slope, my phone rings deep in my backpack. I dig it out, and my heart leaps when I see who it is.

"Lucas, it's Mom! Hello? *Mom?*

"Vivi? Honey? Where are you?" She sounds anxious, and it's like she's talking into a tin can, but she sounds like herself, and the relief flooding through me makes me stumble a little.

"We're at Pacheco Canyon. Brian's okay. We're all okay. Where are *you?*"

"With Brian at the truck." Her voice is breaking up already, but I catch the last words before the call drops: "Una ... Jeep ... meet you all there."

"Mom's here." I look at Lucas, grateful tears blurring my vision. "I wasn't really sure if we'd gotten her out, but she's here, and she's awake."

We scramble back up to the top and sit on one of the boulders, catching our breath. Lucas puts his arm around my shoulders. The sounds of the night forest roll over us in the rain-washed breeze, indifferent to our disappointment, but inside our protective force field, we're warm and safe for the moment.

"Umm, Lucas? Can we not tell Brian about the files? If he hadn't thrown the laptop out of the van, he might not—he might be—"

I can't finish what might have happened to my goofy, brilliant little brother. I can't even think about it.

"You're right. He doesn't need to know. In fact, I don't think anyone needs to know about those files but us. They're gone, so what's the point?" Lucas sighs. "Just like our dads. They're probably dead, but I guess now we'll never know. Talk about epic fail."

"This is not failure," I insist. "We may never find out about them for sure, but they found *us*. They were here tonight. Wherever they are—alive somewhere, or just living in our dreams—they spoke to us. Maybe they will again. We figured out how to dreamwalk together, and we saved Mom and Brian. We were even able to get into Connor's head while he was *awake*."

Our eyes meet. A slow smile tugs at his lips. "And you made him surrender his secrets."

"No one knows about that last part except us," I remind him. "I don't even think *he* knows what happened."

"No one ever will," Lucas resolves, then sighs again. "Maybe it's better this way. It's definitely safer. Connor was right about one thing —this isn't over."

The sound of a car churning its way up the gravel road breaks through the night, and I remember Viktor could be anywhere. If his phone works, he surely called someone. Jackson Connor might even be awake. Two headlights turn in our direction and start closing the mile of road between us. I clutch Lucas's arm as we stand up.

"It's the Jeep," he assures me, and we start down the road to meet it.

"'Bout time you showed up," he exclaims as he opens both doors. He slides into the front seat while I climb into the back. Una holds his chin and inspects his face with a frown.

"Nephew," she says, sternly shaking her head.

"You should see the other guy."

She can't contain her smile any longer. She leans over and hugs him, then pulls back, her face serious again.

"So, where are they? What happened? Brian told us how you got up here and how Vivian rescued him." She shoots me an approving look over the seat as she backs up and turns the Jeep around.

"Jackson Connor's hurt pretty bad. Sprained ankle, maybe broken. Probably got a concussion thanks to Vivian, here. And he's snake bit." Lucas holds up his wounded hand to fend off her alarm. "We did what we could, again thanks to Vivian, and he was alive when we left him. Hopefully he's still at the cabin."

"But we don't know where Viktor went, so can we please get out of here?" I poke my head over the front seat. "Where are we meeting Mom?"

"At the rest stop near the last exit. She's got Brian in the truck."

"She's okay to drive? There's no... after-effects from Jackson Connor?"

"No, none at all, thank God."

"Unlike my mom," Lucas says. His voice unravels with exhaustion. "Una, he's the one that made her... the one who..." He leans back on the headrest and closes his eyes. In the dim light of the dash, I see a tear slide down the curve of his bruised cheek. I rest my hand on his shoulder. Una holds his bandaged arm, and her eyes, too, are full.

"I'm all right. Just really tired," he whispers.

Exhaustion must be contagious, because I have never been this worn out in my life. I close my eyes—only for a minute, I swear—but when I open them again, we are pulling into the deserted rest stop. Well, not quite deserted. Parked by a picnic table is Lucas's red truck.

All three of us tumble together, hugging—Mom, Brian, and me. Mom is totally out of uniform, wearing skinny jeans and a black T-shirt. Two large bags from Blake's Lotaburger rest next to a thermos on Lucas's truck box. The smell of green chile cheeseburgers is pure heaven, and my stomach reminds me with a loud grumble that I haven't eaten since this morning's cereal.

Brian looks at Lucas's bandaged hand. "What happened to you? Did you punch out Jackson Connor *too?*"

"Yup." Like he takes out CIA agents every day and twice on Sundays. "It's a long story, but basically Vivian saved me. She helped me get loose, and I got into a fight with Connor. I hurt my wrist. *He* got bit by a rattlesnake."

"Told you there were snakes," Brian reminds me.

"Then Vivi did the snakebite kit," Lucas continued. "We made sure he was okay, and, well, that's about it. Una found us, and here we are."

Brian turns to me, erupting with questions. "You *cut* him? You cut into Jackson Connor? Gross! *Awesome!*"

"It was absolutely disgusting, so I had to do it with my eyes closed," I joke, and hand the Space Camp box over to Brian. "Assisted by Hamlet."

He high-fives me. "Nice work, V!"

"Brian, go wash up," Mom urges, "and then we can eat. I know you guys must be hungry, and I'm starving." He makes a face, but she shoos him away. "You have not washed your hands all day. Go!" Brian trots off to the restroom, and when he's out of earshot, she motions us closer. "After we eat, you have to get out of here," she says calmly, handing Lucas his keys. "They're already looking for you two."

"What? How do *you* know?" I burst out. "Jackson Connor told us they might, but—"

Ninja Mom looks at me, her eyes reflecting eighteen years of Stargate surveillance and living as off-the-grid as possible. "Someone 'Unavailable' called my cell looking for Lucas, and hung up when I asked who it was. When I called the number right back, it was no longer in service."

She glances toward the restroom and continues, "I never met Jim Cooper. We only spoke on the phone a few times, and it was so long ago. But there was something about Jackson Connor, something I couldn't put my finger on. I thought if I kept him coming in for readings, I would figure it out, but trying to read Jackson Connor was like running into a big stone wall. And then I started getting sick. I can hardly even remember this past week. I did have the weirdest dream today, though, and when I woke up, Una explained what's been going on. All of these years staying out of the databases, and they still found us." She shakes her head.

In the still of the night, the sound of Brian slamming the bathroom door echoes across the parking lot, and Mom's voice drops almost to a whisper.

"Vivian, you and Lucas need to take the truck and go to Grandma

Lily's for a few weeks. Just until everything settles down and they quit looking for you. They won't find you up there if you stay off the grid."

I'm definitely used to being off the grid, and it will be even easier on the reservation. Cellphone coverage is shaky in those mountains, and there's only Wi-Fi in a few places. They won't look for us without Jackson Connor pushing them, and a week or two up in Whiteriver with Lucas sounds safe. Peaceful. Even... romantic.

Brian reappears and holds up his clean hands for Mom to see. "Can we eat now?" he demands. "I'm *starved*."

We find a table away from the street light and dig into the Blake's bag for a midnight picnic. The burgers are hot and gooey with cheese, the fries are crispy, the Cokes are ice-cold, and I don't think anything has tasted this good ever in the history of cheeseburgers.

Lucas and Brian take turns telling about getting snatched at the bus stop and demonstrate how they managed to send me the picture of the van with their hands tied. Brian reenacts Hamlet's dramatic conquest of Viktor. When he comes to the part about the flying laptop, Lucas catches my eye, and we silently remind each other of the lost files—and the life they saved.

By the time we polish off every crumb and lick all the cheese and ketchup off the paper, the horrifying events of the last twenty-four hours have been framed into a PG-13 adventure for Brian, and I feel almost human. He declares that Hamlet deserves a picnic too, after everything the spider has been through today, and he runs under the street light to catch some June bugs.

I head for the ladies' room to wash my face and braid my hair. When I come out, Lucas is leaning against the Jeep, talking quietly with Una. His long legs are crossed at the ankles, and he's shaking out an old gray T-shirt with a faded Marine Corps emblem on it.

I stop and hold my breath as he peels off the bloodstained nightmare he's been wearing, and it's the Piggly Wiggly all over again. His lean body is a perfect sculpture in the moonlight, and the wave that surges through me is more than chemistry. Chemistry is volatile, tricky, a balancing act that can go wrong at any moment. This is gravity. We belong together.

I can't drag my eyes away, but if I put one foot in front of the other, I can probably make it to the truck.

Mom intercepts me at the sidewalk. She hands me a small gray duffle bag, one that usually lives on a high shelf in the garage. "Take this with you. You probably won't need all of it, but in case you have to stay longer—or leave for some reason."

I unzip the bag and see some rolled-up clothes, a polka-dot toiletry bag, and a pair of disposable phones still in the box. There's a juice pack to charge the phones, a map, and a bank deposit bag from Déjà Vu. Inside that, there's an envelope of cash, minute cards for the phones, and copies of my birth certificate and Social Security card.

I stare at her. Has she kept a Stargate-Ninja-Mom-getaway bag in the garage all these years, ready to flee with us at a moment's notice?

"Don't use your old phone, either. Send me the pictures you want, but then take out the battery and toss it." She points to the dumpster near the bathrooms.

"Mom," I begin, but she puts her arm around my shoulders and walks me to the passenger side of the truck.

"Vivi, I'm so sorry. I should have listened to you. Maybe if I had, none of this would have happened. I was trying to keep you out of it, when you were right in the middle of everything the whole time. You're going to have to stay out of contact while I handle things here, but Brian and I will be fine. He's not the one they're interested in."

"But those guys—what if—" My sluggish brain is still trying to process this new side of Mom, and it must be really obvious because she smiles her patient Summer smile.

"Don't worry. It's been a while, but this is nothing new. Your dad and I always had an adventure bag ready in case we needed to get away for a while." Her voice is light and her eyes are steady, telling me nothing yet telling me everything.

"You better get going, though. Liluye is expecting you by morning. On Monday, I want you to text me and say, 'California is awesome, and Lorena says hi.'" Mom says this like she's making a morning to do list: 1. Water flowers, 2. Take out trash, 3. Evade CIA.

Who *is* this woman, and what has she done with my mother?

Mom reaches into the pocket of her jeans and presses something small and pointed into my hand. My fingers close around Dad's caduceus, and tears prick my eyes.

"Your father would be so proud of you, honey. As hard as it was, you probably saved that man's life. Surgery in the field, *and* you brought Brian home. He would want you to have this."

She hugs me for a long time, and when I close my eyes for a moment, I see that nighthawk again, swooping out over the canyon and back into the shadow world of dreams.

While Mom explains to Lucas how to find Grandma Lily's once we get to Whiteriver, I put the Stargate-Ninja-getaway bag in the truck behind the seat, slip on my father's jacket, then step over to the Jeep to say goodbye to Una.

"I guess we're going now. Una, thanks for everything." That sounds woefully lame after everything she's done to help. Mom might still be asleep if it wasn't for her—or worse.

"Thank you for saving Lucas. *Ashoog*," she says simply.

"*Doo da t'eedah*," I reply. "It's okay." And for a moment, everything really *is* okay.

"Una, there's something you should see. It helped me find my Dad, maybe even Brian and Lucas. It was in the jacket." I draw the feather out from the lining, handing it to her.

Her eyes widen in recognition. "That was in there? The way it's wrapped—it looks like my brother's work. A hawk feather is unusual, but good for a hunter. He must have made it for your father. A nighthawk for a Night Hawk." She holds it for a second then gently opens my hand and lays the feather across my palm. "Maybe you should hang on to it a little longer."

"But I don't feel right keeping it."

"It belongs with you two, for now."

"Hey, V." Brian hops into the back seat holding a Blake's paper bag. Hamlet's midnight snacks are buzzing around inside. To Hamlet, I suppose they're like little flying nachos.

"Hey, B. Guess I'll see you in a couple of weeks." I lean in and give him a big hug. "We're a pretty good team, aren't we?" A big-sister impulse makes me smooch his cheek noisily. "Mmmwah!"

"Yeah." He wipes his cheek quickly, but he nods and refrains from making his usual gagging noise. I guess he's too tired to put up much of a fight.

"Vivi, guess what? I remembered some of that dream I had. Mom was in it, and I was scared. I was calling you, and you came, just like you said. We were flying."

"See, I told you I'd come. And we got out together, right?"

"But it felt like *real*. Are your dreams always like that?" His eyes are huge and anxious in the dark.

"Pretty much. They do feel real, but they're usually not scary. Stars and colors with delicious smells. And more flying."

He smiles. "Guess you aren't the only Night Hawk around here that can fly." His voice drops to a whisper as he says, "You know when I threw the laptop out the window?"

"Yeah, that was a stroke of genius, bro. We never would have escaped if you hadn't."

"Well, I need to give you this." He's holding something in his fist, and I'm relieved it isn't Hamlet. I appreciate the spider's help, but there is such a thing as too much togetherness.

"When Viktor was out looking at the wreck, I downloaded some of Jackson Connor's files. I only had a few minutes, but I got two for sure—Wolfsong and Night Hawk. And another one too, but it's encrypted."

He opens his fist and drops his USB drive into my stunned hand, sending a shock wave through my whole body. "I can't open it, or someone will know. Remember how they found us because of the tablet? You guys better take this. Make sure you open the files on a computer with no Internet." Brian yawns loudly. "And bring me some of Grandma Lily's fry bread, okay?"

"Um, okay... see you soon, B."

"Laters, V."

I don't know how I make it to the truck. I can't feel my feet, and there's a roaring in my ears. Lucas adjusts the rearview mirror as I latch my seatbelt.

"Okay, we've got fresh coffee and a full tank of gas. From here, we just hit I-40 for a few hours, then exit at 77 South." He grimaces, flexing his bandaged hand. "When we get off the main road, you can drive. I guess you don't need any more driving lessons now, but we don't want to get pulled over for something, and you don't have a license."

I can't speak. I open my mouth, but nothing comes out.

He looks at me. "What's wrong? Besides this whole day, I mean."

I set the USB on the dashboard carefully, as if it might explode without warning. "Brian just gave this to me. He... he copied some files."

"Files? What files?" Lucas's quizzical look turns laser-sharp, and he goes very still. "The laptop?"

I nod. "He said to only open them on a computer that's offline."

We watch the Jeep pull out of the rest stop. We don't say anything for a moment. He clasps his hand around mine, and we are warm and strong together. Our eyes meet. A flush of excitement surges under my skin, and I'm not sure if it's because he's so, so near, smelling like rain and coffee, his muscles smooth under his father's ancient T-shirt, or if it's because what we thought was gone forever may be alive and waiting in a thumb drive.

"Okay, then," Lucas says thoughtfully. "I guess the hunt is on. Maybe we'll get some answers after all." His voice is calm, but his eyes are gleaming with fresh hope in the light of the dash, and as we drive out of the parking lot, I can't stop smiling.

I don't know what comes next. Like Mom said, you can't push the river. All I can do right now is be still and see where it takes us. I don't want to get my hopes up—there's probably nothing in that thumb drive but a lot of details about what we already know. Anything more than that is just a dream.

But for dreamwalkers, dreams are as real as being awake.

[*FILE 201 230614 SANTA FE (04:37)*]

Black Sky: Raven. Trigger. Request situation report.

Trigger: Sir. Mission aborted. FUBAR. Van totaled. All targets, location unknown.

Black Sky: Continue surveillance on the mother for a few days, in case they make contact. Where's Raven?

Trigger: No report from Raven, sir. Location and status unknown.

Black Sky: (pause) Find him. You know what to do.

AUTHOR'S NOTE

The Stargate Project was launched in the late 20th century as part of the CIA's legendary program, MK Ultra. According to all official sources, the program ended in the 1990s and is no longer active.

ACKNOWLEDGMENTS

Writing *Dreamwalkers* was one of the most challenging things I've ever done.

Luckily, I was not alone.

First and foremost, I must thank my husband Joaquin, who has loved and supported me for over forty years: I knew when you saved me from that snakebite, it would get into print someday. You found the road through Pacheco Canyon, and your suggestions and patience throughout this process were essential. Most of all, you brought me to the desert and showed me where the magic was hidden.

To my sons Adam and Kelly, who approved the plot twists and the fight scenes, and whose loyalty and love inspired the bond between Vivian and Brian.

To my grandchildren Tristan and Millie, who inspire me to follow my dreams.

The Apache tribal communities are spread out over thousands of miles, and intricate cultural nuances vary widely across those miles. I'd like to thank Beverly Malone, from the White Mountain Apache Cultural Center, for her assistance in art and language accuracy, and Daiiv Sundown for the conversations about the power of dreams, which planted the seeds of this story. Special thanks to Sharon Gloshay, archaeologist and sensitivity reader, for honoring me with her invaluable insights into White Mountain Apache language and traditions. Any inaccuracies in this book are unintentional and completely my own.

Thank you to Carla V. Lewis, my first editor, mentor and fairy godmother. Deepest gratitude to all the *#Unicorns*.

I'd also like to thank Neysa Hardin, book warrior extraordinaire.

To Pamela Thompson, mere thanks will never be enough. My BFF, writer-blogger-foodie-fashionista, who named Déjà Vu and jokes that we share the same brain, you are my best friend, toughest critic, and head cheerleader. I would never have even started this journey if it weren't for you, much less made it this far.

Thank you to Midnight Tide Publishing for giving Vivi's story a new home.

And finally, to New Mexico, the Land of Enchantment: the magic *is* there, when you know where to look.

ABOUT THE AUTHOR

Leslie Rush grew up near Philadelphia, spending much time at the Jersey Shore. She moved to El Paso and fell in love with the desert Southwest. Disguised as a history teacher, she spent years eavesdropping on her future readers. When she's not in her classroom, Leslie can be found on the road with her husband, exploring the desert and the world of dreams.

Leslie loves to hear from her readers. You can find and connect with her at the links below.

Website/Blog: https://leslierushwritingbooks.wordpress.com/
Instagram: @leslierush_author
Twitter: @LeslieDRush

MORE BOOKS YOU'LL LOVE

If you enjoyed this story, please consider leaving a review.

Then check out more books from Midnight Tide Publishing!

The Siren's Song by Heather Kindt

The shadowy folds of Mo capture both souls and secrets.

Catron's father intended to scare her with his words. After all, her mother traveled far from home, losing herself to both the shadows and her wayward spirit. But instead of heeding his warning, Catron longs for more than her life as a glass blower's apprentice. When Dawkin, a member of the King of Mo's illustrious guard, offers her a place at the Vradian Academy, she willingly accepts.

Fivlon would rather gouge both of his eyes out with an iron stick than attend the Vradian Academy. Messing around with his friends is a lot more fun than attending school with a bunch of stuck-up future leaders. Following in his father's footsteps as the head of Ferox isn't a priority. Until one of his friends disappears.

Now at school, Catron and Fivlon face a much larger task than their ethics homework. As students and staff disappear from the academy, they must figure out who is behind it before they become the next victims.

The Vradian Academy is the prequel series for Kindt's *Eternal Artifacts* series.

Available Now

Call of Death by R.J. Garcia

Hannah Priestly is an obsessive-compulsive California girl attending an English boarding school with the usual teen problems. She doesn't fit in at school and is falling in love with her best friend. But when she wakes up knowing the name of a notorious serial killer at large, Norman Biggs, her life goes from complicated to scary, and her visions only grow darker. Rory Veer is Hannah's easy-going, romantically challenged friend, and school crush. When Norman Biggs unexpectedly appears in Rory's reality, terror is set in motion. It is Rory who must acknowledge a past he has denied if the mystery is to be unraveled. Thrust into a terrifying future, they must find a way to change fate before it catches up with them.

Available Now

Marrow Charm by Kristin Jacques

Azure Brimvine lives in a world decimated by magic. One where humans have retreated underground from the overwhelming dangers of the surface. But Below is no safer than Above. Magic borne plagues continue to eat away at the remaining human cities. A sickness that doesn't merely kill, but creates aberrations from the stricken: people twisted by magic into something dark, dangerous, and powerful.

But when Azzy's brother, Armin, is infected and cast out into the Above, she sets out after him, determined to be there for him no matter what he becomes. The world Above is full of monsters, both wild and cunning, some more human than Azzy was led to believe.

Her search for Armin leads her to Avergard, a ruthless city of inhuman lords and twisted creatures. Azzy must find allies and forge new bonds in this broken world, brave the perils of the Above, and reach Armin before his new power is used to open the Gate once more.

Available Now

www.ingramcontent.com/pod-product-compliance
Lightning Source LLC
Chambersburg PA
CBHW070449300726
48975CB00007B/2093